CW01629503

By

Murray McDonald

First Published by Kennedy Mack publishing

Trial

ISBN 978-0-9574871-2-3

This book is a work of fiction. Names, characters, places and incidents are the product of the author's imagination or are used fictitiously. Any resemblance to actual events, locations, or persons, living or dead, is purely coincidental.

For Marie-Hélène

Chapter 1

Kate woke up with an imposing sense of unease. She reached out across the bed, the empty space a stark reminder that it was no longer temporary. A tear welled. Even after three months, every morning hurt almost as much as the first. They said it would get easier. They lied. The sound of the birds singing invaded her thoughts, drying the tears whilst increasing her sense of unease. The sun was up; the birds' vocal abilities were testament to that fact. She checked her bedside alarm clock, but its digital digits remained dark, offering no help in identifying the time. She reached over and grabbed her smart phone, but its display remained black despite her repeated attempts to bring it to life.

"Mom, I'm gonna be late!" shouted Danny, her eight-year-old, invading her bedroom and throwing the curtains open to reveal a beautiful clear blue sky.

"What time is it?"

Danny checked his watch, his father's old watch, far too big for him but one he insisted on wearing in the house.

"It's zero seven fifty-five Tango," said Danny proudly.

Kate hadn't noticed Danny's use of 'Tango' rather than 'Sierra' to define the current time zone as a result of the clocks changing from daylight saving two nights earlier. She'd been too busy pushing past her eight-year-old son to get to the window.

The world had stopped, quite literally stopped.

The reason for her unease unfolded before her eyes.

The freeway was stationary. The airport, her usual early morning alarm call, was blissfully silent. Their elevated position offered an excellent view of the unfolding chaos across the southern side of Boise, Idaho, their new home town. Nothing was moving, nothing. Cars and trucks sat idle on the freeway, but the morning rush hour for once was not to blame. Traffic wasn't nose to tail, it just wasn't moving. Car hoods sat high as drivers tried in vain to restart their vehicles. The sound of the birds singing - a sound alien to her since their move three months earlier - continued.

"Mom?" asked Danny, sensing his mother's concern.

"Where are your sisters?"

Danny shrugged.

"Go get them and bring them here!" she commanded, steel in her voice, grabbing the jeans she had worn the previous day. She pulled them on whilst reaching for the TV remote. She knew before hitting the power button that it would be useless. Power was out, but that didn't stop her trying. Nothing. The only sound invading the peace remained the bird song. She had never heard them sound so loud.

Kate looked at the airport again, she hated it with a passion. Every morning at 5.30a.m. it would wake her, the jets thundering overhead after takeoff, only to be repeated like a 'Snooze' button on her alarm clock every ten to fifteen minutes. Many times, it had been Tim who had woken her, thundering over the house., a house he had chosen, to be as near as he could to the two loves of his life - his family and his aircraft.

"Mom, my phone's not working!" gasped Sophie, tears welling at the thought of her loss.

"Nothing's working, honey," she said.

"God, Mom, pay the damn bills why don't you!" shouted Sophie, storming out of the room and nearly knocking over her younger sister, Ava, in her wake.

Kate bit her tongue. Sophie had been closest to her Dad. His loss had hit Sophie as hard as it had hit Kate. She was struggling; school, friendships, behavior, all had been affected by Tim's death. Sophie was a fifteen-year-old whose rock had left her when she'd needed him most.

"What's up, Mom…Danny said something was happening?" Ava asked. She was twelve, going on thirty. Kate didn't know what she'd have done without her. Her ability to ignore her older sister's outbursts was astonishing and spoke of a maturity that Kate wasn't even sure she possessed herself.

"Whatever it is, it's not good." Her eyes scanned across the panoramic view they had over the city. She had yet to see one single vehicle move. All were stationary.

"I'm going to be late for school!" said Danny, disappearing into her en-suite.

"There'll be no school today…" the sound of the toilet flushing didn't sound right. Kate rushed in after him. The cistern wasn't refilling. The sound of a shower cascading through the wall had her in a panic. She rushed out of her bedroom and down the hall to Sophie and Ava's bathroom. The door was locked.

"Sophie, turn off the shower!" she screamed. Every drop of even their hot water reserve would be precious until power and water supplies were back to normal. She rushed down the hallway, and throwing open the storage cupboard door, quickly turned the valve to isolate the water tank, a tank that Sophie could easily empty with one of her showers. What she found to do in the time she took to shower, Kate had no idea.

"What the…" screamed Sophie from the shower as the water dribbled to a stop mid-lather.

Kate had stopped listening to her older daughter's complaints. The bird song had stopped. An eerie silence had descended. A silence that was no longer possible in the modern world. Somewhere, an engine droned or a motor whirred or a vent expelled. An electrical circuit buzzed. Silence was not something you heard often and when you did, it was a sound you struggled to remember. Total and complete silence. Kate ran back to her bedroom as a streak of light flashed in the distance. She grabbed Ava and Danny, pulling them tight into her body and shielding their eyes from what she sensed would follow.

The mushroom cloud was an image everyone understood and one that no one ever wanted to witness. But here it was, rising ever higher in the distant sky. She knew what it was. The location was North West of Boise. The new nuclear power station at New Plymouth had just blown up. Correction, she thought, taken out. Something had hit it, whether lightning, an asteroid or a missile, something had struck it from above. The house shook gently before the crack of the diminishing shock wave finally hit them almost four seconds after the cloud had risen. Its power was enough, over forty miles away, to rattle every window violently in the house.

"Mom!" Sophie joined them, her hair plastered in soap suds, her eyes transfixed on the image in the distance. Her arms wrapped fiercely around the family as all four clung to each other for support.

Kate pulled them closer. She had no illusion as to how hard it was about to become. Their life, as they knew it, was over. The world would never be the same again.

Chapter 2

Radiation. As the cloud dissipated, Kate's first thought turned to radiation. She turned to her tablet, and picked it up before the realization that it wouldn't work hit her. Over forty miles. Was that far enough? She had no idea. The plant was new, only commissioned two years earlier in 2025.

"Mom, it's okay," said Ava as if reading her mind. "We did this at school when the power station opened. In a catastrophic failure, we're safe. As long as you're more than three or four miles away, it's fine."

"That's right," nodded Sophie. "They told us we're outside the danger zone, no matter what happens."

A banging on the front door made them all jump.

Kate turned to Sophie, her wet towel clinging to her. "Go and get dressed, honey, quick." She watched her daughter leave, her fifteen years hidden in the body of an eighteen-year-old. Both girls were going to be heartbreakers, of that there was little doubt. They already had a number of admirers. Her eyes fell to Danny, the poor boy so innocent and at times, victim to a house bursting at the seams with female hormones.

"Mom, my hairdryer's not working," shouted Sophie, frustration deep in her voice. Ava just shook her head and walked away. Kate considered answering but stopped herself, whatever she said was just going to sound condescending. She took a leaf out of her younger daughter's book and followed her, leaving Sophie to work out the problem on her own.

The door banged again.

Kate waved Ava back. "Who is it?" she shouted as firmly as her nervousness allowed her. She was the parent. She was responsible for keeping her children safe, her alone. Tim had been the undisputed protector of the house, powerful and commanding. She had never once felt nervous of the door being knocked on while he'd been in the house.

"It's Harry, from next door. Just wanted to check you guys were okay?"

Kate relaxed, Harry was their next-door neighbor, a widower in his eighties., a lovely old man who had looked out for them since Tim's death. He had gone out of his way to say hi and throw the kids a smile and do 'man things' with Danny. Letting him tinker with his tools, help out in the garden, ask him about the game the previous night. All things Kate never had an inclination, nor the time to do. Her every waking hour was generally consumed with ensuring she could house, feed, and clothe her children, something, as Sophie was only too quick to point out, she was struggling to do.

Kate opened the door, letting Harry in and ushering Ava to go and get dressed.

"Don't worry about the radiation, we're outside any exclusion zone they'd set up," he said, catching his breath as he spoke. A lifetime of smoking had taken its toll on his lungs.

Kate nodded. "Yeah, the girls were told the same at school."

"Coffee?" she asked.

"How're you making that?" asked Harry with a deep hacking laugh.

Kate thought back to Sophie and the hairdryer. She had been so ready to throw smart ass comments to her daughter for exactly the same mistake.

"Hey, Harry!" said Danny, high-fiving Harry as he

joined them in the living room.

"Hey, Danny!" smiled Harry. "Would you mind giving me and your mom a minute or two?"

Harry waited for Danny to close the door behind him.

"I'll wait with the kids. You need to go and get whatever you can from the store," he said, handing her a handful of bills.

Kate looked at the handout and shook her head. I've got plenty in for the next few days, enough to see us through the next week or so if I stretch it out. I'm sure by then, things will be back to normal.

"I can see it in your eyes. You know as well as I do, there isn't going to be normal anymore. I've been awake since dawn, and nothing's moved or worked long before the power station blew up. That ain't right. Cars don't just stop working, all at once, all of a sudden, for no reason."

"Something hit the power station," said Kate quietly. "Streaked down from the sky and blew it up."

Harry nodded knowingly. "The war in Iran. They said the Russians and that Putin were going to make something of it. We should never have gotten involved."

"You won't hear any arguments from me on that point."

Harry reached across and placed his hand on Kate's. "I'm sorry, I should have thought before opening my mouth."

"Don't be silly, you're just trying to make some sense of what's happening."

"Whatever is happening, you need to take this money and get down to the store. Water and dried goods. Don't waste your time or effort on anything perishable."

"I'll get my keys… God, I did it again."

Harry reached into his pocket and pulled out a revolver, pushing it across the kitchen top towards her.

Kate looked at it and shook her head. "I don't like guns, Harry."

"You're a good-looking woman, Kate…"

"Harry, we live in Boise, not Manhattan, people here look out for one another. You're overreacting."

"Overreacting? If you don't mind me saying, you're being naïve and you've got three kids to take care of."

"I know what my responsibilities are, thank you," she snapped.

Harry held up his hands in surrender. "I'm sorry, but I really think you are overestimating the charitable nature of your fellow humans in a crisis." He pushed the revolver nearer to her.

Kate ignored it, but took the cash. Without it, she had nothing but plastic and without power that was useless.

"Sophie, you ready?" she shouted up the stairs.

"Not without a hairdryer, I'm not!"

"You need to come to the store with me."

"Are you crazy? I'm not going outside with my hair like this!" she shouted with a finality that Kate knew deserved a fight but had little will to enter into.

Danny appeared at her side. "I'll come with you. I can attach my radio flyer trailer to my bike," he smiled. His young mindset had already readjusted to their new reality.

Harry offered her the revolver again.

"I don't like guns!" she said firmly.

Chapter 3

Danny wound the handle to open the garage door, Kate having tried the clicker, much to his amusement. With the door partially open, they rode out onto the street. Kate paused, she'd not have thought twice about leaving the garage door open previously. It was a wonderful neighborhood; safe, secure and a perfect place to raise the kids. Although only a resident for a few months, they had been made her feel welcome from day one, and she'd instantly felt at home in the vibrant and welcoming community.

Sitting in the foothills of the mountains, they were afforded spectacular views across the plain, the city of Boise, and beyond. From their house, they could see across most of the Boise-Nampa Metropolitan area, almost five counties and home to three quarters of a million people; often called Treasure Valley. Bike and hiking trails started just yards from their front door and Tim had made sure the family was well-prepared to take advantage of it. Within a day of moving in, they had each been outfitted with a new mountain bike. Ava's and Sophie's had yet to see the light of day, while Kate's bike hadn't seen the great outdoors since the day she had succumbed to Tim's pleading to join him and Danny. She looked back into the garage. One useless car and three top-of-the-line mountain bikes lay for the taking.

"Honey, would you mind rolling the door back down?"

Danny looked at her quizzically. He'd never shut the

garage door in his life. Once opened, he'd disappear for hours, only closing it if he remembered on his return.

"Kate, everyone okay?"

Kate turned to find one of the more active members of the Warm Springs Mesa community walking towards her.

"Thankfully, yes, Barbara. And you guys?"

"Yes, thank you, all fine, but I can't believe it. It's like…like someone just switched us off," struggled Barbara.

"Even our water's off," said Kate.

"Same as everyone else. I can't find out what's happening. The phones are down. The cars aren't working. Even Gary, over on Rockridge Way, you know, from the Sherriff's department? Well, even his radio's not working. He cycled down there an hour ago. Hopefully, we'll hear more when he gets back."

Barbara lived two streets over from Kate. Her husband, Roger, was a local businessman who was, as all the ladies of the small community were well aware, a player. He had contacted Kate a few times over the previous couple of months, offering his 'support', a support she was sure Barbara knew nothing about, nor a support Kate was in the least interested in, and had made that point abundantly clear to Roger. Kate had come close to outright telling Barbara, but after a couple of hints elicited, a "you know Roger" from Barbara, with a smile that failed to hide a deep hurt in her eyes, it was clear she was not only aware, but didn't want to hear about her husband's antics. She had a lovely house and garden, didn't need to work, and had obviously decided his failings were worth the reward.

Kate could deal with the Rogers of the world. She had deterred many an admirer in her time. Whether before Tim, or while he was on operations overseas, she'd had her fair share of unwanted admirers. Tim had always laughed when she had relayed the stories on his return. 'I don't understand what I'm doing wrong?', she would say, only to be wrapped in his arms and deafened by his hearty laugh. 'That's why I love you so much. You've no idea just how damned hot you are!'

Kate turned away from Barbara as thoughts of Tim flashed through her mind. The house, another reminder. Danny came out of the front door. A small Tim. Everywhere she turned, she was reminded of the only man she had ever loved. The house, sitting above the plain with its perfect views, was *his* dream home. It had cost them every penny they could scrape together, and then some. She loved and hated it in equal measure. Unlike nearby communities, theirs were individually built homes, not symmetrical estates where you got to choose from only one of three or four house types.

"Are you sure you're okay?" asked Barbara.

Kate wiped a tear from her eye. "Yes, yes, I'm fine," she smiled as genuinely as she could, watching Danny jump on his bike. "We're just going to go down to the supermarket and see what we can pick up."

"Roger's there now. The minute he realized the power was out, he was out of here in a second. I couldn't even speak to him; he was in such a hurry to get to the store."

Yet here you are, holding me back, thought Kate. "Anyway, we better get going. See you soon, Barbara."

The cycle to the store was easy, downhill all the way. Kate had never seen so many bikes on the roads but then, she'd never seen the roads with no moving cars either. There were a lot of norms that were going to change, she surmised as they freewheeled most of the way in the late autumn sunshine. Kate was thankful that she had insisted on the windbreakers, as her face bore the brunt of the icy breeze that the low hung sun failed to warm.

If Kate had any illusions that the world would soon return to normal, they were squashed the instant that

Albertson's, their local supermarket, came into view. Police officers surrounded the building, while a large crowd of customers waited angrily for their chance to enter. Kate and Danny joined the quickly growing line that was filling the empty car lot and much like the rest of those in line, kept their bikes by their sides.

"If everybody could just keep calm, please. We're trying to ensure that everyone gets some food and water," shouted one of the officers. Kate counted twenty-two officers protecting the supermarket.

Angry shouts were hurled back. A number of those in the line did not appreciate the police taking control, likening the control to something that the Russians would do.

Kate tried to ignore the shouting and attempted to find out what she could from those around her. An hour later, she had discovered that everyone, including the authorities were as in the dark as she was. Potentially more so, as nobody else seemed to be aware that the power station had been struck by something prior to its explosion.

The crowd had grown steadily in that time and despite the occasional shouts of disdain, people remained surprisingly well-behaved and controlled. Kate could see the line looping numerous times as it snaked through the parking lot, ending up nearly at the main road. She guessed there must have been over a thousand people behind her but thankfully, only a hundred or so in front.

To almost everyone, the current situation was the result of a catastrophic disaster at the nuclear power station. A man nearby was explaining in some detail, to all who wanted to listen, how an electromagnetic pulse could have caused all electrical and electronic circuits to fail. Kate understood little of his detailed explanation and zoned out as he digressed to the banning of diesel engines. due to nitrogen oxide levels ten years earlier, and the fact that they may have survived the pulse effects. As it was, the enforced hybrid generation of vehicles stood little to no chance against such a catastrophe.

"But the cars had stopped before the explosion," said Kate to herself, but loud enough for those around to hear.

"The explosion was over forty miles away. It is a massive site, there must have been others we didn't see. What we witnessed was the final explosion," explained the man.

"But what about radiation?" asked another person.

"Actually, what we witnessed was a relatively low yield explosion, the ultimate height of the cloud was quite low. The height of the cloud determines the scale of the explosion. We're probably looking at a yield of between ten to twenty kilotons. Honestly, even without the extensive safety procedures that are in place to contain any fallout, there is no danger to Boise, or for that matter, anywhere outside of the immediate vicinity of the explosion."

"And what makes you such an expert?" called someone from the crowd.

"I'm a Physics lecturer at Boise University, specializing in Nuclear Engineering."

"Oh, okay, thanks," replied the questioner quietly.

Kate noticed the people around her relax as the 'expert' confirmed they were safe from radiation. It was clear that the majority felt whatever had happened was temporary, a local problem that would be fixed as soon as the State and Federal Emergency plans kicked in. The Governor would be asking the president for help and FEMA, with its billions of dollars of federal funding, would ride into Boise and save the day. Kate was not convinced. They were over forty miles away from the plant. Whatever the expert claimed, that was one hell of a long distance for small explosions to disable every electronic device in Boise. She had not seen one piece of electronics work. Even the police officers' radios were useless. She had watched as notes were delivered to the officers while they waited.

"You don't agree?" the woman next to Kate, had been watching her.

"Sorry?" asked Kate.

"You don't think this was just an accident?"

Kate shrugged. "I don't know what I think," replied Kate honestly, "but I'm going to assume the worst and pray for…"

"Mom," Danny pulled at Kate's jacket, attracting her attention away from the woman.

"I'm talking, Danny."

"Mom," he pulled again, more insistent.

"I'm sorry," she offered to the woman, bending down to Danny.

"That's very rude," she chastised her son for his manners. He ignored her and pointed over to a corner of the lot where a small group of men had gathered. The group was obscured from the police and the majority of the line by the building. In a few seconds, Kate would lose sight of them as the line would take her and Danny around the final loop towards the supermarket entrance. They were nearly there.

"Mom?"

Kate looked around desperately. The last thing she wanted to do was create a scene. She looked over to the nearest officer as she inched out of the group's line of sight and waved wildly for him to come to her.

"Ma'am, you'll just have to wait your turn," he called over.

Kate waved more insistently. The officer nodded to his colleague and headed to her.

"What?"

She leant forward and whispered in his ear, much to the disgust of those queuing around her. She could see how it looked, good-looking woman trying to charm her way to the front or get some sort of special treatment.

However, the looks of disgust were short-lived, as the officer snapped back from Kate's whisper and rushed to his colleagues.

If there were a point that Kate had to define as the point that the world turned to complete and utter shit, it would have been that moment.

Chapter 4

Kate pulled Danny behind her as the first of the group of men burst around the corner. She didn't like guns, but knew them well enough to know that the men meant business. AR-15 assault rifles were aimed at the policemen and balaclavas covered their faces, suggesting they weren't entirely convinced that civilization was completely gone for good.

The police to their credit stood their ground, their service revolvers looking pitiful, in comparison to the assault rifles they faced. Kate counted nine men in balaclavas facing down the twenty or so policemen. As the first screams cut through the crowd, the stampede began. Kate held on tight to Danny, keeping herself between him and the gunmen as the crowd pushed and pulled around them.

As hard as she fought, she couldn't keep her feet and both crashed to the ground. Kate managed to cover Danny with her own body as the crowd stamped and kicked their way to safety.

"Just let us into the store and walk away. Nobody needs to die today," called one of the hooded men, stepping forward. His voice was calm and clear as he pointed his rifle with unnerving confidence at the officers.

Kate and Danny were caught only yards from the incident. The crowd had gone in seconds, dissipating into the surrounding neighborhood. Hopefully, some of them would alert the police and back up would be on the way. However, that wouldn't be any time soon, as the only form of communication was person-to-person and the police headquarters was nearly four miles away in downtown Boise.

Kate tried to move. A police officer waved for her to stop. She was safer where she was, given that the tension between the police and the men was rising. Kate shielded Danny, holding him as tight as the day she had given birth to him.

"Walk away!" commanded the man.

"This is crazy, guys. In a day, things will be back to normal," offered the senior officer, a sergeant who had made his way to the front of his men. "Just put your guns down and we'll forget this ever happened."

The man in charge of the hooded men scoffed, "You have no idea what's happened. Tomorrow, the next day, the day after, this is the new normal." He waved his arms around dramatically. "We're screwed! The sooner you realize that, the greater the chance you'll survive. Get in that store and take what you can for your families. You won't get another chance."

"It's just an accident, the power will be back on soon."

"Look above us," said the hooded man.

None of the officers did.

"It's not a trick. Just you, look above us."

The sergeant looked. "So? It's a beautiful day, clear blue sky."

"Do you think there was a simultaneous nuclear power plant disaster in Washington, Portland, San Francisco, or anywhere else for that matter?"

"I wouldn't have thought so," said the sergeant, still searching the sky for whatever he was missing.

The hooded man joined him in looking up. "So, where're all the planes? Not a one. Not one plane has flown over the city all morning. Not one. There are hundreds of flights supposed to be up there at any time, casting their vapor trails, flying from Seattle to New York, Chicago or wherever, you get my point? Not a one. Not one."

More of the officers began to look up. As did Kate and Danny. She had never really looked to see planes flying high above them before, and wasn't even sure if you would see them, but she certainly was used to seeing the vapor trails.

"The world has changed, you just don't know it yet. Just walk away and let us get what we need," prompted the hooded leader.

The sergeant looked at his men before turning back to the group. "I'm sorr…"

The gunshot echoed around the empty parking lot. Kate threw her hand over Danny's eyes as the sergeant's head bore the brunt of the shot. The look of shock was etched on his face as his lifeless body slumped to the ground. Kate managed to quell her scream, despite it being the most shocking thing she had ever seen.

The police officers were stunned into inaction. All looked to one another for inspiration - fight back or concede? The leader's AR-15 muzzle smoked from the single round it had spent in proving his resolve. It had been a calculated gamble. It worked. The officers weren't willing to die for a world that may no longer exist. Their inaction proved that. They all lowered their weapons and walked away.

"I'm sorry you had to witness that," offered the hooded leader to Kate as his men, grabbing two small trailers, pulled them by hand towards the supermarket. Kate was fighting to keep the contents of her stomach down as the man spoke. His voice was familiar, but she desperately didn't want to place it. She had no wish to know who the cold-blooded killer was. She just wanted to get her son as far away from there as possible.

Running boots preceded the arrival of more men. Kate looked up briefly to see another five, hunting rifles with scopes slung over their shoulders. Pistols were holstered on their hips. Snipers oversaw the operation. Whoever this group was, the men were well-prepared and willing to do whatever had been necessary to secure what they wanted. Fourteen men who, by the looks of them, had money and looked after themselves and their equipment well. Their clothing, Kate knew, was top of the line. She recognized a number of brands, all high-end, all-weather gear. Their weapons weren't cheap either. Kate didn't like them, but knew enough to know quality. These weren't hardened criminals. They were people from the community who obviously felt times had changed, to the point they could gun down policemen, and not have to worry about the dire consequences.

"He was just doing his job," she managed as the sergeant's dead body caught her eye again, and an overwhelming feeling of sickness rushed over her.

"His job's redundant now. He just didn't know it yet," said the hooded leader with little feeling. His mind was already moving on to his next task. He was pointing to a location on a map, and issuing orders to his team.

"And who made you judge, jury, and executioner?"

The leader looked down at her. Although she couldn't see his mouth through the balaclava, she could see the smile in his eyes. He cupped his manhood in one hand and thrust his rifle forward with the other.

"These and this!" he proclaimed proudly, much to his men's amusement.

"Yet you hide your face." Her outrage at his arrogance and belief he could take whatever he wanted was rising.

"Mom," cried Danny. He was shaking in her arms, wanting her to stop. He knew her buttons. He knew that tone of voice when she had been pushed too far. It was a tone that stopped all of her kids in their tracks. A tone that she had just used with the shooter.

"Makes us more menacing!" he laughed.

"Or not sure you're right and hiding your identities from the authorities in case you're wrong?"

"Oh, we're not wrong," he said, peeling off his balaclava.

Kate instantly recognized the man she had seen many times before. Bob Jackson, an assistant principal at the high school, coach of the Little League baseball team, and one of the most prominent members of the community. With his face revealed, the rest of the men removed theirs. These men were confident that there would be no repercussions. Kate recognized a number of the men from the local area, one had even been in her home, a well-respected local plumber.

"I suggest you take what you can for you and your family before you go. You won't get another chance," said Bob, ending their conversation.

"I can give you a hand," said one of the group, offering Kate a hand to help her up.

Kate looked at the man offering his hand. He had hovered near Bob throughout the encounter with the police. A snide grin seemed to be permanently affixed to his face. His hair was slicked back and despite having worn a balaclava, remained perfectly in place.

Kate turned to Danny. "No thanks," she replied loudly, standing and helping Danny up.

The man's grin remained affixed to his face, but the warmth was gone. His eyes scanned every inch of her body, taking in a view he very much appreciated and wished to enjoy.

Kate caught the lascivious look, and the man smiled and winked. The smile held a promise that Kate had no intention of ever letting the man live up to.

"Trey! Leave her be, you hear?" instructed Bob.

Trey licked his bottom lip and winked as he walked away, not taking his eyes off of Kate.

Kate stared him down, offering him no suggestion that she was the least bit intimidated by him. His smile grew, the more she stared him down.

"Be seeing you," he mouthed and blew her a kiss as he walked out of sight and into the supermarket.

"Be careful with him," warned another member of the group as he walked by.

"I don't intend to be anything with him!" she called defiantly, with as much courage and bravado as she could muster. Trey had rattled her. She could see through him. He was a predator. Whether he had acted on his urges before, she didn't know. She guessed not, but with law and order gone, who was going to stop the Treys of the world? Who would protect the Kates and their families from the Bobs and Treys who believed they could take what they wanted when they wanted it?

"Kate?"

Kate turned to the source of her name, one of the snipers who had just rejoined the group.

"Roger?!"

Barbara's husband walked closer, out of the rest of the group's earshot. "I never thought…" he said quietly, looking forlornly towards the sergeant's body. She could see he meant it. Roger, the player, was nowhere to be seen. He was genuinely upset at how events had transpired.

"I can see that," she comforted.

"You really should stock up on what you can," he pointed towards the store.

Kate shook her head, the thought of taking anything seemed wrong. The sergeant's body was a symbol of a line crossed.

"You'd be doing it for your kids," argued Roger. "Trust me, this isn't ending anytime soon, if ever."

"What do you guys know?"

"Not much, but the power went out long before the plant exploded and it was no accident."

Kate nodded. "I know, I saw it get hit by something."

"So you know you need to get in there and grab whatever you can!"

Danny pulled at his mom to do as Roger said. She stood firm, the thought of seeing Trey in there sent a shiver through her.

"Come on, I'll go with you and watch out for Trey. He's a bit of a loose cannon, new to the area, Bob's cousin, just came in from somewhere., wouldn't be surprised if that 'somewhere' was prison, to be honest."

Ten minutes later, they cycled out of the shopping center's parking lot with the radio flyer trailer, backpacks, pockets, and handlebars, buckling under the weight of their haul.

Trey watched them go and turned to Roger once they had disappeared from sight. "You're going to tell me everything you know about that particularly fine piece of ass!"

Chapter 5

Kate breathed a sigh of relief as they cycled out of the center and rejoined the safety of tree-lined Parkcenter Boulevard. Danny was ahead of her, his little legs pushing hard to pull their haul along the road. They had a mile and a half to go and although not a big hill to climb, it was a long, slow rise. She knew it was going to be seriously hard work. The men had loaded them up with canned foods, all extremely heavy, but exactly what her family needed.

She hated herself for taking the food, but under the circumstances, she'd had little choice. She tried desperately to erase the image of the sergeant being shot, but she knew it was an image that would live with her forevermore. Tears began to flow, releasing the tension she had felt, the sadness for the sergeant's death, the worry she had for her family's future. She didn't know which had triggered the tears, but they flowed freely and copiously. She watched Danny fight with every push of his pedals, the weight in the trailer easily twice his own. She thanked God he hadn't seen the sergeant being shot. Being there was bad enough, and seeing the body was traumatic, but nowhere near as bad as witnessing the moment of impact - seeing a man transition from life to death in the blink of an eye, the bullet extracting life as it passed through him.

"Mom, you ok?"

Tears were streaming down her face, she wiped her eyes with her sleeve. "This cold wind is making my eyes run!" she said, forcing a smile.

A movement to her right flashed in her blurry vision.

"Freeze, don't move!" A police officer had jumped out of the tree line. It was the officer she had called over to in the parking lot to tell him about the group. She noted his name tag. Miller.

"You did ok," he quipped, surveying her haul from the supermarket.

A number of his colleagues joined him, all looking disdainfully at Kate's proceeds, following their colleague's death.

"After you abandoned us…" began Kate.

"Tactically withdrew," corrected a more senior officer, joining the conversation and dismissing his subordinates. "I believe you alerted my officers to the threat?"

Kate caught sight of more police officers in the park next to the road. They were dressed in tactical gear and carried rifles, similar to those the hooded group had. The police were not, as first suspected, rolling over and giving up.

"Oh thank God, you are doing something!" She could have hugged them all. "Yes," she reverted to answering the question. "Well actually, it was Danny who spotted them first."

"Well, thank you, son," the officer smiled at Danny. "I'm Lieutenant Faulkes."

Danny sniggered.

The lieutenant looked at Kate, not seeing the joke.

"Your name is Faulkes, he thought you said Fox. Our name is Wolfe."

"Uh, oh, okay." After losing a fellow officer and facing a heated gun battle, it was clear he wasn't in a joking frame of mind.

"So, there are nine men, all armed with AR-15 assault rifles?"

Kate shook her head. "No, fourteen men. Well, at

least fourteen. Nine armed with rifles and the other five with hunting rifles. All have pistols and knives as well."

"At least fourteen?" the lieutenant looked at officer Miller, who Kate had initially warned. He shrugged. He had been unaware of the five 'snipers'.

"Would they have brought all their lookouts down to help?" asked Kate.

"Highly unlikely, which means we have a far bigger problem than we thought we had. Without vehicles, we have little or no cover, certainly not against high-powered sniper rifles."

"Any idea who they were?" he asked, almost as an aside.

"Sorry, yes, the leader and shooter is Bob Jackson, he's…"

"Coach of the Little League, Bob Jackson?" asked the lieutenant, genuinely shocked.

"His cousin, Trey…and I recognized a few others," added Kate, listing off the men she'd recognized. Both officers stood in silence as she named a number of known local citizens.

"But they were all hooded?" said the officer.

"They were, but they took them off when I suggested they were hiding, unconvinced of what was happening."

"What do they think is happening?" asked the lieutenant.

"They think this is it. Civilization is over. The Russians or whoever have nuked us into the dark ages."

"Yeah, he told us to look for the planes overhead. You know, the ones going cross-country, flying high over us and leaving vapor trails?" added the officer.

The lieutenant looked up. The sky was clear, no vapor trails were visible.

"And they're so confident they're right, they exposed themselves after killing the sergeant?"

Kate nodded.

"What do you think?" he asked her pointedly.

"The plant was struck by something before it exploded."

"I've heard a couple of people suggest…"

"I saw it myself. Something came down from the sky just before the plant exploded. This wasn't an accident."

The lieutenant nodded but merely listened, not divulging his thoughts.

"Well, thank you, and I'm pleased you managed to get something for your efforts. It can't have been easy for you. My guys were pretty shook up at what they saw." The lieutenant ruffled Danny's hair. "See you later, Wolfe!"

"Best you both get as far from here as you can. This may get quite nasty, and high-powered rifle rounds can travel quite a long way."

Kate didn't need to be asked twice. She hurried Danny forward, wishing the police well in their efforts.

"Lieutenant?" Officer Miller prompted his commanding officer.

The lieutenant watched Kate and Danny cycle away, replaying what she had said in his mind. He looked to the forty officers that were preparing themselves in the small park. What if the group of men were right, what if this was an attack? What if the power didn't come back on, the water stayed off, and there were no more deliveries of food? Not one truck or car had made it into the city since early that morning, and hours had passed. Where was the traffic that was driving to Boise from two hundred miles away, far out of the reach of any effects of the plant's explosions, or shielded by the mountains? He looked up, where *were* the planes?

He had a wife and two sons, both of whom were on Bob Jackson's Little League team. He knew Bob well. He was a popular guy, and the leader of a militia group that the police had looked into a couple of times. He couldn't remember what they were called, but recalled they stood for minimal authority and were strong advocates of the second amendment. He also remembered, most importantly, they were all well-trained. A number of the members were ex-military and the group trained regularly. He looked back at his men and up into the sky. If the world had gone to shit, he was sending his men into a firefight where many could and probably would be killed or injured. They had families like his waiting at home and who would need them more than ever, if that were the case? He thought of his wife and child.

"Lieutenant?" prompted Miller again.

The lieutenant snapped out of his thoughts. He looked around at the community, a community he had sworn to protect and defend.

"Okay, men, here's what we're going to do!" he said proudly for all to hear.

Chapter 6

Kate recoiled as the sound reverberated across the surrounding hills, the slopes of the rising hills working like an amphitheater for the plains below. She looked back as the sound repeated, before increasing in regularity to the point she couldn't make out the individual shots. A full-on firefight had broken out. She and Danny were almost home and well out of the danger area, but that didn't make it any less frightening. Both pedaled faster, increasing the distance between themselves and the gunfight.

***

The lieutenant had split his men into four groups of ten. They were going to attack from all four points at once. His biggest problem was going to be communication. They didn't have any. With timing their only way to coordinate their attack, it was imperative all four teams were in place at the allotted time.

Teams North and West would lay down cover fire across the open parking lot from whatever cover they could find, distracting the militia group while Team South, led by the lieutenant, would attack from the rear and Team East, led by Miller, would infiltrate from the East. With a fifteen-minute countdown underway, the four groups moved stealthily towards their allotted positions. With twenty seconds to go, all were nearing their final positions when the first shot rang out.

A sniper atop Gordman's department store had followed the progress of two of the teams. He was one of many spotters watching the police position themselves for their assault. Another atop Albertson's, tracked the progress of the Southern team. Bob Jackson tapped his sniper as he joined him.

"How many?"

"Ten per team, and looks like four teams," replied the sniper.

Bob scanned around the rooftops. His snipers were positioned across the Southshore Shopping Center's buildings. A loose collection of commercial properties and banks spread across three parking lots. At its heart, sat Albertson's grocery store. His snipers had eyes on every potential route towards the supermarket, positioned on the roofs of buildings at the periphery of the small shopping complex, each with a clear line of sight to one another. They knew exactly what was coming and when.

Ideally, they'd have been at the supermarket before the police and would have avoided the interaction, having taken what they'd needed and bugged out as their plan dictated. However, the shit hitting the fan during the night had taken them by surprise and the majority of his men hadn't appeared until eight that morning, when they'd realized the TEOTWAWKI event that Bob had been predicting had occurred. Bob had had to contain his excitement when he had first awoken to the realization his predictions had come true. The world as they knew it was over. It was time for a new dawn, a new world, where those who were prepared and ready to do whatever was needed would survive. Those who were strongest, both physically and mentally, would prevail. The time for 'live and let live' and liberal nonsense was finally over.

He had made his way to the storage bunker, arriving at 6.30 a.m. as he had ordained. By seven, ten of his men had arrived and he had been tempted to make the run to the supermarket then, but every time he thought he'd set off, another couple of stragglers had arrived. By eight, he had thirty-six of his sixty-two members and they watched the power station take a hit before exploding, eliminating any doubts that they were living through an end of the world scenario. The world, as they knew it was over, and new rules applied. Life was now about survival and only those prepared to do whatever was necessary would prevail. With all doubt removed, supplies needed to be secured. Leaving six men behind to plan and prepare, and to bring the stragglers up to speed, he'd moved out.

Obtaining supplies and securing their base were crucial. The base could wait. It wasn't going anywhere. Supplies, however, were vital. As soon as people realized what was happening, stores would be emptied in the ensuing rush. Over the next few hours, the major stock sources would be emptied, leaving him with piecemeal supplies, available from house to house sorties, a protracted and inefficient use of his resources. Winter was coming and he needed to secure foods for the new community that his men would form.

The delay had cost them. The police were in situ and were controlling access to the supermarket and rationing goods, something he could not allow. He needed to show resolve. He needed to show he was a leader who would do whatever was required. He took no pleasure in killing the sergeant, but he was sure that the message it portrayed to all those who'd witnessed it would save many lives in the future.

Bob indicated to his sniper where to shoot first. The sniper nodded. Bob tapped his shoulder as he took aim, delaying the shot.

"No suppressor," he said, having noticed the man's HK417's adornment.

"Gotcha," acknowledged the sniper, removing it and reacquiring the target. Bob signaled to his surrounding snipers, counting down from three. He had instructed the sniper next to him to fire on one and not wait for the final signal.

As he reached one, the single shot echoed across the empty and silent lot. The amphitheater effect amplified the crack for all of Boise to hear.

***

The lieutenant checked his watch as he directed his men into their final positions.

"I've got movement on the Albertson's roof," advised one of his marksmen. "Two men, one is signaling to others by the looks of it."

"Have you got the shot?"

"Yes!"

The lieutenant checked his watch, it was too early. His men weren't going to be ready.

"Sir…" prompted the marksman urgently. The signaler had just lowered one of three raised fingers.

"Take it!" instructed the lieutenant.

The impact of the sound knocked him to the ground. A second distinct shot rang out before the noise became one. The lieutenant tried to get himself back on his feet. His mind was willing, but his body resisted. His head rose, but his body remained down. He looked down at a wetness swelling on his shirt. His breathing became labored as his mind suddenly caught up with his physical state. He had been hit, the first shot, center mass. His head slumped back, the strain of holding it up was too much.

"Put pressure on it!" he heard, but felt nothing. He could sense motion, but felt nothing. His view changed, he was being pulled into cover. He couldn't feel anything below his neck, his spine most likely severed, he thought. He stared at the only place he could - straight up. He looked for the vapor trails, anything. Nothing. What had he done? His wife and kids would be lost without him. If the world was over, he had left them defenseless. He searched the sky, desperate to see something, praying that he could see something to prove Bob Jackson wrong. Desperate to see that his wife and kids would be okay without him. Life as they knew it would be restored.

"Why's he smiling?" asked one of his men as the lieutenant gasped his final breath.

Nobody answered, only the lieutenant knew. The tiniest flash of light was all it had taken, the slightest of glints in the clear blue sky.

***

As Bob's third finger fell, the head of the sniper to his left, snapped back. The police had returned fire instantly. Bob ducked down, content in the knowledge that the senior officer he had directed his sniper at was also down. He grabbed the sniper's rifle and rolled across the roof. His snipers on the outer edges of the shopping center were having an easier time. The police had missed them, in their focus to surround the supermarket.

With the police pinned down, Bob signaled to his men from below, up and into the fray. They spread out across the roofline. The police were about to experience another unpleasant reality. Bob signaled to open fire. The AR-15s joined in the action and opened fire, each having been modified to fire on full auto. The high-capacity drum magazines out maneuvered the police who were now outgunned and out of options. They retreated en masse, taking more casualties as they fled.

Bob watched as his men marveled at their new toys. With the rule of law over as far as he was concerned, he had cracked open the special arms case that morning. In peace time, handing out the modified AR-15s would have ensured that he spent the majority of the rest of his life in prison and penniless. The gunsmith who had prepared them was, he'd been assured, one of the very best and as he watched the performance he couldn't disagree. Not one rifle jammed or kicked inadvertently.

With the last of the police officers disappearing out of sight, Bob signaled for his men to cease fire. It had been a salutatory and difficult lesson for the police to learn. They lived in new times and there was a new law in town. Bob's law.

Chapter 7

The final few hundred yards were a killer, the steepest part of the climb and a part that neither of them could have cycled. Even on foot and pushing the bikes was a struggle with all the additional weight. As much as the shooting rattled her and upset Danny, she couldn't help but wonder if without it, there would have been more people on the streets and their trip home more eventful, given the attention that their supermarket haul would have drawn.

While Danny rushed through the house to open the garage door, Kate kept watch over their supplies.

"We were worried," said Harry, coming out on hearing Danny enter the house.

Kate looked down towards the supermarket. "It was awful," she said, her voice wavering. Safely home, the full extent of what they had witnessed began to sink in. Harry let her talk, not wanting to interrupt her. She explained what had happened and how the fighting they'd heard would have been the police fighting back.

The garage door opened, allowing Harry to avoid having to answer her question. "How'd you think it would have gone?"

Badly, he was sure. What he'd heard was sustained automatic gunfire, not something the police were likely to do. The police had taken a beating. He also was extremely concerned that not only did the group now know who she was, but through Roger, they knew exactly where she lived. As Kate pushed the first bike into the garage, he checked his revolver. He hadn't known the Wolfes long, but they had shown him more kindness than anyone had in many years. Even through their grief, a grief no family should have to suffer, they had kept him in their thoughts, as he had them. They were more family to him than his hopeless son and bitch of a daughter-in-law, who only ever came calling when they needed money.

Danny rushed past him and gathered up his bike and pushed with every ounce of his body weight. Harry snapped himself back into action and helped the youngster. The weight of the trailer was buckling the axle and Harry marveled at how Danny had made it home at all, as they both pushed it the final few yards into the safety of the garage.

Kate rolled the door closed and surveyed their haul. It looked far less when stacked on the garage floor.

"Girls!" she shouted.

Ava appeared almost instantly, Sophie didn't. After a minute and three more shouts, Kate went looking, telling everyone else to stay where they were. She wasn't in the mood for Sophie's histrionics, not after what she had just witnessed. She walked into the kitchen, a large family room that was the heart of their home. The view across their back garden and across to Boise never failed to take her breath away. Yet today, all she could see was the lack of movement. The roads and streets flowed like veins and arteries on any normal day. The city was dead, quite literally dead. Without electricity, it was lifeless. Just like a heart, it needed electricity to jumpstart it.

"Sophie!" she called again. Nothing. Her anger began to manifest into panic. She raced through the house. It wasn't a large house, just four small bedrooms, a lounge, a family kitchen, a two-car garage, and a small garden. The views had sold it to them, particularly Tim, who would sit and watch the aircraft land and take off all day long, given half the chance.

Sophie's door lay open, so there was no reason she hadn't heard Kate's shouts. There was no music to play and the house was deathly silent. Kate heard her before she saw her, deep gasps of breath, a noise she recognized from herself. Tears from a deep dark place, a truly desperate cry. Sophie lay curled in a ball at the end of her bed, hidden from sight. Her body heaving with each gasp as the heart-breaking tears flowed. Kate dropped beside her and wrapped her largest baby in her arms.

"Baby, what's wrong?"

Sophie could barely speak between drawing breaths. "I heard the shooting… and… you, you… weren't here," she managed.

"But we're fine, baby. We're home safe."

She calmed slightly, but the tears continued to flow.

"I know, but I thought about Dad, what he went through, hearing those gunshots…"

Kate pulled her close. "Your Dad wouldn't have felt anything. He died instantly, honey," she lied. She had kept the truth from them since the day she had been told of his death. It was bad enough she'd had to hear the truth. Why they hadn't lied to her, she didn't know. The grief counselor had suggested it was always better for the truth to be known. Kate disagreed, her kids would never know the truth.

"Come on," she guided Sophie up and down to the garage. "See what your brother and I managed to get."

By the time they reached the garage, Sophie had wiped her eyes but in the process, caught sight of her hair. Her focus was diverted, and a new drama unfurled. "We need to get the hairdryer working, Mom!"

"I'll make it top priority," promised Kate.

"Thanks, Mom."

Kate rolled her eyes as she pushed open the door to the garage.

Whilst away, Harry, Ava and Danny had been busy. The collection of cans and dried foods were displayed across the floor, along with the bottles of water and packets of seeds.

"Seeds?" asked Ava, "it's November, Mom. You planning on gardening anytime soon?"

She shrugged. She hadn't noticed the packets of seeds and there were a lot of them.

"Roger helped me get stuff. He must have put them in our packs."

"He must know something we don't. You don't plant these until March."

Kate ignored the seeds and looked at the stockpile of food. It was barely a two-week shop at any normal time. Her cupboards were fairly well-stocked, a Costco trip the previous week had unsurprisingly nearly bankrupted her and laden them with multipacks galore of stuff they didn't really need, at least not then.

She looked at Harry. He had the same look of worry she knew she was projecting.

"I've got more than I need back home," he offered with a knowing and apologetic smile. "We can share whatever I have."

"No, that's not fair. You need to take some of this."

It was thanks to Harry that she had made the run to the supermarket. She hadn't even thought of going until he'd insisted.

"I'm an old man with an old dog, we've more than we need already," he assured unconvincingly.

"No…" began Kate. A loud knocking at the front door froze her. Her immediate thoughts turned to Bob Jackson, Roger, and Trey.

Danny immediately reacted. He was always first to answer the door. Kate caught his arm mid-run and stopped him in his tracks. "Hey!"

"What's wrong, Mom?" asked Ava and Sophie in unison. Harry's hand moved towards his pocket and the revolver.

The door was knocked again. A hard and insistent knock. Kate held her finger to her mouth. Her children looked at her wide-eyed, not knowing what was going on.

Chapter 8

"Kate?" came a shout. "Anyone home?"

It was Carol, the neighbor from the other side of Harry.

"Sorry, just coming!" shouted Kate, ignoring her children's questioning looks.

Carol paced nervously as Kate opened the door.

"Have you seen Harry?" she asked.

"Yeah, he's here," she said, stepping back to let her in.

Carol stayed where she was. "No, but thanks, we're just doing a check on everyone. We're checking on the more vulnerable first. Harry wasn't answering. We were worried."

"We've got another couple not answering, Mrs. Somerville and Frank Hurley, have you seen them since…"

Kate shook her head. Mrs. Somerville lived in the last house on their street. She'd never even heard of Frank Hurley. Carol was their street's representative on the Neighborhood Community Association. Ten streets, working together to build a better community, or something like that. Kate couldn't remember exactly what the shiny brochure had told them when they'd moved in, but it was clear the people in Warm Springs Mesa wanted them to be a part of a friendly and welcoming community.

Harry appeared by Kate's side, just in time to hear mention of Mrs. Somerville.

"I've got a key for Hilary's. She had workmen there a few months ago and she asked me to let them in. She told me just to keep the key."

"Kids, I'll be back in ten minutes," shouted Kate. She felt bad that she had not thought to check on anyone else herself.

As they stepped onto the street, the quiet was disconcerting. It was a beautiful day but no lawnmowers, trimmers, kids playing or cars spoiled the peace that she would normally have craved. She'd expect something to be going on to fill the silence. It was an overwhelmingly young community; family homes in a safe neighborhood. Only a few elderly residents remained. The hilly nature of the neighborhood made for spectacular views, but being built on a slope and on the outskirts of the city made it less favorable for the less mobile. There were a few Harrys and Mrs. Somervilles dotted around the community, but they were by far the exception.

"I've never seen anything like it," said Carol as they paused outside Harry's house.

Both looked out across the city below. It remained static.

"Is Mike home?" asked Kate as they waited for Harry to find the key. Mike was, if Kate remembered correctly, a regional sales manager for an engine manufacturer.

Carol shook her head. "Seattle on business. Due back tomorrow," she smiled.

"Fingers crossed," offered Kate.

"They'll have us back up and running soon, I'm sure," said Carol cheerily. "God, I almost forgot, did you hear all that commotion earlier? Must have been some people set up a range somewhere. All that shooting."

Kate looked at Carol. Her husband was out of town, and her two kids were at college out of state. The truth, if Kate was right about the power and what was to come, could wait.

"I know, what a terrible noise."

"What was a terrible noise?" asked Harry, holding the key for all to see.

Kate answered quickly, hoping Harry would cotton on. "Whoever the folks were that set up a gun range."

"Yeah," he threw her a wink, he understood.

The street consisted of twelve homes. Six either side, either built on the up slope or down slope. All were built to take advantage of the views across the city. Being on the down side, it was the back of Kate's house that faced the street. While those on the up side, their main rooms faced the street. Despite the closeness, shrubbery, and the slope, each of the homes had plenty of privacy. Mrs. Somerville's home was on the up slope, the opposite side from Kate. Her blinds, they could see from the street, remained closed despite the time nearing eleven in the morning. Nobody expected anything other than bad news as they turned the key in the lock.

Carol insisted she go first, just in case Mrs. Somerville was in distress and in no position for a man to find her. Harry stepped back and let Carol pass as he opened the door.

"It's okay, you can come in," shouted Carol.

Kate and Harry walked into the bedroom. Mrs. Somerville lay perfectly still in her bed. Her eyes were closed in what looked like a peaceful sleep.

"She's gone," confirmed Carol as both looked to check that she wasn't just sleeping. "Just passed in her sleep, bless her."

"And so peacefully," added Kate, noting the bedclothes were perfectly in place. Mrs. Somerville had not even moved before her death.

Kate's attention was caught by the classic art deco alarm clock by Mrs. Somerville's bedside. The Bakelite flip clock was a classic and probably worth more than it had been new. "You think this thing still works?"

"No way to know until the power comes back on. Don't see why it wouldn't if it's still plugged in," said Harry, following the power lead.

Kate pointed to the time. "Well if it does, we now know when the power went out." The numbers had stopped flipping at 5.27. Only six hours earlier.

"Oh God," Harry turned to face Mrs. Somerville's body and his face fell. "Hillary had a pacemaker, you don't think…" he said, hoping both would tell him he was being silly.

"And Frank?" asked Carol panicking.

"I'm not sure, maybe," said Harry, sitting heavily in the chair by the bed. "But I do know a lot of other people with pacemakers."

"We don't know that's what happened," offered Kate as cheerily as her convictions would allow. She wasn't convincing either of them. It made perfect sense. Every other piece of electrical or electronic device had stopped working, so why would the pacemaker be any different?

"Hello? Anybody there?" came a shout from the front door. Kate pulled a sheet over Mrs. Somerville's head as Carol left to break the bad news.

Kate and Harry walked through as Barbara was confirming the worst. "Frank as well, peacefully though," added Barbara.

"We think it might be pacemakers, do you know if Frank…" began Kate, joining the conversation.

"Kate, hi! You're back and you're okay," interrupted Barbara, realizing it was Kate. "You didn't see Roger, did you? He's still not back. There was all that shooting at the supermarket and I'm getting really worried."

Carol swung towards Kate. "I thought you said that was just a gun range?"

"Did I? Oh, *that* shooting," said Kate flustered. Both women stared at her, waiting for more.

A red-faced Danny burst into the house. "Mom, you have to come quick!" he managed between deep breaths.

"Sorry!" said Kate, pushing past her inquisitors and following her son out of the house. "What's wrong?" she asked as they rushed back home, with Harry following as fast as he could in her wake.

"Zach appeared. You told me I was to let you know if ever Zach and Sophie were ever alone together in a room."

Kate smiled and thanked God for teenage hormones and child spies.

Chapter 9

"Sophie!" called Kate as she opened the front door.

She checked behind her. Harry and Danny were going to check on Hank, Harry's dog. As soon as she had heard it wasn't a life or death scenario, she had slowed Harry down and asked him to keep Danny company while she dealt with her daughter. She had a feeling that Sophie and Danny would be best kept apart for the next few hours. Poor Danny was totally unaware of how he was, in his sister's eyes, ruining her life. Zach was a senior, captain of the football team, and the boy every girl wanted to be seen with, let alone be with. Sophie was a sophomore and the envy of every girl in the school. Zach lived two streets over and most definitely had a thing for her.

"Hey, Mom," said Ava, appearing in the hallway at the base of the staircase, blocking Kate's progress. "What should I do with the freezer stuff?

Kate looked at her quizzically. "Really, you're running interference for her?!"

Ava shrugged her shoulders and smiled innocently.

"We'll talk about this later," promised Kate. "Sophie!"

Sophie appeared at the top of the stairs. "What's up?" she asked, as though butter wouldn't melt in her mouth.

Kate looked up and had to do all she could to stop herself from laughing. "Apart from your t-shirt being inside out?"

Sophie's face blossomed into a deep red.

"Tell Zach to get down here!" advised Kate sternly.

"I'm going to kill Danny!" said Sophie, storming into her room.

Zach appeared shortly afterwards, suitably embarrassed with the situation. He was a handsome young man, reminding her of Tim in his youth. She tried not to be a hypocrite, the situation wasn't dissimilar. Tim had been a couple of years older and they too had started dating when Kate was just fifteen.

"Let's have a chat," said Kate, steering Zach into the kitchen and stopping Sophie in her tracks. "No, just Zach for now."

Sophie huffed and puffed, but knew better than to argue with her mother when she was in the zone.

"Take a seat, Zach," she ordered, closing the door on her two daughters.

Zach sat down. He looked around the room, concerned as to what was about to happen.

"Zach, you know my husband, Sophie's father, died recently."

He nodded.

"Sophie was his baby, his first child. Tim was a wonderful father, a former footballer like you. Although, he was bigger, a lot bigger. He was a man that feared no man, nothing scared him. Well, that's not entirely true, there was one thing he feared…"

Zach edged forward on his seat as he waited to hear what scared Sophie's father.

Kate left him hanging, turning to look at the plethora of medals and ribbons of Tim's that adorned one wall of the family room.

"What?" asked Zach, not able to wait until Kate's pause was over.

"Pissing me off!" she said, the tone in her voice changing. It was her 'no nonsense, you've gone too far' tone.

At only five feet four inches to Zach's six two, he dwarfed her. Even seated, he was taller than Kate, but he had no doubt whatsoever looking at her that she was telling the truth. She had an inner strength that he could see in her eyes, a strength that far exceeded her physical attributes.

Kate's physical attributes were deceiving. She'd been a gymnast from a young age and throughout her college years, her strength belied her petite size and frame. Had it not been for a young and unexpected pregnancy, there had been every chance that Kate would have gone on to represent her country, such was her ability. She could train harder and longer than almost all of her teammates, and fight through pain to achieve whatever was necessary. She had a resolve and belief that few possessed. She had, as one of her coaches had told her, 'it', that special something that champions had, that extra something that the 99.9% of the population had no idea even existed. He'd struggled to explain what 'it' was to her, other than it was an inner strength, resolve, and belief that drove the very few to achieve extraordinary things.

"Ma'am, I'm sorry. I will not disrespect your house again," offered Zach.

"Good, I'm pleased to hear it," she dropped her tone and smiled warmly. Zach visibly relaxed. "And please, call me Kate!"

"Yes, ma'am," replied Zach.

With another situation resolved, Kate went back to the garage. Ava's blocking strategy of asking about the freezer goods was a good one and one that had Kate thinking. The chest freezer sat at one side of the garage. If she remembered correctly, it would keep the contents frozen for about twenty-four hours if, after the power went out, you kept the lid closed. Seven hours down, she thought. If she cracked the lid, what did it mean? Did it half the twenty-four hours or did it just take an hour off? The important question was simple. Did she think the power would be back on within the day? If not, there was a lot of produce that she was going to have to cook and use or try to store in other ways. If there even were any other ways. She was in fact, hopeless when it came to knowing how long foods lasted. She went by store dates, throwing out food she was certain was perfectly fine, but the date suggested otherwise.

"See? We do need to think about the freezer stuff," said Ava, joining Kate.

Kate turned to her daughter, the questioning look on her face was enough for Ava to crack.

"Okay, maybe I was helping Sophie out," she admitted. Ava was not a liar. She was incapable of lying, especially to her mother. "But we do need to do something or it'll waste."

Kate walked over and gave her a hug. While Sophie was thinking about alone time with Zach, and Danny just thought about having fun, Ava was thinking about the long-term practicalities. She was the sensible one. She was Kate.

"It all comes down to how long do we think the power will be out?" mused Kate.

"Best case, a few days, I'd guess," said Ava.

"In which case, let's get this open and see what we can salvage!" suggested Kate, opening the lid.

"Salvage how?"

"Cook and eat what we can over the next few days."

"Cook how?" asked Ava.

Kate held the lid high, wishing she hadn't broken the airtight seal. Cook, the reason she was worrying about the freezer was because they had no electricity, the same thing that powered their stove and oven. She really wasn't getting with their current situation at all.

"That's a good plan," said Harry, joining them.

"Cook it before it goes bad."

"Cook on what, though?" asked Kate, holding a pack of frozen meat in her hand.

"Cool, barbecue!" said Danny, following in behind Harry.

Ava and Kate shared a look. Why the hell hadn't they thought of that? They were supposedly the brains in the house.

"Do you know how we can maximize the life of what's here?" she asked Harry.

Harry joined her and scanned through the contents. "To be honest, I'm no expert, but I'd say cook it all and consume it over the next two to three days."

Kate looked at the amount of food. It was far in excess of what they needed for the next few days. "Well, I guess you're eating with us for the next few days then," she smiled.

"You sure?"

"Well, it's either that, or a lot of this will go to waste."

"I've got a few things in my freezer and fridge, not a lot, but I'll bring it over and we can cook that too."

"Sophie?!" shouted Kate.

"Yeah," she appeared sullenly, a defiant and angry look, following Kate's earlier intervention in her love life.

"Do you want to ask Zach to stay for lunch?" asked Kate, ignoring the mood.

"Yeah, okay," she huffed and walked back to Zach.

Kate listened. "Hey, my mom wants you to stay for lunch," she said happily.

An urgent knocking at the front door drowned out Zach's response.

Kate turned to Harry whose hand moved to his revolver.

"Kate, it's Roger!" accompanied the next urgent

round of knocking.

"Can nobody just knock a door normally anymore?" she asked, as she approached the front door.

"Are you alone?" she asked through the door.

"Yes," replied Roger, sounding relieved. Kate waved Harry away. He had followed her with his revolver at the ready.

"What, Roger?" she asked, opening the door carefully just in case he had lied.

"Thank God you're okay," he gasped, on seeing her.

"Why? I'd have thought you were more likely to be hurt than me!"

"I didn't stay. I got out of there after you left. I never signed up to kill anyone."

"So what did you sign up for, Roger?"

"It was a bit of camaraderie, weekend hunting trips, some fun with the guys, you know. We shared similar views and gave me an outlet for my frustration at the government..." he paused, trying to think why he had joined Bob Jackson's militia. He couldn't. "It all seems so stupid now."

"And deadly. Just as well you didn't stay. All that gunfire earlier was the police restoring order."

Roger shook his head. "I'm afraid not, the police attack failed. Bob was prepared for them."

"Oh, God," gasped Kate, remembering the faces of the policemen she had spoken with. "But wait, why are you worried about me? If you know the police were beaten, you were there long enough to know I was out of the area."

"Trey, Bob's cousin. He was very interested in you. I'm worried he…"

"What? That he comes here? But how would he know where I live, unless…"

Roger couldn't have looked any more sheepish. "Trey's a very scary guy. It's one of the reasons I left them.

There are a few that are just, well, they're just not right in the head. Unhinged."

"So you gave him my address???!!!" she shouted. "Are you out of your fu…"

"Roger, is that you?" The shout came from further down the street. Barbara had just spotted her missing husband.

"Oh, God," panicked Roger, as his wife rushed towards him. He looked at Kate. "Please don't tell Barbara…"

The crack of gunfire cut his pleas dead.

Chapter 10

Alex threw his hand in the air and clenched his fist. The man by his side stopped instantly.

"What can you see?"

"Utter- -chaos!"

"And more precisely?!" asked Nick as he grabbed his backpack and retrieved his binoculars.

"I've got a group of men, at least twenty, and they…well…" he struggled to understand what he was seeing through his binoculars. "They seem to be forcing people out of their homes at gunpoint. And I mean forcing, literally throwing them into the street. Men, women, and kids."

Nick followed Alex's line of sight towards the small group of houses clustered at the very edge of Boise, just under a mile away. Large homes with perfectly manicured lawns and gardens created an affluent estate, built on the banks of the river. As Alex had said, a group of men were throwing the homeowners out into the street. A large group stood in the middle of the street with their guns at the ready, while smaller groups cleared the occupants out house by house. It was clear that those being thrown out were terrified. Their screams and shouts echoed across the hillside and Nick could see the fear in their faces.

Alex and Nick had flown into Boise the day before. A last minute, unexpected change of plans had given them the opportunity to visit an area neither had visited before. A quick tour of the Boise outdoor retail emporiums supplied the men with the finest all-weather hunting gear that money could buy. A further trip to Boise Guns ensured they were adequately armed for their unexpected excursion. They both loved the outdoors and despite the late hour, had hiked up into the hills and set up camp, high above the city below.

The explosion that morning had rocked them to their core. The mushroom cloud rising in the distance, a sight neither had hoped ever to envisage, had them both checking their kits to ensure they were adequately equipped for what both knew was going to be a longer and harder trip than expected.

"Oh shit!" exclaimed Alex

"What?" asked Nick, swinging his binoculars to where Alex had focused his attention.

The crack of gunfire answered better than Alex ever could. Nick watched as a property owner fell to the ground, the handgun in his hand spilling across his driveway.

"We should do something!" said Nick.

They were just less than a mile way at the brow of a hill, with little or no cover other than their camouflaged fatigues.

"There are at least fifteen civilians out in the open…" argued Alex, "and over twenty heavily-armed gunmen."

Nick grabbed for his MacMillan Talon .340 Weatherby Magnum rifle. "We can't just sit here and watch!"

Alex glanced at his Dakota 76 Safari .338 before looking back to the scene below. There was no doubt the rifles they had purchased were up to the job, but not without endangering the homeowners who faced an overwhelming force at close range.

As a second gunshot rang out, Nick chambered a round and took aim, he couldn't sit back and watch as unarmed innocent civilians were gunned down in front of them. Their only crime, defending their home.

Alex laid down his binoculars, unable to watch any more as a second homeowner fell to the ground, "Nick?"

"I've got the shot!" said Nick, tracking one of the killers.

"All you'll do is make us a target. There's nothing we can do. You can't take that shot."

Another gunshot, another murder below.

"Those are innocent people being slaughtered down there. What if that were your family and there was someone deciding not to help them?"

Alex reached over and raised Nick's rifle gently, aiming it away from the targets below.

"Damn," said Nick. "We need to help."

"You know we can't!" said Alex. "It's as hard for me as it is for you! There are probably thirty heavily-armed men down there. We are two men with bolt-action rifles and no working communications. All we'll do is get ourselves killed and for what? Something we had no power to stop in any event."

Gunfire erupted below, and the screams echoed up the hillside as the sustained fire cut through the homeowners. Both men felt sick to their stomachs.

Alex glanced at his watch. It was just after 10 a.m., two hours since the explosion and less than five hours since the power had gone out. Nobody had envisaged such a quick breakdown in law and order. Not even the wildest modeling had predicted anything like they had just witnessed.

"We're screwed, totally and utterly screwed!" whispered Nick, cradling his rifle and watching the events unfold below.

Alex nodded gently.

"We need to do something," said Nick exasperated.

Alex reached into his backpack and withdrew a notepad and pen. "You're right, we do need to do something. Take notes, as per our orders."

Nick looked at him, and just stared at the heartlessness of the situation. "Sir, yes Sir," he mumbled, taking the pad and pen.

Chapter 11

The small estate, one of the newest in Boise, consisted of twenty homes built with the most advanced building materials available. Superb insulation ensured heat was retained or kept at bay, depending on the season. The tiles on the roof were not merely to keep the weather at bay, they were solar panels. The roof itself became one large solar panel, producing more energy than each house required.

On the very edge of Boise, the only road beyond the estate led to a dam. A bridge over the River Boise offered access to a large housing estate to the front while behind lay hundreds of miles of forest and mountain. The road that followed the river led back towards Warm Springs Mesa and a few smaller estates. The bridge was key, as the main threat to them lay across the river in Boise, not the small communities that lay on the narrow strip of land on their side of the river and in the foothills of the mountains. Tactically, Bob didn't think he could have chosen better as he looked around at their new homes.

"Probably best we killed 'em," said Trey with a smile. "They'd have always been resentful of us taking their homes, always a threat. This way, we have no personal vengeance to worry about."

Bob couldn't argue. He hadn't planned it that way, but when the owner had appeared with a handgun, it'd been necessary for him to show his resolve and leadership. His men needed to see once again, he was going to do whatever it took. He looked back at the homes. They really were perfect and Trey was right, he smiled to himself, they were far more secure this way. Killing kids wasn't something he had considered, but it seemed winners really could do whatever was needed when the time came. Two of his men had paused when they had aimed at the two children amongst the homeowners. But once again, he had proven his leadership and hadn't flinched as he'd shot the two. It was a new world and Bob was going to be someone. It was a world for winners and Bob had proven throughout his life, he'd do whatever necessary to win.

"What about the bodies? Toss them in the river?" asked one of his militia.

Bob shrugged. "We're upstream, the dam's behind us, our water will be fine. Yeah, saves the hassle of burying them or smelling the corpses."

"Bob, you got a minute?" asked another militia man, coming out of one of the homes.

"Yeah, Charlie, what's up?" he asked of his electrician. Bob had had a strict selection criteria for his militia. None realized a number of their memberships rested partly on their trade. Charlie was an electrician. Bob had covered most bases with his selection from medicine to plumbing. There wasn't much that could go wrong that one of his guys couldn't handle. Being single was a major plus, followed closely by unhappily married. Happily married with kids was a definite no. He wanted a strong, focused militia, not men who worried about their wives and kids first, and their duty second. A propensity for violence and time spent in a correctional facility most definitely helped.

"These homes are dead, d-e-a-d," he spelled out.

"Come again?"

"Even though they're off the grid, their electrical circuits are completely gone, fried."

"And you can't fix them?" asked Bob, following a headshaking Charlie towards the house and its electrical system.

Charlie pointed to the circuit boards. You didn't need to be an electrician to know they were useless.

"They need complete new circuitry," he pointed to the board. "These'll all have to come out and be replaced, and I'd imagine we'd need to get them from out of the area. Everything in Boise is gone. I've not seen a board anywhere where the circuits have not been completely burned out and irreparable."

"Oh well, it would have been a bonus, but it's still a great location." He managed to keep his smile, while inwardly wanting to scream in frustration. The main reason he had scouted the location was the ability to have power in exactly this scenario. No power, diminished the benefit of the location significantly. If he had known the power situation, he'd have gone for the Warm Mesa Springs community where there were more houses closer to downtown, with the added benefit of an elevated position.

He headed back out to find Trey. It wasn't too late to change their mind.

"Where's Trey?" he asked.

"Helping dump the bodies in the river."

Bob raced down towards the river. He caught himself, stupidly checking that no traffic was coming, before crossing the road. The succession of splashes as he reached the bank told him he was too late. The bodies were already making their way out into the main flow of the river. It had been a stupid idea.

He considered ordering his men to pull them back out, but didn't want to contradict himself. He looked back at the estate. They'd make do in the short term. He certainly wasn't going to move downstream towards Boise with all of the bodies in the river. It would soon be the only source of water for the city. With no one upstream of the estate, they were at least going to have clean fresh water for the foreseeable future.

He watched the bodies float away. His first mistake. He promised himself there would not be anymore.

Chapter 12

Kate slammed the door in Roger's face as the gunfire, once again, echoed around the hillside. A shiver shot through her as the image of the sergeant being shot, just a few hours earlier, flashed through her mind. The gunfire continued as she updated Harry on Roger's admission. Concern was etched across his face.

"This Trey guy sounds dangerous," he said, toying with his revolver.

"I've dealt with Treys all my life." She waved away his concern. "They're all talk." Deep down, she had a feeling Trey was different. She was worried, but wasn't going to show it.

"Come on, we need to help the kids," she prompted. They had a freezer and a fridge full of food to cook. Zach had already fired up the barbecue, by the time they made it to the back garden. The view was as spectacular as ever, but Kate couldn't help feel that the loss of flow had diminished it. Although beautiful, it looked soulless, which in a way it was. The city of Boise as she knew it was dead.

"Are we going to discuss the water situation? I, like, really need to go!" asked Sophie, out of earshot of Zach. Kate smiled, the sight of her daughter gently dancing on the spot, was a welcome interruption to her deathly thoughts.

"Use the toilet in the main bathroom, if it's yellow…"

"Okay, okay, got it, I'll be flushing though!" she raced away.

Kate followed her into the house. She needed to

switch the water back on. She detoured via the garage, and grabbed a bucket. They could fill the toilet cistern with water from the hot water tank, their only source of water in the short term, and using the 'if it's yellow, let it mellow and if it's brown, flush it down' mantra, they'd hopefully last a while before they needed to work out a long-term solution.

As she walked through the house, she couldn't help but notice items that may no longer have a purpose in their lives. Everywhere she looked, she was reminded of the immense change that was transpiring. Electricity, running water, things that civilization took so readily for granted, and then cleanliness, sanitation, and entertainment. She paused, those were luxuries. She hadn't even focused on the basics; food and clean water. They'd bought food in stores and from reading the labels, little of it was ever local. Fresh vegetables came from all around the world, transported by planes, trains, and trucks. So, if there were no planes, trains, and trucks, was there even enough food locally for the population and if there was, where was she going to get it? She had three kids to take care of on her own. How was she going to feed them, take care of them? The more her mind considered the implications, the faster her heart raced. Her breath started to catch. She had to calm herself. She'd manage, she told herself, she always did. Over the last few months, she'd proven that to herself, if no one else.

Kate regained her composure and joined the cooking party. Zach was proving to be a useful addition to the party. His father had clearly trained him to use the barbecue. The more they cooked, the more ridiculous the amount of food they had to eat over the next few days became apparent. There was easily two weeks' worth of food under normal circumstances, but without refrigeration, she and Harry guessed it would last three days, just to be safe.

"Well, Harry, it looks like you'll be eating with us for the next few days," she said, piling another mound of chops onto the growing pile.

"You know, we should get the food into the basement. Keep it as cool as we can, and keep it good as long as we can," said Harry quietly. He knew it was a touchy subject.

The basement had been Tim's area, his man zone and somewhere, Kate had been unable to visit since receiving the notification of his death. His call-up had been so unexpected that he'd had no time to prepare. 'His man cave,' he'd said 'was a pit. Sorry, babe, I'll tidy it when I get back'. She couldn't bring herself to go down there. Tidying just felt so final, an admission to herself that her Tim was not coming back. He'd said he'd tidy it.

"I'll take it down," offered Harry.

"Don't be ridiculous, Harry. You're not fit to be carrying all this up and down stairs. I'll just have to man up and go down there. Tim's gone, I just have to accept that," she said with a finality that she had struggled to accept before. The sight of a lifeless Boise below and the situation that faced them was such that she had to let go. For the good of her kids and herself, she had to move on.

"But first, we eat!" she announced as another crack of gunfire filled the air.

"Perhaps indoors?" she suggested as another two cracks were issued in response. Nobody argued. Apart from the cool breeze eliminating the heat of the sun's rays, the sound of gunfire, a sound not normally so common, was unsettling.

To describe the feast as substantial would have been unjust. The Romans would have had a hard time beating the amount of food they consumed.

"We need a vomitorium!" said Ava, holding her stomach as she stuffed down another mouthful of ice cream. Kate had foolishly mentioned that it may be some time before they had the chance to have ice cream again.

With that sort of threat, not one drop of three tubs from the freezer was going to be wasted.

"What's that?" asked Danny.

"It's nothing, honey, just a word your sister made up because she feels sick," said Kate, making it clear that no one was to tell Danny what it really meant.

"Do you think school will be back tomorrow?" asked Danny, thankfully moving on.

"I was going to go down after lunch," said Zach. "We've got a big game next week and I wanted to check what the plans were if the power's not on."

"I'll go with you. We can ride down together," said Sophie.

As the sound of gunfire once again echoed across the city below, Kate intervened. "Let's check tomorrow morning. Things are getting a bit crazy out there today."

"We'll be fine," argued Sophie, glaring at her mother. The idea of riding down and being seen with Zach at school was not something to be missed.

"I think your mom's right. Best to stay home today. With no power or water, there's no way school will be open," said Harry. His words held more sway than Kate's, if only for his advanced years, and Kate and Tim's instilling in their children a respect for their elders.

"Best we stay here," said Zach, winning a smile from Kate, although that dropped quickly as another burst of gunfire cut through their conversation.

"That sounded very close," panicked Sophie.

Chapter 13

"We need to pack what we can carry, and leave!" pleaded Roger.

Barbara had jumped to the wrong conclusion on seeing him at Kate's door. After an hour of shouting and arguing, she had finally let him into the house. Explaining that they had to leave their home as a matter of urgency hadn't made his welcome any warmer. Barbara loved her house more than life itself. She'd put up with Roger's flirting and philandering knowing that apart, they couldn't hope to keep it. She had put her life and soul into making it the home she had always wanted, a perfect example of the American home. Even Martha Stewart would have struggled to do better.

"I don't believe you. This is all rubbish."

"These men are killers!"

"And they're going to kill you, why?"

"They'll kill us both!"

"Don't be ridiculous, Roger. If you need to leave, go. To be honest, I'm not sure I can take the humiliation anymore anyway."

"I can't leave you here alone. When they come for me, they'll kill you."

Barbara stormed out of the room. She was convinced that Roger had just screwed the wrong wife and an irate husband was on the warpath. She wouldn't listen to his warnings about Bob and his militia. Roger checked his watch. It had been three hours since he had snuck away from the militia, and ninety minutes since the gunfire he was sure came from Bob's new estate. He couldn't bear to think of what had been done to the homeowners. Their only crime was owning the homes that Bob had targeted.

Leaving the militia was not an option. That had always been made clear. Very clear. Roger was party to information that Bob would not want anyone else to know, making it even more important that Roger shouldn't leave. As soon as Bob noticed he was missing, he'd be hunted down.

"Barbara, please, we need to leave!" he knocked gently on the bedroom door that she had locked.

"Piss off, Roger!" she screamed.

He recoiled. In all their years together, she had never once sworn at him. There had been many heated arguments, but Barbara had never sworn.

"I can't leave you here alone," he pleaded.

"That's your decision, but I'm not leaving my house."

"I won't leave you alone. They'll think you know where I am."

Despite the affairs and the wandering eye, she was his soul-mate, the only woman he ever wanted to spend time with outside of the bedroom. As much as he hated what the militia had done that morning, a life with the militia meant life without Barbara, something he just wasn't willing to do.

He collected his hunting rifle and made his way outside. He wasn't going to go down without a fight.

***

"Where's Roger?" asked Bob.

With the bodies of the homeowners dumped and the estate secured, he had called his militia to order. In all, fifty-seven of his sixty-two men had reported for duty that day.

Two had been lost during the battle with police and another three slightly wounded. A cost he was happy to bear. Losing only two men, in exchange for control over South Boise was far better than he could have ever hoped. He had no fear the police would be back. Without vehicles or communications, they were lost, a spent force. Within a few days, they'd realize things weren't getting fixed and their focus would swing towards their own families and their own survival. Of the missing five, he didn't worry that they had deserted him and the militia. He imagined they were either caught out of state or still making their way to him, or even more likely, sitting in jail. What he did worry about was some losing their stomachs for what was needed when they realized Bob was for real. He practiced what he preached.

Only thirty of his men stood in front of him. The loss of all vehicles was not something they had anticipated. Bob had illegally sourced a few old diesel trucks, storing them for just such an event. Spending hours each week, sourcing the constituents and preparing biodiesel fuel in small batches, he'd created a stockpile of the fuel, as diesel was no longer commercially available. However, despite their best efforts somehow, what had happened had managed to disable their supposedly indestructible diesel engines. An alternative was needed and Bob wanted to be ahead of the game. After securing their food source, housing and transport were his next highest priorities. Whilst he secured the food, he had sent another twelve men to secure transport. Bob had specifically chosen the men for each detail and Roger was supposed to stay with him at all times. Roger wasn't supposed to be out of Bob's control at any time. He was the quartermaster. He knew where every item they had stockpiled over the last few years was stored. Whether it be medical supplies, ammunition or gold, he knew where some of their most treasured resources were hidden.

Shrugs from the group were not an acceptable answer. "I said, where's Roger?!" he shouted angrily.

"Not seen him since Albertson's," said a number of the members.

Bob turned to Trey. "You saw him?"

"Yes, but not since he was helping that woman at the store," he said, smiling at the thought of Kate.

"Do I need to remind you how important he is?" whispered Bob angrily to his cousin.

After a few more mumbling answers, it was clear that Roger had not been seen for some time.

"He didn't look comfortable after we shot the police sergeant," offered Trey quietly.

"Nor with you ogling his neighbor!" spat Bob angrily, needing someone to blame for his lack of focus. He should have spotted Roger's disappearance much sooner. He had gotten caught up with himself. Roger was one of the softer members of the militia, a CPA with no convictions. Bob doubted the man had been in a fight in his whole life. The militia for him was a fantasy, a place where he could pretend to be something he wasn't. He hadn't met the criteria that Bob had insisted upon, but his skills were needed by the group. He was their token suit man and he had done exactly what Bob had feared he would do, run at the first sight of violence. He could kick himself. Another mistake.

The sound of his transport arriving improved his downwardly spiraling mood slightly. At least now they could start transporting proper quantities of supplies across from the supermarket, a short distance away. Ideally, they'd have located nearer the supermarket, but as their very existence dictated they were all located amongst large urban conurbations, that would have lacked the security their more secluded spot ensured.

The clip of the horses' hooves on the tarmac grew as

the first group of men arrived back with ten horses and a horse-drawn carriage, an excellent replacement for their truck. The carriage was more than capable of holding a significant haul of supplies.

"There are another fifteen behind us and two carts," called Neil, with a smile. "I've no idea what the third group have." This meant the militia had at least twenty five horses and the only transport anyone would have for the foreseeable future beyond pedal power.

"Much trouble?" shouted Bob over the sound of the hooves.

"Nothing we couldn't handle with these babies!" Neil held aloft his AR-15 proudly.

"Any comeback?"

"Nobody left to comeback," said Neil, jumping down next to Bob and receiving a pat on the back.

Neil had been a stable hand at a ranch for most of his life. Trailer trash to most, he had led a Jerry-Springer-guest's life. He'd been raised by a single mother who'd had more boyfriends than he could remember, a number of whom had used both of them as punch bags or worse. A disastrous education resulted in him dropping out before graduating, ensuring his life was destined to remain tough, finding whatever job he could without a formal education. Booze, drugs, and the occasional woman were his only escapes until, after a weekend in the cells, he had found his calling. He had joined the militia after a chance meeting with two other members who had been arrested in a drunken brawl.

Neil had quickly proven himself and had not only helped add numbers to the group, but had become one of Bob's right-hand men. Neil had found the home and family that his life had lacked. His story was not dissimilar from the vast majority of the militia who treated Bob as a father figure and a leader they could believe in and respect.

Bob Jackson, Assistant Principal and Little League coach, should have had little or nothing in common with the group of men facing him - manual laborers or tradesmen with countless convictions for everything from DUIs to attempted murder and rape. Few had not had at least one violent conviction or charge to their name. The Bobs of the world didn't mix with these guys, they mixed with the Rogers of the world, with their perfectly manicured wives and homes. But then Bob Jackson was a fraud. Bob Johnson was his real name, a convicted felon who had spent twenty-five years of his life behind bars in neighboring Nevada for attempted murder, amongst other convictions. During this time, he had been introduced to the survivalist beliefs of an end-of-the-world scenario. Where others viewed it as preparing for the worst, Bob, in his twisted mind, saw it as a once in a lifetime opportunity not to be missed. For men of his resolve, it would be a time to grab power and control that would otherwise never be theirs.

Neil had three horses strung out behind him, all saddled and ready for action. Bob pointed to two men he knew could ride. "You two, with me and Neil."

"Trey, you're in charge," he said loudly, jumping on a horse and heading out of the estate with his rifle over his shoulder and pistol in its holster. As they moved onto the open road, he picked up the pace with the other riders keeping up behind. He needed to get to Roger before he did anything stupid. He knew exactly where he lived, having been invited over for dinner a few times. Roger's wife, Barbara, had even tried to set him up with her sister. As much as he had wanted to seduce the uptight bitch, his body was covered in prison tattoos, not the ornate and delicate ones that had become all the rage. His were harsh, rough, and bold statements that many found offensive. Fortunately, he had favored his back and chest. He'd always kept his arms, neck, and face clean for no other reason than to keep his options open in the future. Bob had always been a forward thinker; a planner. Getting to know the sister too well would've threatened to expose himself to the type of people who would ask too many questions.

After his release from prison, he had skipped parole. With two strikes under his belt in Nevada, his first thought upon release had been getting out of the state, and avoiding the third strike scenario, of which he had little doubt he would fall foul. From there, his transition from Bob Johnson to Bob Jackson had taken shape with nothing more than sheer luck, and an extremely lax referencing procedure in the Boise Education Department.

With fingerprints that would consign him to prison for the least inconsequential interaction with the police, Bob Jackson had become a model citizen and pillar of the community. The setting up of his militia gave him an outlet for his wilder side as he waited for what he believed would come, and he trained his men to believe the same – the inevitable: TEOTWAWKI - The End Of The World As We Know It scenario. That would be his moment to shine.

When the conflict in Iran had escalated, with Russia siding with the Ayatollah, he had upped the readiness of his men. Russia, under Putin, had throughout the twenty-twenties increased defense spending, far in excess of its wealth. There'd been little doubt in many people's minds that Putin had expansionist plans, but with China and the USA forming an alliance to deter him, it seemed unlikely he would risk the wrath of both. Bob saw in Putin some of himself. He knew better. Putin wasn't the type of guy to back down. If he wanted something, he'd take it, and be damned with the consequences, just like he had done in The Crimea, followed by Ukraine a few years later.

Bob directed his men towards Roger's street. Their appearance on the horses caused quite a bit of interest as they galloped past bystanders, the interest waning quickly as the rifles and holstered pistols were spotted on the heavily-armed riders. The streets emptied quickly. Whatever the men wanted, nobody thought it'd be good. The look of determination on the riders' faces just added to the panic that had begun to race through the area.

Bob held his hand high. The four horses came to a stop. He thought back to the old western movies, the hero riding into town to save the day. He laughed to himself, he wasn't the hero, he'd have been the guy in the black hat, riding in to take care of business while the townsfolk cowered, peeking out of their windows to try and see what was happening. But that was then, and this was now. The world wasn't the same place. He could change the narrative and he *could* be the white-hat-wearing hero. He could be the John Wayne character. He could be the 'Duke', the 'Duke of Boise', he thought. He liked it! Duke… he'd work it into this plan. 'Bob' seemed a little too familiar. He needed a title, something for the men to call him, to show their respect. He'd speak to Trey when he got back.

"It's the next street over. We'll leave the horses here," he called out.

"What if someone takes them?"

Bob eyed the man with derision. "Really? The same people who watched us and ran like cowards would dare to steal our horses?" Bob thought back to the westerns, where they'd tie their horses to a railing without fear of their horses being taken, mainly since the punishment for that was hanging. So he shouted out that fact. The fact that he himself had stolen the same horses didn't even enter his mind. He couldn't steal what he deemed was his for the taking.

"Hanging? They don't hang people anymore!" argued the man.

"Jerry, these are new times," rushed Neil, seeing the look on Bob's face. "Bob, Jerry didn't mean no disrespect.

He's just not quite understanding the scale of what's happened yet. He's not the brightest."

Bob watched as Jerry reacted to the fear in Neil's eyes. He was one of Neil's recent additions. An excellent rider and stable hand, he was going to be valuable moving forward, given their new mode of transport. However, Bob had to exert his authority and his men had to respond to his orders unquestioningly.

"Yup, what he said," said Jerry quickly. The deference in his voice and his inability to return Bob's imposing stare were rewarded with a temporary reprieve. He'd deal with Jerry after they had dealt with Roger.

"Well, let's go get our deserter!"

"What's the punishment for that?" asked Jerry eagerly.

Bob smiled and leaned over, patting Jerry on the back. He had just won a permanent reprieve.

"Still to be decided…" began Bob.

The gunshot cut through his words, pushing him to the ground, a large pool of blood spreading all over him.

Chapter 14

Roger had taken up position atop their garage, a monstrosity built at the request of his wife. The pyramid roof complete with bell tower, was for once in its existence, proving its worth. He had complained bitterly at the additional cost and height of the garage, but she had wanted a feature that he was finally appreciating. The fake bell tower, although flimsy, offered him an exceptional shooting position to see down the street. Their house, the largest on the street, sat at the far end, set back from the rest of the houses and on the upslope, affording it frontal views out across the city below.

Roger had heard them coming. The moment he heard the horses' hooves crashing against the tarmac, he knew it was Bob. The man was nothing, if not resourceful. He had half-expected them to have appeared on mountain bikes. Bob was a big guy, an imposing man, it would have been a comical sight.

Roger put his eye to his scope, tracking the noise, waiting for the horses and their riders to appear. His M1A M21 Springfield was ready to propel its .308 cartridges to wherever he pointed with deadly accuracy. A horse's head come into view first, poking above the fence and beyond the house at the end of the street. Roger's body tensed at the sight. There was still a chance it wasn't the militia. He had the faintest of hopes that he was wrong. Then Bob rode into view, his image filling the scope briefly, to be replaced by three other horses and riders, blocking his view. In a fraction of a second, he had missed the shot. He chastised himself as the horses continued to protect his target.

He could see the men talking as they jumped down from their horses. They were unaware of his bird's eye view, his line of sight allowing for an angle over the fence they thought was shielding them. They had no idea that he was ready for them. Bob came back into view and Roger couldn't afford not to take the shot again. Without Bob, the militia was nothing. He squeezed the trigger, the rifle exploding into action, pulling up and pushing back into his shoulder. He pulled it back onto target, but Bob was no longer standing. He scanned down to see that Bob had been propelled backward into the open and was on the ground, kicking and flailing wildly.

***

"Get him off me!" shouted Bob as he struggled against Jerry's dead weight on top of him.

Patting Jerry on the back had saved his life and ended Jerry's. The slight movement, combined with Roger's hastily-aimed shot had caught Jerry perfectly center mass and propelled his dead weight forward, crashing into Bob and sending them both tumbling to the ground.

Neil had reacted as soon as he'd heard the shot, catching sight of the gunman's location. He ducked out of the gunman's line of sight, an elevated position allowing him a clean shot over the fence line of a home a few yards behind them. Neil crawled forward, keeping low. He grabbed Bob's boot, pulling at it with all his might. Vince, the other rider, quickly caught on and keeping low, helped with Bob's other boot. Between the two men, they were pulling over four-hundred pounds of dead weight, two-hundred pounds of which had no inclination, nor need to move. Bob inched towards them as another crack of gunfire echoed across the estate. Neil felt the whiz of the bullet as it cleared the fence behind them. He felt the world had slowed right down as he pulled even harder, despite already pulling as hard as he thought possible.

***

Roger had no idea who he had hit. He could see two bodies on the ground, blood spilling out from beneath them. All he knew was that Bob was still moving. He lined up the headshot and squeezed the trigger once more. This time, he was ready for the kick and was surprisingly more calm. The first shot had been, as they'd said, the hardest. He kept his eyes on the target and followed the bullet.

"Shit!" he screamed, as somehow Bob's prone head slid away at the very moment the bullet struck the sidewalk. He looked for another shot, but the fence now blocked his line of sight. The body, still visible, was unmoving. His first shot had killed whoever had been standing next to Bob. He'd had the shot and had rushed it.

***

"Jesus, that was close," gasped Neil as the bullet tore into the tarmac surface where Bob's head had been just moments earlier. Bob was sitting with his back to the fence, patting himself frantically to ensure the blood that soaked him was all Jerry's and not his own. After a few seconds, he turned and smiled at the two men next to him. They too had their backs to the fence, offering only Jerry's corpse as a target.

"Things are getting fun now," whooped Bob, a manic look on his face. The adrenaline, after two near misses, was pumping through him. He grabbed his rifle and checked it was good to go.

Neil and Vince readied their weapons.

"What's the plan?" asked Neil.

"Kill that deserting blood sucker!" said Bob, moving up to a crouch. He edged his way along the fence line towards the end and snuck a look down the street. He could see Roger's shooting perch, a ridiculous appendage atop his garage. He wasn't even sure what it was supposed to be. A bell tower or something but it had no bell, just a little pitched roof above a balustrade. He ducked back.

"He's got absolutely no cover up there. Vince, you draw his attention and I'll take him down."

"How will I do that?"

"You're gonna make a dash for the horses." Bob pointed to the horses which were tied to a railing beyond the safety of the fence.

"I'd rather not," said Vince, looking at what he guessed to be a ten-yard kill zone between him and the horses.

"I'm not asking whether you'd rather do it, on three! 3…2…1…"

***

Roger's eyes caught the movement at the side of the fence, but whoever had looked was already gone by the time he had a chance to shoot. They had seen where he was, of that he had little doubt. His hide was exposed. He turned and sat on the steeply sloping roof, sliding down on the far side, out of sight of the attackers. His feet slowed him as he neared the guttering at the base of the roof. A few tiles were damaged in his haste, but that was the least of his concerns. A seven-foot drop to the driveway followed. Fortunately, his foreboding visions of twisting or breaking his ankle didn't come true. He landed in a crouch with his rifle slung across his back and raced into the house, just as a burst of gunfire tore his wife's bell tower to shreds.

Barbara was waiting for him, tears streaming down

her face and a bag at her feet.

"I'm ready to go," her voice wavered in fear.

"Too frigging late! Get down in the basement and lock the door! Come out for no one but me!" He bolted past her and up the stairs, towards the loft. A small feature window at the top of the house, almost invisible from the outside due to the shadow cast from the overhanging roof, offered a view back down the street. He got to it and watched as an attacker darted diagonally across the street, working his way towards him. They were still a few houses away. Roger took aim and squeezed the trigger as the attacker attempted his next diagonal.

***

"Damn, he's not there any longer," shouted Bob as he emptied his magazine into the small tower.

Vince thanked God he'd reached the horses and promptly ran back to cover.

"Okay, we'll work our way down the street, darting from house to house, moving up one house at a time."

Neil and Vince both nodded.

"Okay, go!" Bob slapped Neil on the back, whilst holding Vince back. As Neil reached the cover of the next house, Bob waved Neil onward.

"Go!" he shouted to Neil. As Neil ran to the next house, Bob raced to the first house. Two men running as fast as they could across the street, Bob crossing the opposite way from Neil. Another pause and Bob, back with Vince, pushed him onwards again. Vince had the short straw. He was making the crossing on his own, offering Roger no confusion over who to target. One target, one shot.

A shot rang out and Vince fell, followed almost instantly by a burst of gunfire. Bob had used Vince's movement once again to take aim. He had remembered the small window at the top of the house, almost indiscernible from a hundred yards away, in the shadows of the overhanging roof. He had thought it an excellent vantage point looking back down the street when he had visited previously, and he hadn't been wrong when he saw the flash of Roger's rifle firing from the shaded darkness.

Roger failed to return fire. Bob knew there was little chance he ever could. He had returned fire instantly towards Roger's line of fire. A hail of bullets tore into the only place Roger could have occupied.

Vince's screams cut through the otherwise silent street as the shooting stopped.

"D'you get him?" asked Neil from across the street.

"Yep," replied Bob, despite not actually seeing the kill shot.

Neil raced out to check on Vince. Bob followed a little more cautiously, his eye remaining on the shaded area beneath the roof.

"Oh shit, it's bad. He's taken out a chunk of his lower spine," explained Neil, as Vince writhed in pain.

"Can you move your legs?" asked Bob, kneeling at Vince's side, his eyes constantly checking Roger's house.

"I can't even feel them."

Bob stood and fired a round into Vince's head without so much as a pause or a goodbye before walking towards Roger's house.

"What the hell?" struggled Neil, not sure whether to console the now dead Vince or chase after Bob.

"This isn't a world for invalids. If he'd lived, he'd never walk again," said Bob without a backward glance.

Neil had a choice to make. Follow Bob or make a stand for Vince. Vince was dead, but Bob had survived two attempts on his life and had killed another two men. He was also the man who had given him a purpose to what had been a shitty life. He stripped Vince of his weapons and ammo and hurried to catch up with Bob.

***

Another hit, thought Roger when he spotted Bob. His mind raced to get his body to react. The lightning speed of his thought process slowed catastrophically as his physical processes took over. He knew what he wanted his body to do, it just couldn't do it anywhere near fast enough. His feet felt the force of his leg muscles pushing them into the floor as the first bullet struck, his M1 taking the full power of the shot, adding additional momentum to his moving body. The second bullet took out his scope, merely a tenth of a second later. To his racing mind, it felt like a lifetime before the third bullet struck, directly above the top of the scope, mid-forehead, a perfect kill shot. All thoughts instantly stopped.

***

Bob stood over Roger's corpse which lay in a strangely contorted position.

"It would have been better if he were still alive," said Bob, frustrated at how good his return fire had been.

Neil searched the body and discarded the M1 in frustration. "Ruined," he said, throwing it and the shattered scope aside.

"We need to find his wife," said Bob urgently.

"Why? She's not done anything wrong," said Neil.

"He may have told her things," said Bob, stomping away, his mind preoccupied with the frustration of not being able to torture out of Roger whatever he had known.

"What things?"

Bob spun around, his eyes flaring in anger. "If you needed to know, I'd tell you! Just find...," he shouted, stopping mid-sentence and lowering his voice. "What was that?" he whispered.

"What?" asked Neil, hearing nothing as his ears still rung from Bob's tirade.

Bob stood at the top of the narrow staircase that led into the loft area. It wasn't what he had heard, he too had heard nothing over his own voice, but he had felt a vibration through his foot. Somebody had stepped onto the staircase below. Bob stepped back, the entry to the staircase was below him to the left, around two ninety degree turns, four steps, a small landing, a straight run to another landing before turning another ninety degrees and a final four steps into the loft. The staircase was one complete unit and unlike the rest of the house, which was on show to the world, was not the best money could buy, but a functional and cheap set of stairs, knocked into place and hidden out of sight to all but the homeowners themselves.

***

Crazy didn't even begin to describe how Gary's morning had been. The Sherriff's office had no working communications, no vehicles, and no idea what was happening and quite frankly, from what Gary surmised, no clue as to what to do. He had stuck it out for most of the day but as reports of violence were relayed, it became clear there was little or nothing they could do in response. By the time they had received the report, to the time they could get help to the area, the incident was over and or far too dangerous for two deputies on mountain bikes to deal with. With no communications, calling for back-up wasn't an option.

The jail itself was a mess with no electricity, and although it was November, the prisoners were overheating without air-conditioning. The toilets had backed up within hours of the water going off, and with sanitary conditions worsening by the minute, it was clear the situation was only going to get worse. Without transport, food for the inmates wouldn't arrive. All in all, it was a disaster. Without sanitation or food, the Sherriff had no choice other than to order all but the most serious offenders to be released. One thousand and twenty-three inmates became eighty-seven, as lunchtime came and went without food being delivered.

Gary and the other deputies had managed to scrape together enough to feed the eighty-seven. With far less strain on the toilets and with some shuffling around of cells, they'd managed to rehouse the more serious offenders in almost humanitarian conditions. Dinner and the following morning's breakfast were catered for, but beyond that, nobody knew what they were going to do. There was already talk of releasing everyone but the five murderers, and that was less than ten hours after the power, water, and everything had stopped working. Ten hours, thought Gary, and it was already messed up beyond comprehension. He headed home for a few hours' rest and to check on his family before going back to work. The Sherriff wanted them to maintain high visibility as much as possible, and as such was authorizing overtime, something Gary hadn't seen in a long time.

It was only as he hit the hill at the bottom of Warm Springs Mesa that he realized how exhausted he was, or more accurately, how unfit he was. The hill, although not steep, was long and slow. The view behind him of the unmoving Boise was not one he wanted to linger over. He kept his head down and pushed on the pedals. All forward momentum had all but stopped when the first shot rang out from ahead. His head automatically snapped to the direction from which the sound had come. It was from the same direction as his house. He pushed on the pedals and began to move faster and faster. He had a wife and a three-year-old at home. A second shot rang out. He pedaled harder. He reached the first street in the community to see his neighbors scurrying into their homes at the sound of the shot. While they ran away, Gary cycled towards it, two streets away, two uphill sections still to mount. He pushed on, his holster flap unclipped, allowing quick and easy access to his Sig Sauer P226 pistol. He didn't care that he was alone, his family was in danger.

The body next to four tied-up horses had his heart racing as he entered the street. Another body lay opposite his house in the middle of the street. He cycled with every ounce of energy he had left to his front door, jumping off his bike as he mounted the sidewalk and driveway. The momentum carried him through his front door at a full run. His wife threw her arms around him.

"Thank God, you're home," she cried.

"Where's Debbie?" he panicked, looking around for his daughter.

"She's fine," she calmed him. "In the back playroom."

"Bob Jackson, the Little League coach?" asked Gary for the third time as his wife described what she had seen.

"Yep, but with the meanest look on his face. Pure evil. He shot that man," she pointed into the street. "Without a thought, and he was with him!" she stammered between tears.

Gary looked out of the window and squinted to see Roger and Barbara's house, which sat at the end of the street. All was quiet. He pulled out his pistol and checked it was ready.

"What the hell are you doing?" asked his wife.

"My job."

"Your job is looking after your family!" she commanded.

"I've sworn an oath, and Roger and Barbara need

help."

"And who's going to help us if you don't come back?"

"I'll be back," he said confidently, opening the door and closing it behind him.

Gary worked his way along the front of his neighbors' homes, but none of them came to his aid. Grown men cowered with their families from the evil that was on their street, outside their own front doors. He shook his head as he made it alone to Roger's front door. It lay open. He could hear voices from upstairs. He climbed the stairs carefully, his pistol leading the way, ready to take down whoever came at him.

"Just find…" As the volume of Bob's voice rose, Gary made his move. The first stair to the loft creaked under his weight. He wasn't worried about the noise with the shouting, but he could have sworn the staircase moved. Bob's shouting stopped instantly. Gary paused before moving onto the first small landing. He was still out of sight.

"Who's there?" came a shout from above, Bob's voice. He knew Bob well. He was a larger than life character who'd kept himself to himself.

"Gary. I live a few doors down. I'm a sheriff's deputy."

"There's nothing for you here, Gary. Now head on home."

"Bob, there're two dead bodies outside that tell me otherwise."

"What they should tell you, Gary, is that things have changed here today. Best go on home. I know you've got a lovely wife and daughter who'll be needing you."

"Are you threatening me?" asked Gary, his temper flaring.

"I'm just telling you how it is now, Gary. The world's

screwed. The sooner you accept that and move on, the better."

***

Bob signaled to Neil as he spoke with Gary, directing him to a spot on the floor and pointing his AR-15 to indicate Neil should shoot through the floor where he believed Gary stood below.

"Where's Roger?" asked Gary.

"You can't help him anymore, and he's the one that killed the two guys outside."

"Well, that isn't quite true, is it?"

"I just finished what he started. Vince's spine was half blown out, He'd never have survived."

"So you just put him down?"

"He was suffering. You wouldn't let a dog suffer, would you?"

Bob held up three fingers.

"Where's Barbara?"

"No idea. Not here, I don't think," said Bob, dropping one of his fingers.

***

Gary looked at his pistol. There were at least two men upstairs with fully automatic rifles. The world was screwed. He'd witnessed that already. The jail would be uninhabitable in two days. They were already letting prisoners go and before long, the murderers were going to have to be let go. Roger was dead and had shot two guys himself. What exactly was Gary going to do if he did capture Bob? Lock him up? He'd be out in two days, at the rate the world was falling apart.

Falling apart, thought Gary. Words Roger had said

himself, when the 'world falls apart, he'd be fine'. He'd been in some sort of group. A bunch of guys who liked to play weekend warrior, but Gary couldn't be invited. No law enforcement and invitation-only, Roger had told him one Saturday while loading up his jeep. Gary had pushed for more. But the most he'd gotten out of Roger was that it was a tough bunch of guys you don't mess with, and who you'd want on your side when the brown stuff hit the fan.

***

Bob dropped another finger as he waited for a response from the silent Gary.

"You're not going to cause any more trouble in Warm Springs, are you?" asked Gary.

"Got what we came for," shouted Bob, holding his single finger up for Neil.

"And Barbara?"

"If we see her, we'll tell her that you're looking for her."

Gary stepped back, keeping his pistol at the ready as he backed down and out of the house. He walked back towards his house. There'd be no overtime that night. No work anytime soon, at least not until he had some proof the world wasn't, as Bob obviously believed, falling apart.

***

Neil raced over to the window as they heard the door close below them. He raised his AR-15 and took aim at the sheriff's deputy walking away from them. He lined up the shot and squeezed the trigger.

"Stop!" shouted Bob, suddenly realizing what Neil was doing.

Chapter 15

"It sounds as though it's stopped," said Kate, pausing with a bowl of cooked chicken fillets in her hand. She snapped the lid on top and added it to the pile to be transported down to the coolness of the basement. With the shooting so close, she had kept everyone in the kitchen, which was on the opposite side of the house from where the sound had been coming from. Gunshots also rang from the city below, but at least those were out of harm's way. The shooting from behind them sounded like it was just a street or two away. It had been over five minutes from the last burst of gunfire.

"I should go check on my parents," suggested Zach, extracting his hand from Sophie's.

"Not yet, you're not. Give it some time for things to calm down, okay? The best thing you can do for your parents is to stay safe," warned Kate as a single gunshot rang out.

"We should get this down to the basement," said Harry, eyeing the mound of food that would be their rations for the next few days.

"Let's just label it first," said Kate. "Some will keep better than others." She opened the 'everything else' drawer and extracted a roll of sticky labels and a marker pen.

"No problem," said Harry, knowing it was nothing more than a stalling tactic. The food was stored in clear containers, and everything was visible.

Ten minutes later and with no further shooting, her excuses were dwindling.

"I'd really like to check on my parents," said Zach, who had become increasingly anxious over the last few minutes.

Kate shook her head. Harry walked over and took her aside. "I'll take him. You go down and spend a little time on your own down there. By the time I get back, you'll be ready to move the food down there," he whispered, squeezing her arm gently to show his support.

Kate looked towards the basement door. "I can feel him down there."

"Zach, come on. I'll take you home," said Harry.

"Will you come back later?" asked Sophie.

Zach looked at Kate. She nodded it was fine. She wasn't sure she could say another word without breaking down into a blubbering wreck.

Harry guided Zach out, quickly recognizing Kate's situation. She steadied herself against the kitchen counter and breathed deeply to compose herself. With the front door closing behind them, she moved towards the basement door. She reached into her pocket and extracted a key she'd had on her since the day they had been notified, inserting it into the keyhole. She paused, feeling a presence behind her. She turned and looked back down the hallway to the kitchen. Danny, Ava, and Sophie were lined up, one behind the other, their breaths held. It was a big moment for them as well. Tim had been their father, not just her husband.

"We'll all do it together," she said, the three shuffling towards her as one. Kate reached out and turned the key, the lock slipped back easily. Her hand hovered over the handle. Ava reached out and helped Kate take it. They pushed down together. The door pushed inwards and as a waft of stale air blew outwards, they all started to cry at the smell of Tim, perhaps, they all realized, for the last time.

Kate stepped forward and then quickly stepped back. "It's very dark down there," she said, bursting into laughter.

Such a silly little thing had cut the tension that had been building up for so long.

Danny rushed off and appeared back with his flashlight, flicking the switch with no luck.

"You need batteries?"

"These are new ones, it's not working."

Kate walked back to the kitchen and her 'everything else' drawer and took out a small penlight torch. It too was dead. She had one last option, one that wouldn't fail. She went to the garage and retrieved a box of candles and matches from her trusted drawer on the way back through the kitchen.

Ava disappeared as Kate lit the first candle. By the time she had the fourth one ready for Ava, she was back with four rough-cut circles of paper in her hand with two small nicks in the center of each. Ava took her candle and pushed the bottom through the nicks, pushing the paper up the shaft of the candle a few inches. She then held the candle shaft under the circle of paper.

"It'll stop the candle wax from dripping on our hands," she smiled.

With all of their hands protected, Kate led the way, down into the depths of the basement. At the bottom of the stairs, she stopped, her three kids adding more light as they joined her. The basement was pristine, not a thing out of place. No mess, not the pit that Tim had warned her about. His desk, normally strewn with papers and mail, sat empty except for four sealed envelopes, one with each of their names on it.

Kate felt a lump form in her stomach.

Chapter 16

Bob rushed over and pushed Neil's rifle up as it fired. The bullet sailed harmlessly into the sky.

"What the…"

"We have an agreement," Bob said, pushing Neil roughly away from the window, and waving out towards a very confused and concerned Gary. "Went off by mistake!" he shouted.

Gary waved back half-heartedly, but picked up his pace in his effort to get home.

"Agreement? He's a cop!" spat Neil.

"We're going to rule this city, and if we are, we're going to honor agreements we make, and sure as hell won't be known as the gang who shoot people in the BACK!"

"Hanging horse thieves and not shooting people in the back? What is this, the Wild frigging West?"

"You're catching on, son. We're living in a whole new era! Let's go find the wife!"

"But you said…"

"Yep, I know what I said, 'if we see her, we'll tell her you're looking for her'."

Neil smiled. "Ah, I see. That's why you're the boss!"

It took two minutes to find her, in the only locked door in the house, the door to the basement. One kick and a quivering wreck of a woman was discovered, tucked away in the corner, hiding. Her teary breaths gave her away in the darkness. Neil pulled her out into the daylight of the kitchen and pushed her into a dining chair. The house stood at the end of the street with the kitchen at the rear. There was nothing but landscape off into the distance behind them.

"Barbara, you know me?"

She nodded her head.

"I'm so sorry about this, but your coward husband ran off and he knew things. I need to know if you know those things too, and whether anyone else does."

"I don't know anything," she said, pleading with her eyes for him to believe her.

"I should be having this conversation with Roger but well, he can't talk anymore."

"Anymore?"

"He's dead. But if he wasn't, he'd be sitting here instead of you."

"I swear…I don't know anything," she managed between sobs of pain for her lost husband and fear for what was to come.

"Tie her to the chair," instructed Bob, before opening the kitchen drawers and removing an assortment of utensils and knives.

Barbara struggled wildly against Neil's bindings as Bob produced implement after implement.

"Barbara, you have the most amazing set of knives," he said, running his finger along the blade. "Japanese?"

She nodded.

"I'm a 'Made in America' type of guy myself, but I do appreciate quality."

He selected a small paring knife, picked up a paper napkin, and ran the cutting edge across the top. It sliced through the paper with little effort.

"Impressive," he offered, walking around the island that separated him from the dining table.

"NO!" screamed Barbara, her scream muffled as Neil filled her open mouth with paper napkins.

Bob approached her slowly and began to remove each of the buttons of her blouse with the knife. It flapped open to reveal her bra. He sliced through the bra to expose her chest.

"That's a nice rack," appreciated Bob. "It's a shame to waste the work someone's put into them." He placed the knife blade against her nipple. Barbara's eyes pleaded with him as she stopped moving to protect herself from injuring herself against the razor-sharp blade.

Bob kept the knife in place and instructed Neil to remove the napkins.

"Everything he did with the militia, he kept in a file in his computer. But he kept paper copies in his cabinet. There's a magnetic key on the back right-hand side if you feel around."

"And he told you all this?"

"No, he tells me nothing. He hasn't even noticed these!" she looked down at her new breasts. "But I know everything he does, every sordid little secret he kept. The women he banged," she spat. "Everything!"

"I'm so sorry to hear that," said Bob. He withdrew the paring knife from her nipple and slashed it across her neck. Blood spurted over him as her eyes opened wildly in panic. Her mouth moved to scream, but the only sound was the bubbling of blood though her open throat.

Neil looked away, his body convulsing. He hadn't expected the brutal killing. Watching men die in a gun battle was one thing, a woman tied to a chair having her neck slit, an entirely different matter. How it differed from shooting someone in the back, he didn't understand.

Bob wiped Barbara's blood off of himself and the knife with a napkin, replacing the knife in its block.

"Gary's looking for you," he called back as he guided Neil towards Roger's office. "See? Agreement honored," he smiled.

Chapter 17

Harry returned without Zach, whose parents weren't for letting him out of sight as darkness loomed. He had taken his dog, Hank, with him and Zach, but dropped him home before returning. He had knocked on the door, and to no reply, had turned the handle. The door was unlocked. Harry's heart began to race, something he most definitely could do without. With a number of scares under his belt, his doctor's words rang in his ears, 'just make sure you take it easy, no stress or excitement and you should be fine'.

"Hello?" he shouted to silence. The house was still.

He walked into the hallway. The twilight was taking its toll on the light in the house. Where he could once see clearly, the shadows cast darkness.

"Hello?" he called, walking in further, hesitantly. The door to the basement lay open, a dim light visible from below.

"Hello?" he called down.

"Harry?" Kate called back through tears.

Harry carefully worked his way down the narrow staircase. The candlelight offered him little visibility until he neared the bottom step. A concentration of light in the far corner led him to the family huddled together, their quiet tears barely audible from across the room.

He rushed across as fast as his eighty-year-old frame would allow.

Kate stood up and hugged him, seeing the angst and worry etched on his face. "It's okay, nothing to worry about," she said, tears streaming down her face. "We just each got a letter from Tim."

Harry's face turned to confusion.

"He left them here," she said, pointing to the desk. "In case he didn't make it back."

The rush in leaving had resulted in many things being forgotten. One thing he hadn't forgotten had been personal messages to each of them - touching memories of the best he saw in them all, and the future he hoped for them, were he not able to share it with them. Each letter was personal to each of them, written entirely separately, no sentiments were copied or regurgitated between them.

Kate read through hers three times. Each time touched her more and proved just how extraordinary a husband, a father, and a man, her Tim had been.

While the kids engaged with the last words of their father, Harry decided to make a start, bringing the food down. The temperature, as hoped, was cooler in the basement and would hopefully extend the perishable food by at least an extra day or perhaps more.

As he turned back towards the stairs, his eye caught a door with a wheel in the middle of it. In the dimness of the candlelight, he struggled to make out what it was.

"Previous owners left it behind," said Kate, startling him.

"Did they leave it full?"

"I wish. No, it's empty. Tim used it for his guns."

"I thought you didn't like guns?"

"I don't. I hate the things."

"And Tim?"

"Loved them!"

"Fighter jets and guns, he was a big kid at heart," she smiled. "Anyway," she steered him towards the stairs. "Come on, kids, time to get that food down here," she ordered.

With the food in far more able-bodied hands, Harry

bid them goodnight.

"Oh, and don't forget to lock this door after me, unlike earlier."

"I did lock it," said Kate, the joy of finding Tim's letter dropping in an instant.

"But it was unlocked when I came back from Zach's," he said, reaching for the revolver in his pocket.

Kate put her hand over Harry's to stop him from bringing out the revolver. "Kids, did anyone go outside after Zach left?" she shouted out.

"I went out to get my windbreaker," shouted Danny.

Kate relaxed. "That boy's never locked a door behind him in his life!"

"Times are different now," warned Harry, a burst of gunfire from the city below proving his point perfectly.

Chapter 18

DAY 5

Nick lay awake as the sun rose over Boise below him for the fifth morning since the explosion. Ninety-six hours had passed and still not one vehicle had moved anywhere within their field of sight. Nothing, no traffic in or out. He had given up even looking. The first few days he had stared down the highway, willing himself to see a vehicle head towards them, something to prove that the rest of America was functioning normally. Nothing.

Over the previous few days, they had watched the unfolding chaos below. It was a sobering sight and one that had him spending more and more time worrying about his own family, over two thousand miles away. Not knowing whether they were suffering the same fate as the people of Boise was insufferable.

Each night, as darkness fell, they willed the lights to kick on. A population of over 750,000 lay before them, yet as the last chink of dying sunlight faded, the city was enveloped in a darkness unlike anything he had witnessed in the modern world, a true darkness where all that was visible shone in the unpolluted sky and vastness of space – a reminder of just how insignificant one little planet could be.

As the sun had risen each morning, he had hoped things would improve but day after day, the city below had failed to show any sign of life, anything, a vehicle moving, just something to show that the lifeblood of the city had been restored. But as each hour dragged by, his heart sank further. Whatever had happened, things weren't improving, things weren't being fixed. More importantly, it didn't seem like people were even trying. Boise was a great American community, heralded as one of the friendliest, safest, and most welcoming cities in all of America. If this had happened to Boise in four days, God help the rest of the world.

They had maintained their position over the home-stealers, or as they had renamed them, the Boise militia, for the first few days. Alex had been fascinated as to how organized the group was, in comparison to the vast populace and had insisted they stay in situ. Thirty-two horses and five carts had been acquired by the militia within hours of the power outage. A corral was being constructed behind the estate while the carts, with a significant contingent of outriders as guards, ferried back and forth with supplies from a local supermarket, which they could only assume the militia had taken control of. The brutality of their acquisition of the estate and ability to secure so many resources suggested that law and order, within just hours of a catastrophic failure of all power and communication, had effectively ended, at least for these men and the area they inhabited.

It had been a mind-blowing revelation. No one had thought for a second any of that would happen so quickly, but the militia had obviously assumed the worst and their survival instinct and plan had been initiated and executed with devastating efficiency and brutality.

Within two days, the food supply runs ended and the storing of goods and products was complete. Every garage, shed, and spare room had been filled. The carts had been redirected and building materials had begun to appear, including wood, nails, tools and sand. A number of the militia were obviously builders and carpenters, as a barn began to take shape. On the perimeter, sandbags were filled and machine gun nests were installed, each with a clear line of sight to the next and a hundred-yard killing field in front. Another two nests adorned the bridge that separated the estate from the main city. No uninvited guests would be getting anywhere near the estate anytime soon.

Within three days, they had secured a base of operations that would allow them a stronghold over the city of Boise. It was, as Alex commented, a truly remarkable and impressive feat, whilst also one of the most chilling and depressing things he had ever witnessed. With the base secure, points were being identified in the hills above for lookout posts. At that point, it had become apparent they'd have to move. Alex had insisted they wait one more night, a night they both wished they'd never have to relive.

Unlike the previous two days, as the sun began to set, the carts set back out for the city, the outriders once again accompanying them. They crossed the bridge and unlike previously, they turned right into the large housing estates that lined the opposite bank of the river and stretched off into the distance, and not left towards the commercial buildings. An uneasy feeling had swept through them, as the sound of gunfire and screaming echoed across the hillside. The last wisps of light allowed them to see the carts arriving back, filled with a new range of supplies. The women that filled the carriages were tear, blood, and fear-stained. It seemed that food and building supplies were not the only things the militia were planning to take as they pleased.

Alex and Nick began urgent preparations to move, as there was only so much they could stomach. The mass rape of innocent women was most definitely way beyond that point. The thought of listening to the screams of women being raped throughout the night was not one either could bear, and with over sixty militia members in a highly secure base, there was nothing either could do to stop them, certainly not without endangering themselves, or more importantly, their mission.

Three miles later, and with not one word spoken, they stopped high above Warm Springs Mesa, a larger community in the foothills of Boise. It was there they had bedded down and where Nick, as the sun rose, prayed for some semblance of normality.

He lifted his binoculars and with a heavy heart looked down on the community, expecting the worst. He scanned the various streets. There were no machine gun nests, no sign of violence or unrest. It looked like any neighborhood would at that time in the morning. His heart began to lift as the first signs of life erupted from the houses. Neighbors were talking with each other, kids appeared on the street, taking full advantage of their impromptu school vacation. Watching plates of food being transported between houses after their previous view had a smile breaking on his face for the first time in days. The world hadn't quite descended into chaos after all. America and the city of Boise did still have its heart and soul.

"What're you seeing?" asked Alex, awakening to Nick's movements.

"Hope!" replied Nick.

Chapter 19

With complete darkness falling just after seven, it had been amazing how quickly their body clocks had accustomed to the situation. Once darkness set, there was little that could be done. Candles were already a rationed resource, and with no other light source, sleeping during the hours of darkness became the norm.

Danny and Ava seemed to be coping with the change far easier than Sophie, who had always been a night owl. Never a great sleeper, she had struggled and dreaded the long dark nights, particularly without her tablet, which had been a constant source of tension between her and Kate over the previous few months.

Kate only wished they were still having those fights as she woke up to another powerless morning, the sun edging its way into the sky. They had stretched the perishable foods out across the first four days, longer than expected. She rose and washed herself with cold water, a cloth, and small amount of soap. They'd had to reconsider everything they did. Every resource they used was finite, whether it was the water in the storage tank which was quickly emptying, bottled drinking water, food, gas for the barbecue, deodorant, candles, or even soap. They only had so much and as each day stretched on, the likelihood of ever being able to get more diminished, as did their resources.

Kate dressed and made her way down to the basement. There were a few items of the cooked food still left. If they were lucky, it would stretch to breakfast and lunch. They had enjoyed huge meals up until then, but as she opened the door, it was clear the feasts were over. Rationing of the longer life food was going to have to begin. Her ever eager helper, Danny, appeared by her side.

"Oof! That stinks!" he wafted the smell from his nose.

Kate closed the door. "Yeah, we won't be eating that anymore. Did you sleep okay?" she asked, bending down and giving him a hug.

He nodded. He didn't have a worry in the world to stop him from sleeping. He was blissfully unaware of how bad the situation was becoming. Danny wasn't party to the talk from the neighbors. As the days passed, the stories of the breakdown of the society they had come to love worsened. The hospitals were, as one neighbor described, worse than any he had seen in a war-torn city. People were lying in their own filth while gunshot victims were dying as they waited for the dwindling number of staff to attend to them. Medicines were already running out and morgues were overflowing with decomposing bodies. The message was clear and simple. They were fast becoming no place to go if you were sick.

With the militia effectively stealing the local supermarket in its entirety, those not as quick to stock up had had to resort to finding other stores and supermarkets in the wider area. By the end of Day 2, the police were just about managing to control the unrest at each of the stores. By Day 3, and as the last remaining food sources emptied, the dwindling number of officers, who were still attending for duty, had effectively given up. By Day 4, none of the neighbors ventured out. The situation in the city below had become too dangerous. Gunfire had become so common that Kate had stopped flinching each time she heard a shot.

City Hall and the council offices had closed on Day 3. A hand-written note from the Mayor wished the citizens of Boise the best of luck through those trying times. With no transport, communication, water or power, there was nothing that could be done. Even the fire department had closed its stations. Without vehicles, water or communication, there was little they could do and like everyone else, the fire officers had families to look after for themselves.

Day 4 had been a wakeup call for many of those who assumed the power would be back on soon, that the authorities would fix the problem and that life would go back to normal. Day 4 had been the day the local authorities themselves had given up on Boise and gone home. Day 4 saw the last police officer walk out of the final station that was still manned in the city. Day 4 witnessed the murderers being let loose from the county jail where the officers had held on dearly to try and keep them longer, but with no food or water, they'd had no choice but to let them go. Day 4 was the day the warden, who had ordered the release of the murderers, became a killer himself, gunning down the murderers as they walked out of his jail, before turning his gun on himself.

Day 4 had been the day many households ran out of food and water as they'd failed to comprehend how dire the situation really was.

Day 5 was a day Kate was not looking forward to. Day 5 was the day people would appreciate their new reality. A reality that the vast majority had no idea how to survive in, just like Kate.

"Ouch!" said Danny. "You're squeezing me too tight."

"Sorry, just needed an extra big hug."

He squeezed her as tight as he could in response. "There! Better?" he asked.

She nodded, a tear welling in her eyes. "Let's get some bags and we can get rid of the food before it stinks the whole house out," she said, not wanting him to see her upset. Day 5 was going to be tough. They would have to start rationing food and as much as she didn't want to think about the problem, they had to find a solution to the bathroom, as the toilets had finally become blocked.

Ava joined them as Danny was being dispatched to Harry's with the smelly food, for his dog, Hank.

"Should you let him out on his own?" asked Ava.

"It's 7.30 a.m. and he's just going next door." Kate defended herself against her twelve-year-old.

"Well…," began Ava.

"Fine, I'll go with him," huffed Kate, following him out. She hated being out-parented by her daughter, but Ava was right. With no law and order, the streets were no place for an eight-year-old on his own, even just after sunrise.

Kate knocked on Harry's door and waited. Hank barked, an old gruff lazy bark, he was a twelve-year-old lab and acted it. Everything was done slowly. Hank didn't waste energy he didn't need to. 'Old and wise', Harry liked to call it.

"Coming," shouted Harry after a few more seconds. A few seconds that had Kate panicking. Danny couldn't have been more than thirty seconds ahead of her. Harry should have just been letting Danny in, for him and Hank not to be near the door. If Danny wasn't in Harry's house, where was he?

As Harry began to unlock his various locks, further proof that Danny wasn't already there, Kate looked wildly around. The carrier bag with the leftover food for Hank, the dog, lay strewn in the street. "Danny?" she called desperately.

Chapter 20

Nick picked up his binoculars and scanned the streets below. It was a welcome sight after the previous few days.

"Don't get to emotional just yet," cautioned Alex, he pointed back towards the militia base just a few miles to their east. "It'll be like that here soon enough!"

Nick shook his head. "You're wrong, these people are looking out for one another. This is the real future!"

Alex shrugged, it was too early for an argument and he didn't care whether Nick believed him or not. The truth would be evident soon enough.

"Sleep well?" he asked, changing the subject.

Nick didn't reply, he kept his eyes focused on the community below.

"What?" asked Alex.

Nick pointed to a quiet street, halfway down the hillside.

"Shit!" exhaled Alex.

Nick was lifting his McMillan Talon rifle from his kit when Alex stopped him.

"No, the kid's struggling too much, and from this distance and the way the wind shifts down the hillside, it's too risky."

"I'm not standing by and watching this!" warned Nick, lining up the shot, the orange jumpsuit with ADA COUNTY JAIL filling his scope. The young boy's face bounced into view as the man ran off with the boy held tightly to his chest.

"You can't shoot!" said Alex definitively.

"He's got him off the street and they're on the trail now," said Nick. "The boy's not been able to call for help or alert anyone to his situation!"

Their bird's eye view over the scene below allowed them a line of sight above the obstacles that those at ground level would be obstructed by. Although only a hundred yards from his house, the boy was effectively out of sight to all those below.

"Danny!" a desperate plea echoed the mile up towards them. The stricken sound and sight of a mother looking for her child in a lonely street when they could see where her son was, was not an easy sight for either of them.

Alex looked through the binoculars, scanning to where Nick directed him. Their position allowed them a view that even someone six feet from the situation would struggle to see. The man was hiding with the boy in a gulley, almost shrouded in shrubbery. Alex grabbed his pack and extracted a pair of denims and a t-shirt.

"What you doing?" asked Nick.

"I have my limit and that's it," he said sternly.

"But our orders, I thought we were to avoid all contact with the locals?" asked Nick, setting his rifle aside and pulling out his own clothes.

"We can't expose ourselves for who we are. We'll keep out of sight and if anyone does see us, we're just two guys out for a walk."

Nick threw a camo sheet over their equipment and rushed after Alex. With their H&K 45Cs holstered on their belts and hidden under their tops, they looked like two walkers out for a morning stroll.

Alex put the binoculars to his face and checked where they were heading. He broke into a run.

"What?" asked Nick, racing to keep up.

"Let's just say the boy needs us there now!" he replied, breaking into a full sprint.

Chapter 21

"Kate? What's up?" asked Harry, joining her in the street.

"Danny, he…he…he's," she stammered. "…missing!"

"Since when?"

"Just a minute but…"

"Mom?" Ava joined them in the street as Gary, the sheriff's deputy, rushed towards them, responding to Kate's desperate plea. "Everything ok?" he asked, pulling his mountain bike to a stop.

"Danny's missing!"

Gary didn't reassure her, he simply looked to the two men following him and issued a signal to them. Both turned and cycled off at speed.

"What?" asked Kate.

"There was a sighting this morning of a guy in an orange jumpsuit."

Kate shrugged, that meant nothing to her.

"Orange jumpsuits are issued to sex offenders at the county jail. The description matched that of a known pedophile," said Gary quietly, as though it would lessen the blow.

"Oh, dear God," Kate looked around wildly, not knowing which way to search first. "Danny!" she cried in despair.

The cyclists appeared back a minute later, their messages were conveyed and being passed through the entire community. After the killings of Roger and Barbara, the community had realized all too late that law and order was no longer protecting them. Protection was down to themselves. A hastily-arranged community meeting had appointed sheriff's deputy Gary as Head of Security and he had, with the support of the community, formed a small volunteer security force to protect the families and properties of Warm Springs Mesa.

Receiving a nod from his team, he turned to Kate. "Please, don't panic. We've got a search party on the way. The alert has been raised."

Gary's newly-arranged communication and security process was about to be tested. A number of keywords alerted neighbors to the danger they faced, no long explanations as to what was happening. One word would illicit an immediate response and the passing on of the message to their neighbor. In this case, it was the 'Amber' warning and meant exactly the same as the national alert system of the same name. A child was missing and a search party was urgently required. As the message spread through the community, the search party grew. Within minutes, the first community members arrived and after ten minutes, forty people were beginning the search for Danny. It was an impressive display of the community's effort to ride out the storm and survive through their darkest days.

"What's happening?" asked Sophie, rubbing her eyes as she joined the commotion outside of her house, "You woke me up!"

"Danny's been kidnapped. Wait here and shout if he comes home!" barked Kate, rushing off with one of the search parties.

"We don't know he's been kidnapped," cautioned Gary, chasing after her.

Kate wasn't listening, her baby was in danger. Breaking off in four separate directions, four teams of ten people began the search. Kate joined the group heading to the nearest trail at the end of their street. As directed by Gary, on reaching the trail, they spread out and began a slow and meticulous search for any clues. Kate charged on ahead, "Danny!"

While they continued their meticulous search for clues, Kate was already out of sight, her eyes darting from side to side, covering every inch of the trail and its surroundings.

***

Alex and Nick raced down the trail, slowing as the shouts from whom they could only assume was the mother, from the desperation in her voice, began to near them.

"Where was that spot?" asked Alex, looking back to where they had come from to try and work out where the hiding spot was.

Nick looked back with him, both struggling to pinpoint the bushes under which the boy and man were hiding. Down at eye level, it all looked the same.

"Danny!" the shout came from just around a bend in the trail.

"She's getting very close. She can't see us, and we can't explain who we are. She may think we took him!"

"Shit, I hadn't thought of that!"

"Danny!" the shout was even closer.

A rustle in the undergrowth to their right caught both of their attentions. A flash of orange amongst the greenery was all either needed to act. They both dove into the bushes, almost knocking each other over in their eagerness to save the boy and avoid the mother.

***

Kate's heart raced as she turned the bend and was faced with the undergrowth shaking wildly in front of her.

A muffled oomph was followed by the bushes calming and the sight of Danny appearing before her. All thoughts of why the bushes were shaking left her as she grabbed her child, checking him for any injuries, while holding him tight.

"Are you okay?" she asked, her breath catching on itself.

He nodded his head, tears were rolling down his cheeks.

Kate pulled him even closer, wiping the tears from his face.

"What happened?"

"A man grabbed me and ran in here with me. He had me in those bushes until the other men came just now!"

"What other men?" asked Kate, the search party was behind her.

Danny shrugged. "No idea!"

Kate looked at the bushes as the voices of the search party closed in behind her. She waited, having no intention of leaving Danny.

"You've got him!" said Gary with relief as he rounded the bend.

"Yes," said Kate, pointing to the bush where he had come from. "A man had him in there!"

Gary withdrew his pistol and with two of his security volunteers, moved cautiously towards where Kate had pointed. They carefully peeled back the undergrowth and bushes to reveal the small gully. A man lay awaiting them, his orange suit shining all the brighter as the morning sun shone through the exposed bushes.

"Well?" asked Kate.

Gary holstered his pistol. "Nothing here, best head home. We'll keep looking."

His two volunteers were about to speak when he hushed them.

"You sure?"

"Nothing here!" said Gary with some force, looking at the man whose body lay face down while his face pointed skyward. Whoever had broken the man's neck had done so with astonishing force and technique.

As Kate, Danny, and the search party dissipated, Gary answered the questioning looks of his volunteers. "People are scared enough without a kidnapping and death on our doorstep."

"How is that even possible?" asked one of his volunteers.

"I've no idea, but whoever did it, we have to thank them, I know that guy from county. He was one sick son of a bitch."

***

"Jesus," said Alex, "Could you not just have knifed him? Breaking his neck like that, you know, no one can ever know who we really are!"

"I didn't want to traumatize the kid."

"So you spun the guy's head around like an owl?!"

Nick shrugged. "No blood."

Alex pulled him deeper into the undergrowth off the trail. "Come on, let's get out of here before they spot us."

"That's the wrong way."

Alex looked down towards the city below. "Time to find out what's really happening down there!"

"But I thought we were strictly covert?"

"We are," said Alex, looking at their jeans and polo shirts.

Nick looked at Alex. He was indeed dressed in jeans and a polo shirt, but it did little to hide his demeanor or physique, nor that general look that screamed special forces, no matter what they wore. They had a look, a look they'd honed to intimidate their opponents, but not one they could easily shed when required.

"Just don't talk and we'll be fine!" assured Alex, leading the way down towards the bridge that would take them into Boise.

Chapter 22

Kate didn't let go of Danny on the walk home. Smiles marked their route home as neighbors who had come to the rescue were relieved that, on top of everything else, a tragedy had been avoided.

Locking the door firmly behind her and with her family around her, she sat Danny down and remarkably, he smiled back at her. His age had saved him from fully understanding the implications of what could have happened. Danny was a fun-loving boy who lived to play. He hadn't befallen the social media or video gaming trap, he was happiest playing outside in the wonders of the outdoors. He'd been warned of strangers and knew the dangers, but had no idea what those dangers were and from his demeanor, thankfully still didn't. Kate still wanted to know every detail and looked him straight in the eye. "Danny, you need to tell me exactly what happened."

Danny described being grabbed by the man and how he had clamped a hand over his mouth to stop him shouting for help. He had fought but the man was very strong, and when he heard shouting, made them run towards the trail and hide in the bushes. Then, two minutes later, two men appeared out of nowhere, didn't say a word, pulled Danny clear, and took him back to the trail.

"And you heard nothing?"

"I heard a loud snap, but nothing else."

"And the men weren't combing through the undergrowth? They just came to exactly where you were?"

Danny nodded.

Kate thought about it. You couldn't see anything beyond the trail. The undergrowth and bushes were so thick, they'd never have found Danny. Even from a few feet away, he would have been invisible.

"What did the men look like?"

"The man who took me was really smelly and was wearing an orange suit."

"No, the men that helped?"

Danny paused as he tried to recall what they'd looked like.

"Like guards."

"Guards?"

"You know, like the guards at our old house."

Kate looked at her two daughters to see if they could make any more sense of what Danny was saying.

Both looked as confused as she was.

"You know, the base guards, like big, serious, and scary."

Kate recalled their old home. A place they had spent many happy years raising their children in the safety of Mountain Home Air Force base and where they had fallen in love with Idaho. Danny venturing outside had never been a concern. The base guards were the only people who scared him, as they didn't respond to his boyish charms and antics. Steadfastly vigilant, they would never crack a smile or give him an inch, where others were putty in his childhood hands.

"So, they were dressed like soldiers?" asked Kate excitedly. The military had not been seen since the power had gone.

Danny shook his head. "No, they were just dressed normally, I think."

A loud knock at the door interrupted the interrogation. Kate told him not to move as she left the lounge and opened the front door. It was Gary.

"How is he?" he asked quietly.

"Remarkably fine. I don't think he fully understands what danger he was in."

Gary nodded knowingly. "Thank God for that. He was one nasty piece of work."

"Was?" queried Kate. "I thought there was nobody there?"

"Oh, he was there. I just didn't want Danny to know."

"So, what, you killed him?" Kate stepped back, visibly shaken.

"God no! He was already dead. His head was twisted around a-hundred-and-eighty-degrees. He was staring up at us even though his body was facing down. Did Danny say who saved him?"

"Yeah, two guys."

"From where?"

Kate shrugged. "Come ask him yourself," she said, stepping back.

"Hey, Danny!" smiled Gary, entering the lounge.

"Hey, Sheriff," smiled Danny in return. His close call with danger already forgotten.

"Great to see you're okay, buddy!" he said, tousling Danny's hair. "The two guys that helped you, did you recognize them?"

Danny shook his head. "Nope."

"He said they reminded him of the base guards at Mountain Home, big and scary," offered Kate.

"So, they were military?"

Danny shrugged. "Don't know. They were dressed normally, so I don't think so."

"Did they say anything?"

Danny shook his head. "No, they just took me to the path and my mom."

"There was no sign of them when we got there," said

Gary.

"But that was less than a minute after Danny appeared. Why not make themselves known? Why not take the credit for saving Danny? If they were military, why are they hiding from us?" asked Kate. None of it made sense. The total lack of military or of any other federal help after five days was wearing on every citizen. Each day, they thought someone was going to come to their rescue. Each new day would hopefully bring the help they were all certain was coming. Yet each day, nothing came, nobody came to help or even tell them what was happening to the world.

Kate shuddered as a thought hit her. "What if they *were* military?" she asked with concern.

"And that would be a bad thing, why?" asked Gary, seeing her worried look.

"Because they might not be *our* military!"

Chapter 23

The trail they picked took them past the Warm Springs Mesa estate and delivered them to the bridge that crossed the Boise River. Nick and Alex both stopped as they crossed the bridge - the smell of decaying human flesh, a smell that once experienced was never forgotten. A look over the bridge into the water below explained the smell. A rotting corpse caught in a swirling pool at the base of one of the concrete supports, bobbed in and out of sight. The eyeless body already victim to opportune feeders.

Nick looked further upstream. Another body lay tangled in bushes at the water's edge. He shook his head in disgust. This was a modern, civilized American city, not a war-torn, third-world state. Could things have really gotten that bad so quickly?

They kept walking. The street remained deserted. They knew the road led to a shopping area, a supermarket, restaurants, and banks just a few hundred yards ahead.

"You don't want to go down there!" called an elderly lady from her backyard. She stood at her waist-high fence, a shotgun tucked under her armpit, ready to bring up if required.

"Good afternoon, Ma'am," offered Alex, walking over the grass verge that separated her yard from the main road.

"Afternoon. Not seen you fellas before." she eyed them suspiciously.

"We're from Nampa, just out for a walk."

"Yeah, whatever," she said, not buying it. "Nothing

left down there," she said. "All gone, some militia emptied out everything they could, and killed anyone that got too close."

"Everything?" asked Alex. From their map, it looked like a large store.

"Pretty much. What they didn't want would be no use to you, but didn't stop folks taking it. TVs, washers, you name it, it's gone. As soon as the militia were gone, that place was stripped bare."

"What about the police?"

"Militia broke them Day One, shot them to hell and back. Big gun fight. We haven't seen a policeman since."

"That's terrible," offered Alex.

"Better in Nampa, is it?"

Alex had to think quick. He had no idea what it was like in Nampa, but being closer to the explosion, he'd have to imagine not. "Nope, similar."

"Yet here you are out for a leisurely fifteen-mile walk to Southeast Boise? While folks here are scared to venture into their gardens?"

Alex was going to have to improve their cover story before moving on. Alex took a long pull on his water bottle, changing the subject. "I couldn't bother you for a refill, could I?"

The woman looked at him like he was crazy. "Now, I know you're not from Nampa."

Nick and Alex looked at her quizzically.

She pointed to his bottle. "We've not had power or water for four days."

"No water?"

"Went off same time as everything else. So, where you really from?"

"Nampa," said Alex, not deviating from his cover, but indicating to Nick that it was time to leave.

"I'm struggling to place your accent. Definitely not

from anywhere 'round here. Lived here all my life!" quizzed the old lady.

"Nice to meet you," offered Alex, walking away and pulling Nick with him. It was time to leave before the old lady embroiled others in her questioning.

"No water and the river contaminated with dead bodies. That is not a good combination." said Nick, as they walked past the deserted supermarket. Trash and discarded crates and boxes littered the parking lot. They watched from a distance as a few stragglers ducked into the supermarket, appearing just minutes later empty-handed.

"So, what next?" asked Nick.

"It's gonna get dark soon. Think we'll call this recon quits and come back another time." A movement in the sky above caught his attention. He looked up, the tiniest of glints catching his eye.

"Is that what I think it is?" asked Nick, following his gaze.

"I think so," said Alex, fishing in his pocket and pulling out a small flash drive type device, which for the previous five days had failed to show any signs of life. A small diode blinked steadily on the top. It had made contact.

"About time!" said Nick, squinting for a better look.

Alex looked around for a private location, his eyes focusing on a small strip of stores at the entrance to the shopping center.

"I'm just going to try the restroom in here," he pointed to the café, its door sitting open. "Keep a lookout, will you?"

"Will do," said Nick.

Alex walked into the café, his weapon drawn and scanning for threats. The stench allayed his concerns almost instantly. He hadn't been the first to consider using the café, its public convenience had been used to exhaustion. No surprise there. He was sure households nearby had no water to flush their toilets and even if they did, the sewers would only work for so long without water flowing. Pipes would back up to the point that even with water, the waste would have nowhere to go.

He pressed the flash drive as instructed, and the red diode turned green. Contact had been made with the drone flying silently high above and almost invisible. His report was concise and to the point, explaining everything they had witnessed over the previous five days. As he spoke, a number of reassuring thumbs up were thrown at him from Nick outside. All was clear. The flash drive recorded everything he'd said, compressed it into a tiny file and sent it in the tiniest of data bursts to the drone above. Finally, they had checked in.

As the light blinked quickly three times, Nick signaled to him wildly from outside and raced off. The message had been sent. Alex raced out after him. Two teenagers were running away from Nick.

"They were in the back of the café! They crawled out the restroom window!" shouted Nick back to Alex who was struggling to catch up as the teenagers raced away.

Alex screamed at himself in frustration. He had just assumed the smell would have meant the café was empty. He hadn't checked, he should have checked. They must have heard everything he'd said.

"What should I do?" shouted Nick from almost fifty yards ahead.

"You know what to do!" shouted Alex.

Chapter 24

Kate flinched as the succession of high-velocity rounds echoed from the city below. It wasn't the random gunshots that had become so prevalent she barely noticed them anymore. These were different. Perfectly spaced, almost indiscernible from one another. Double taps, professional shots. She hated guns, she thought, trying to divert her mind from the vision of whoever had been executed. She had no illusion that was what had happened. Some people had just been executed, in all likelihood, innocent people going about their lives and trying to survive in a new world, where up until then, law and order had kept them generally safe and secure from the less savory elements of the community.

"What's wrong?" asked Sophie, seeing the look on Kate's face.

"Nothing," she said, forcing a smile. She was getting good at it. Sophie smiled back.

"Zach's coming over, that okay?"

"Yeah, just no closed doors!" she warned. Zach spent most of his time at their house. In all honesty, she enjoyed having him around. He had already helped collect and chop more wood than she and the girls could have hoped to in a month. Kate was planning ahead. She had always been the homemaker in the house. Tim did the easy work. He flew planes while Kate ensured he and the kids had nothing to worry about, other than what they were going to wear that day. Even then, with Tim, that was a given. He wore his uniforms and on his off days, Chino shorts or trousers, depending on the temperature with either sandals or boots, again dependent on the weather.

Kate was afraid to ask how much wood he had collected for his own family. Given the amount of time Zach had been at their house, she guessed very little, if any. But then, she was, she was fairly certain, ahead of the curve. Her mind had always focused on the future rather than the present. Although getting colder, the coldest days of winter were still ahead of them. Many believed help was just a day away. Over the space of five days, the belief had barely faltered. Kate wondered how long before that day became a week, or even a month and the reality finally hit home. Something catastrophic had befallen their world. Whatever they were living through, it wasn't just Boise. It couldn't be, not after that amount of time.

"Mom, we need to talk about the, you know…"

Kate turned to Ava who had walked into the lounge. She looked awkwardly towards the arriving Zach. Kate knew what the 'you know' was. The toilet situation. She smiled. Zach's timing seemed to be extremely unfortunate for her daughters.

She would chat it through with Harry later, he may have some ideas. She pulled Ava aside and spoke quietly. "I know, in the meantime, there's a bucket in the garage. Put some water in the bottom and use that, we'll deal with it later."

"Eww. That's gross!" moaned Ava, turning her nose up at the idea.

"Yet, that's the best option you have and it's better than it'll be in the future!"

Ava's eyes snapped to her mother's. "What do you mean better than the future? Things will get fixed!"

Kate wished she hadn't opened her mouth, as much as she harbored concerns that they were facing a new normal, she hadn't shared them with the kids, they needed hope.

"I'm sure they will. I just mean over the next few days."

For all of her kids to slip up with, Ava wasn't having any of her backpedaling.

"No, you didn't. You think this is it!" Ava shouted. Hearing her mother's voice, her thoughts had only added to Ava's own worries. Worries that were similar to her mother's, but without hearing anyone else voice them, she'd managed to keep believing that things may still go back to the old normal.

"What's it?" asked Sophie, joining the discussion that Ava had opened up to the house with her emotional outburst.

"Mom thinks this," she dramatized, waving her arms around in a circle. "Is not going to get better!"

Sophie looked at her mom for a few seconds before breaking into a smile and turning to Ava. "Don't be silly, things will start getting better soon. The power will be back on any time now, you'll see. Won't it, Zach?"

Zach stayed at the entrance of the lounge, not wanting to embroil himself too closely with a family argument, but with Sophie's beckoning, he moved slowly forward.

"Well, it is a bit strange that nothing is happening. You do begin to wonder..." he mused, not able to deny what was staring them all in the face.

"See? We're all thinking it, we're just not saying it," said Ava, tears streaming down her face. Kate moved forward to console her, but Ava brushed her aside and stomped off. Kate heard her in the garage. Ava was accepting the worst and moving on.

Sophie watched her sister stomp off, shaking her head. "What the hell? Can somebody tell me what I'm missing?"

Kate and Zach exchanged a look, a brief look, but one that said more than a hundred words could. He had it, he'd break the news to her gently. They didn't think her hairdryer or the shower would be working any time soon, if ever again. It wouldn't be taken well, but he obviously felt an enormous amount for her and was keen to protect her from as much of the hardship as he could. Whatever he was doing for Kate and the family was primarily for Sophie, and not just because he was a good Samaritan. Sophie had her Tim. Kate just hoped Zach had his Kate. Sophie could be slow to catch on, but it was no indication of the intelligence that lurked beneath her dottiness, and her heart was in the right place.

Through it all, Danny had sat oblivious, lost in his favorite comic book. His encounter earlier already a distant memory. A knock at the door was followed by a "Anyone home?" The voice was Harry's.

Perfect, she thought. She'd pick his brains about the toilet situation. She had some ideas, but he was old enough to have some historical perspective, or at least she hoped he did.

***

"What will we do with the bodies?" asked Nick, looking down at the two teenagers he had taken down.

"Leave them where they are," said Alex. "Come on, we need to get out of here."

"They were just two kids. We need to bury them, or something," argued Nick. He couldn't take his eyes off of the two. He guessed no more than sixteen. One boy, one girl. He'd had no choice, if they had repeated what they'd heard. He didn't even want to think about what could have happened.

"Come on, we had no choice!"

"We could have taken them with us."

"You know we couldn't. We have orders, and taking prisoners is definitely not among them. Staying covert and keeping our mission a secret is critical. Deadly force has been authorized to keep our mission details secret. You were following orders."

"Yes, but if you had swept the café pro…"

"Yeah, it's my fault, the kids are on me. Now, can we get the hell out of here before we have to kill anyone else?!"

Nick closed his eyes and whispered a prayer for the two. He knew he should have felt worse, he had just killed two innocent teenagers for overhearing Alex's report. But in all honesty, with the future that lay ahead for them, a small part of him felt he had done them a favor, a quick and painful release versus what, for the vast majority, was going to be a slow and painful path to an inevitable and very early death.

Chapter 25

"Duke?"

Bob turned to face his cousin, Trey. The use of his new name and title pleased him greatly. He smiled back at his cousin. He could not have envisioned a better transition from the old to the new world order. His order. His world. His base was secure and his men revered him. He had delivered his vision, as promised, only far quicker and more completely than his wildest imagination. The scale and speed of the collapse was, he had to admit, way beyond his most extreme predictions. The world had quite literally stopped at a precise moment in time, five days earlier.

Their numbers had already swollen, more men had begun to arrive after the third day, having seen what the militia had achieved and built. They wanted the security the militia offered. Beyond their acceptance lay a brutal training regime, where failure resulted in a merciless death. Bob had made an example early in the process, walking up to the last recruit to have completed the initial three-mile run required to prove their fitness and without a word, shooting him in the head. Two had, at that point, decided the militia wasn't for them. They met a similar fate at Bob's hands. Once accepted into the militia, Bob had declared, whether recruit or fully-fledged member, death was the only way out.

"Yes?" replied Bob.

"We've got another batch asking to join up."

Bob turned from watching the recruits they were already putting through their paces. "Show me!"

Trey led the way. The base was a flurry of activity as

militia members went about their tasks feverishly, particularly at the sight of the Duke walking amongst them. The builders were already well ahead of schedule on the barns and outbuildings that would be used to house and secure the horses and supplies over the coming winter months. Security was tight, as lookouts and sentry points were manned, and their respective militia members diligently fulfilled their duties. The Duke smiled as he wondered at what he had created, what he commanded.

Trey guided him towards the main security checkpoint at the front of their base and out towards the road and the bridge that separated them from Boise. Fifteen men awaited them in front of the two machine gun nests. A collection of weapons that the potential recruits had brought with them lay uselessly on the road. Bob and Trey walked beyond the security of the machine gun nests and their sentries, and stood before the weapons littering the bridge's road.

Bob looked at the collection of weapons, mainly handguns. The potential recruits had followed the instructions of the sentries, dropped their weapons and retreated back ten yards.

"You!" Bob pointed to a man standing at the back of the group.

The man pointed to himself to confirm that it was himself who Bob was indicating.

"Yes, you. Step forward!"

"Yes, sir," said the man, stepping forward and standing to attention.

"What's your name?"

"Charlie, sir."

Bob looked down at the pile of weapons. "Okay, Charlie, take your gun and shoot one of the men behind you."

"What?"

"Shoot one of the men behind you!"

"But why? We all want to join."

"Vince," Bobby looked to one of his sentries. "Shoot one of those men."

Vince leveled his AR-15 and shot the man directly behind and to the right of the man Bob had chosen.

The man fell to the ground, a bullet having passed clean through his forehead.

Two men broke off and ran back across the bridge towards Boise. The rest were too stunned to move. Two shots rang out and the two runners fell to the ground, dead.

"Charlie, do you know why Vince shot that man?"

Charlie shook his head, barely able to concentrate on what was being said. His mind was telling him to run, dive into the river and swim for his life.

"Because I told him to. That's the only reason. He doesn't need to know why!"

"So, Charlie, pick up your gun and shoot one of the men behind you. You've already cost me three recruits, don't make it anymore!" he said with a smile.

Charlie walked forward, his body forcing him, his mind screaming at him not to, but his survival instinct driving him on. He glanced at the bridge's railing. It was six yards away, and with at least three AR-15s leveled at him, he'd never make it. Whatever he did, someone was going to die, just so long as it wasn't him.

Charlie picked up his gun and paused. The thought of shooting Bob ran through his mind, but his sense quickly resolved against that option. It was a suicidal move. He wanted to live.

"Oh, and Charlie, you have to shoot them until they're dead. We only shoot to kill!"

Charlie turned and eleven men faced him. Three seemed relaxed. They knew Charlie and were correct in thinking he wouldn't kill them. Of the eight remaining, three were white, two were Hispanic and two were black. The Hispanic and black recruits were by far the more nervous of the remaining eight.

Charlie began to raise his pistol.

"Oh, and Charlie, don't take the easy route and shoot the minorities, or someone you don't know," cautioned Bob, his smile widening.

As the color drained from his three friends' faces and their expressions changed markedly, it was an easy spot as to who Charlie knew.

"Okay, Charlie, one of your friends is about to meet his maker," said Bob. "If in the space of the next five seconds you don't make a choice, all three will die. And you too, of course, for failing to obey an order."

"Five…four…three…two…"

A shot rang out and a body fell to the ground. Charlie's friends looked at one another, all three still stood. They looked at their friend who had taken his own life rather than choose one of theirs. All breathed a sigh of relief and remorse for their friend.

Bob nodded, and three shots rang out. The three friends joined Charlie, dead on the ground. His sentries having taken the shots to fulfill Bob's order.

"Alive or dead, if you fail your orders, I'll follow through on my promises!" he cautioned to the eight men that stood before him.

Fifteen had become eight. Bob turned and waved Trey back with him behind the safety of the machine gun nests. "I've got room for four. Grab your weapon and kill a man and you're in!" he offered as he walked.

The rush of feet was followed by the scraping of metal on concrete before finally a number of shots rang out. Bob turned and smiled at the four new recruits to his militia. Two Hispanics and two blacks. He was all about diversity.

"Make sure they're useful," he whispered to Trey. "And get rid of those bodies. I don't want pigs stinking up our bridge!"

"Pigs?"

"Charlie, he was wearing police-issue boots!"

Trey looked back at the bodies on the bridge.

"All the white guys?"

Bob shrugged. "Who knows, but he was the only one stupid enough to wear his boots!"

"We'll be more careful!" advised Trey.

"Make sure you are!" cautioned Bob ominously.

Bob walked off, pausing, "The new recruits?"

"Yeah?" asked Trey.

The time for thought as Trey responded was enough for Bob to change his mind. "Get them into the training program, but no sentry duty for them anytime soon. Let's face it, some of our guys aren't going to be overly pleased with our new diversity hires!"

"Got it!"

"Oh and Trey, if anybody speaks out publicly about our new hires, you tell me!"

"Will do, Duke."

Bob walked back to the main estate and the core of his base. He hoped the new recruits would be accepted without question, but if he were to rule over all of Boise, he needed to have a diverse group. Racial tensions would lead to unnecessary conflicts. He had seen more than enough of that crap in the prison system without having it in *his* Boise. It was far easier for your authority to be accepted when you represented all of those you ruled over. The blacks and Hispanics wouldn't react well to an all-white militia dictating to them in the future. A Boise Militia had to represent Boise, and as much as he didn't like it, he knew it was for the best. His authority had to remain without question. He just hoped that none of his most trusted or loyal men spoke out. He'd hate to have to publicly kill them, but leaders had to step up and do what was necessary whenever called upon, and looking around at what he had achieved in just five days, he had no doubt how powerful a leader he was.

Chapter 26

The darkness, like the previous few nights, when it came, descended with an unsettling finality. There was no escape, and the candles barely ate into the all-encompassing blackness that surrounded them. The city ceased to exist below. The candle power, if anything, failed to progress beyond the curtains and blinds that kept the homeowners as secure and warm as they could be, given the circumstances. As she had before, Kate watched the highway below, willing a vehicle, anything to move, but the darkness and sharp edge of the tarmac stretched off into the distance, a shade darker than its surroundings, highlighting its almost useless existence.

Kate closed her curtain and retreated to bed. Danny was there already sound asleep, stretched out across Tim's side of the bed, a child's worriless sleep. What she would give for the ability to switch off her responsibilities and sleep as soundly as Danny, just for one night. What had weighed on her since Tim's death had been nothing compared to the stress and burden she felt bearing down on her then. Ava would join them too. . Not any time soon, but she knew at some point, the door would crack open and Ava would squeeze in next to her brother. Waking before dawn, she would sneak back to her room. For whatever reason, she didn't want to admit that she needed them and for the time being, Kate wasn't going to question it. She loved having her babies nearby.

"Mom?" a knock at her door was followed by the flickering of candlelight as it consumed the vacated darkness when the door pushed open.

"You okay?" asked Kate, as Sophie, her eldest, entered the bedroom.

"I just wanted to check and make sure Danny was okay."

It had been a traumatic day for everyone, except for Danny who remained blissfully unaware of the danger he had been in.

Kate looked at him, her mini-Tim, sound asleep, with not a care or worry in the world.

"Come on, jump in," said Kate, pulling the covers back.

"No, it's fine," she said sheepishly.

"Get in here. I think tonight, we could do with being together."

Sophie shrugged, blew out her candle and hopped in. Kate could almost feel the sense of relief emanating from Sophie. "What about Ava?" asked Sophie.

"Don't worry, I'm sure she'll join us soon enough."

Sophie's breathing fell quickly into a deep sleep and, Kate stared into the darkness of the ceiling. It had been an eventful and traumatic day. The thought of losing Danny had hit her hard and had been a stark wake up call to their new reality. How long would the community hold together?, How long before the willingness to share resources and help one another waned? The reality was that the help so many still expected to come, wasn't coming. Five days had passed, not one vehicle had moved, not one aircraft had been spotted overhead. Nothing worked and it obviously wasn't just Boise. The nuclear plant had been taken out, whether by the Russians, Iranians, or whoever, and it obviously wasn't the only one, as their country, their lives, as they'd known them were gone.

The afternoon had been spent digging a hole and fashioning an old tent over the hole to form a new toilet. A pile of dirt lay ready to fill the hole, as and when a new hole would be dug and the tent moved to a fresh site in the garden.

"What happens when it's freezing outside?" asked Sophie.

"You'll learn to be quicker!" laughed Zach, much to Sophie's embarrassment.

Storming off, Zach chased after her. Kate couldn't help but hope Sophie calmed down. Zach had been such a help, he'd be sorely missed if he and Sophie fell out. She needn't have worried, for five minutes later, love's young dream was in full flight. Sophie, without a doubt, had fallen hard and if Zach's enthusiasm to help was any gauge, he had also.

Kate was snapped out of her thoughts as her bedroom door brushed open. She closed her eyes, although why she bothered in the total darkness, she wasn't sure. Ava was a proud girl, and for whatever reason, wanted her nighttime visits to remain private.

"Mom?" Ava whispered urgently, reaching Kate's side of the bed.

Kate feigned sleepiness. She had a role to play.

"Mom," Ava whispered, shaking at her mom.

"What's wrong?"

"There's someone trying to get in!" replied Ava breathlessly.

Chapter 27

The sounds of laughter cut through the darkness almost as much as the screams. A new batch of entertainment had been brought in during the day. The Duke wanted his men fresh and ready for action when called upon, so ensuring their hormones were kept in check was just as important as ensuring they were physically capable for their duties. Trey looked around at the selection. There were a couple that he liked the look of, but to him, the fight was as important as the conquest and none of the women looked like they had much fight left in them. After two nights of disappointment, he wasn't particularly bothered and walked back out into the chill of the night air. His mind wandered back to the feisty redhead at the supermarket. She'd be a woman he'd enjoy. She was a woman he knew he'd have to fight and fight hard to tame, if he even could, which for him was all the better, unbreakable, perfect.

He looked across in the direction of Rogers's estate, off in the distance. It blended like every other area of Boise into the darkness. A black mass of civilization indiscernible, invisible for half of its existence.

He remembered the address Roger had given him. He had memorized it without effort, stamped into his mind for eternity. He licked his lips as he watched her cycle away, knowing he'd have her one day. He felt his loins stir just at the thought. Something he'd struggled to do the previous two nights with naked and almost willing women laying before him.

Two horsemen trotted past him.

"Where you going?" he quizzed.

"Patrol."

"On whose orders?"

Both looked at each other in the dimness of the lantern lights that struggled to offer even the faintest of detail in the base compound.

"Yours, I think. We have to have six riders patrolling the perimeter twenty-four-seven. We're just about to relieve two of the six."

"Is that you, Neil?" asked Trey, recognizing the voice rather than seeing the man's features. Neil was one of the main stable men and one of Bob's key men.

"Yeah," replied Neil. "And Eddie."

"Excellent. Get me another horse," commanded Trey, his smile hidden in the dimness as his plan formulated in his mind.

The six outriders extending their perimeter was overkill, and once the sentry points and machine gun nests were in place, really should have been discontinued. If nothing else to allow the horses a good rest through the night.

A few minutes later, he pulled himself on to a horse and joined Neil and Eddie as they rode out to relieve two militia members.

"Okay, you four, maintain the perimeter," Trey instructed. "Neil, Eddie, you're with me." As his eyes grew more accustomed to the darkness, he picked up the speed, the clop of the hooves on the tarmac echoing off into the distance. With little background noise at night to cover their progress, the sound of the horses was deafening, but any other route in the darkness was not only impractical but eminently dangerous.

"Where are we going?" asked Eddie as they cantered along the riverside road.

"Wherever the hell I tell you!" was Trey's answer. His focus was almost entirely on the prize that lay ahead. After twenty minutes, they slowed. The road took a sharp left and in the distance, Trey could just make out the bridge ahead.

"Whoa!" he commanded, bringing all three horses to a halt. He looked around in the darkness. Only the sharp blackness of the tarmac offered any real idea of their reference point.

"What are you looking for?" asked Neil carefully, conscious of Trey's previous reaction.

"Warm Springs Mesa," replied Trey, continuing to try and see beyond the darkness.

"Oh yeah, no problem. That's up there," pointed Eddie.

Trey could sense the man was pointing, but couldn't see where. "Lead the way!" he commanded.

"Be careful, we just have to get down on to the old road," cautioned Eddie, striding forward before slowing his pace. Waiting for the others to catch up, he weaved around what Trey guessed was a gate before once again, picking up speed. The blackness of the road broke off in three directions. Eddie took the right and they immediately started to climb. Trey's smile returned along with the growth in his loins. "East Hard Rock Drive,'" advised Trey.

"Yep, I know it."

"You know the area well?"

"I was a cabbie, so I hope so!" replied Eddie.

"Wait a minute, Warm Springs Mesa. I was at the supermarket, it's not that redhead, is it?" asked Eddie.

Trey could hear the excitement in his voice.

"She's mine. I'm sure we'll find you boys someone else to amuse you up here!"

"You know Bob said we wouldn't cause any more trouble in Warm Springs Mesa," said Neil warily. Damned if he did, damned if he didn't, he was stuck between two guys that scared the shit out of him. He didn't know much about Trey, but knew enough to know he was a loose cannon. The only person who had any control over him was Bob. How real that control was and how much was show in front of the militia men, he didn't know. To the outside world, the two were tight, real tight, and getting in between them was not somewhere Neil had any intention of getting.

"I'll let you know what Bob does and doesn't need to know about what I do!" replied Trey. Neither Eddie nor Neil missed the threatening tone.

"I was just sayin'," offered Neil with his hands raised, not that Trey could see them, it just felt like the right thing to do.

The rest of the ride was in silence, both of Trey's companions having been put in their place.

"It's the next street on the left," said Eddie, breaking the silence.

"Stop here," commanded Trey, bringing his horse to a halt and hopping down.

Neil and Eddie complied, following Trey's instructions and joining him at the end of the street on foot.

"She's number six. We'll approach quietly. Wouldn't want to spoil the surprise," chuckled Trey. Neither Neil nor Eddie joined in the humor, it had been made clear they were along for support, there wasn't going to be any reward for them.

With each passing day, the sun dropped earlier in the evening sky, lengthening the hours of darkness as winter edged ever nearer. It was barely nine pm as they slipped past the houses, all in darkness. Candles were a finite resource and the inhabitants of the street were already becoming accustomed to their new regime. With no entertainment on offer outside of books to read, which required candlelight, darkness meant sleep. With everything requiring more effort to achieve, it seemed sleep had become almost second nature, even to those who'd previously suffered insomnia. Minds were far less cluttered when all you had to worry about was food, water, warmth and sanitation. Worries about jobs, money and the future were already fading, and not even a week had passed.

Trey tapped Eddie on the shoulder and sent him around back. Their eyes struggled against the almost complete darkness. Only the blackness of the house against the night skyline, gave any hint as to their location. Trey waited for Eddie to get in position before moving towards the front door. Again, blocks of darkness led the way, the driveway's solid lines giving little help as to where they were.

"Shit, it's dark!" said Neil needlessly as they edged towards where they believed the door to be.

A scuffle before a thump emphasized just how dark it was. "Fu–"

"Shh…" warned Trey as Neil fell to the ground.

A dog barking next door stopped them both in their tracks, a slow deep lazy woof, slowly followed by another.

Trey rested his hand on Neil's head, stopping him from moving. Three barks, Trey waited for another. When it never came, he released Neil and let him stand up.

"A bike or something, I think," whispered Neil, explaining himself. Trey was not interested. He was already edging towards the door. His hand reached out for the handle and twisted it gently. Unsurprisingly, it was locked.

The sound of locks being opened cut through the silence. Trey stepped back and looked to his left. A door creaked open. The slow deep drawl of the elderly dog barking escaped into the night sky.

"Who's there?" came a shout, the voice as old as the dog's bark.

Chapter 28

Kate slipped from the bed and gathered her children around her, shushing them as she woke them. She looked to her bedside table where she knew the phone sat useless while pulling her kids in close, not that it was going to be of any use. She stood. She needed to act, not cower. Keeping the kids safe was the priority. She stumbled forward, leading the way to the basement. She remembered Tim telling her how secure it was, the door was solid wood and opened outwards. Meaning unlike most doors, a well-placed boot and sheer force wouldn't get through. It had to be pulled open and with a couple of large bolts for added security, should the need ever arise, that'd be no mean feat.

The only problem was that the door to the basement lay downstairs and near the front door. If they made it before whoever was prowling around gained entry, it would be fine, but if not… she didn't even want to think about that scenario. She'd be delivering her babies into the face of danger.

"Quick!" she whispered, ushering them as they felt their way in the darkness down the corridor and towards the stairs. Hank's barks gave them an added incentive. He rarely interrupted his sleep. If he was barking, there was definitely someone around.

Kate led the way tentatively, taking each step carefully and ensuring her weight was spread before taking her next step. The kids followed suit, and all four descended silently towards the unknown. They could only hope their home had yet not been breached.

"Who's there?" Harry's voice carried through the night. Hopefully, his very presence would scare whoever they were away. If not, Kate was sure his double-barreled shotgun would be backing up his shouts.

"Get back inside before you get yourself hurt, old man!"

The angry shout came from just outside the front door. Whoever was there was at their house. Kate's heart pounded in her chest. Up until that moment they'd been random prowlers. Now, she knew they were at her house and were a danger to her babies. She cleared the bottom step and it was just a few yards to the basement door. She felt for its handle in the darkness.

"Get away from there before I…"

Hank's barking drowned out the rest of Harry's words, his slow lazy woof had suddenly turned into a frenzied assault, unlike anything Kate had heard from him before.

Footsteps outside began to crash, quick and heavy, not those of an old man. The sound diminished with each step. More than one man. Whoever they were, they were rushing towards Harry. Kate couldn't worry about Harry, she had to get her babies safe. After that, she would do what she could. Her hand fell on the handle and she pulled the door open, but it stopped after a few inches.

Kate screamed and pulled with all her might to get the door fully open.

Eddie, who had made it through the back patio doors with ease, had walked into the hallway just as Kate had started to open the door. He couldn't see in the darkness and had assumed he had walked into a wall until it started pushing against him, throwing him off balance and knocking him to the ground.

A blast caught everyone by surprise and silenced Hank's wild barking, at least for a short while. Kate shoved

Sophie, Ava, and Danny into the basement, kicking wildly at the man at her feet.

"Lock the door!" she screamed, pushing the door closed as the man grabbed her ankle and pulled her down on top of him. Kate wasn't going down without a fight. She angled her elbow and ensured the point met the man below her with her full weight and every ounce of strength behind it. A satisfying expulsion of air was proceeded by her ankle being released. Kate sprang to her feet. Her attacker was still struggling to work out what the hell was happening, while Kate ensured her kids had bolted the basement door. She pulled on the door, but it didn't budge so much as a fraction of an inch. With her kids safe for the moment, she rushed to the front door. She couldn't leave Harry to deal with the trouble on his own. After all, he was protecting them and not himself.

She pulled open the front door and rushed outside. Two flashes in the darkness lit up the scene before her as the sound waves echoed out across the valley. Harry's shots must have been a warning to the prowlers, both seemed unhurt. Unlike the return fire they sent back, both bullets hit Harry, making his body contort one way then another. Kate's scream was answered by Hank's pitiful howl, thanks to a boot from one of the prowlers which landed with a sickening thud. His whimpers in the darkness were all that remained as the violence ended. Harry lay silent. Even in the darkness, his lack of movement was visible.

Kate sprinted back into the house, slamming the door behind her.

"Come back for Eddie, have we?" asked the prowler. His teeth eerily visible through the darkness.

Kate felt as agile as she ever had. Although she knew her competition days were well behind her, her fitness levels had been maintained, not necessarily out of choice but of necessity, a mother's work was never done. She launched herself towards the teeth and threw out her foot. She wasn't any martial arts expert, but she had the moves and capability to do with her body what most people couldn't. For her height, she could jump far higher than most. Her gymnastic skills came to the fore, her leg swung out, locking at the knee and her full force travelled through her foot and into Eddie's face. His body collapsed beneath Kate, her momentum carrying her on and over his body, landing almost noiselessly behind him. He hadn't seen a thing, nor had any idea where she was.

"Bitch!" he screamed, sweeping his arms out in an attempt to catch her within his grasp.

A kick to the front door sent it crashing into the hallway wall.

"Where's that little cutie?" crowed Trey as he entered.

"Guys!" a panicked shout from behind Trey, caught his and Eddie's attention. They both looked out and the darkness had gone as a few oil lanterns tried desperately to cast their light across the area, making their way towards the house.

"Put your gun down!" commanded a voice from behind the lanterns.

Trey shut the front door, leaving Neil outside to cope with whoever was there. He had all he needed. Kate was there and she was just as feisty as he had hoped.

"It looks like there are quite a few of them," warned Eddie, noting the number of lanterns.

"It's dark and they'll not want to harm the family. I'll have my fun and we'll be gone out the back before daybreak."

"And Neil?"

"He can look after himself. Now, where is she?"

"In the kitchen, I think. She put her kids in the basement before I had a chance to stop her," he replied, picking himself up uneasily. She had caught him perfectly on the chin and there was every chance, from the pain going through his jaw, that it was broken.

"Kids? More than one?"

"Yeah, she's got two daughters and a son."

"What age are the daughters?"

"One's quite young, but the other, she's a fine…"

The clang of the pot hitting his skull echoed through the enclosed hallway, but the damage was already done. He had revealed that Sophie was in the basement. She didn't know who Eddie was, but he obviously knew her from before. There was no way in the darkness, he could have known about Ava and in particular, Sophie.

Trey laughed heartily as Eddie hit the floor for a second time.

"I'm going to screw that spirit right out of you," he shouted down the hallway towards the darkness of the kitchen. "But I think I'll practice on that daughter of yours first!"

Trey felt his way to the basement door and pulled, but it failed to move. He raised his pistol and shot into the lock, it still failed to move. Screams escaped from below as the holes in the door let the sound flow.

"Trey's comin'," shouted Trey eerily, lifting his pistol and emptying a clip into the hinges. The door fell away from the opposite side. Whatever Trey was, he wasn't going to let a door get between him and his goal. He ripped the door back to reveal a dim light, the candles below lit up the staircase. Before he'd taken a step, he was forced down the hallway, crashing onto the carpet. The sweet smell of woman covered him. He became instantly erect as she thrashed wildly at him.

"Eddie?" he said calmly as punch after punch landed. Suddenly, the livewire was being hoisted off and a wildly flung kick caught him square on the nose, and he felt the cartilage give way. It wasn't its first break, but it was the first time he'd enjoyed it.

Eddie tried to stand with his legs apart as Kate continued to swing her legs wildly in an attempt to connect with whatever she could. Her arms were held aloft as Eddie struggled to keep her restrained under her constant struggle.

"Put your guns down and come out!" came a command from outside.

"Take her down to the basement," commanded Trey. He'd had enough of being told what to do. "And remember, she's mine!"

Eddie smiled, noted loud and clear, which meant the daughter could be his.

Another kick from Kate landed on his shin. He winced and threw her unceremoniously down the rest of the stairs. Kate landed with a crack, her world suddenly dulled as the force of the impact made her world spin. Her kids' screams as Eddie progressed slowly down the stairs faded into the background as the darkness consumed her. She was aware of a sustained gunfire from above, but her mind was struggling to make any sense, until it couldn't.

Chapter 29

"Wake up!"

The banging at the door increased, the urgency of whoever was knocking was growing by the second.

"Gary, will you wake up?!" pleaded his wife. It had been a long day for the sheriff's deputy, ensuring that Warm Springs Mesa remained safe and the darkness had been a welcome diversion.

"Wh...wha…what is it?" he rubbed at his eyes, the banging on his front door below bringing him straight into the present. "What the hell…" he jumped out of bed. The candlelight his wife had lit failed to offer any help in identifying who was battering at their door.

He grabbed his sidearm and raced downstairs, pulling his pants and shirt on as he negotiated the pitch-dark stairs at breakneck speed.

"Who's there!" he demanded as he reached the bottom step. He remained behind the stair wall, keeping it between him and his front door.

'Gabe. I'm on night watch duty. Three horseback riders have breached our perimeter!"

"Give me a minute!" Gary shouted, pulling his boots on.

"Honey, lock the door behind me!" he instructed before joining Gabe on his doorstep.

"How many men have you alerted?"

"We should have about ten."

"Good, where are the riders?"

"East Hard Rock Drive."

"Ahh, shit!"

"What?"

"I've an idea what they're after. Somebody mentioned one of Bob Jackson's men has a thing for Kate Wolfe and after the day they've already had with Danny being abducted…God, I don't even want to think about it."

Gary led the way, meeting up with the rest of the community volunteers that had been roused to deal with the intruders. With three oil lanterns between them, the eleven men walked steadfastly towards the street. Each was armed with whatever weapon they could lay their hands on, whether it was a hunting rifle, a pistol or a shotgun. They knew the militia outgunned them. Their weapons were no match for the militia's automatic rifles. But what they lacked in firepower, they made up for in numbers and resolve. This was their community, their families. They were defending against a tyrannical force that had no place amongst them.

There was no doubt in Gary's mind they had right on their side. Bob and his militia had already committed countless acts of the most heinous atrocities across the city. With each day, their power had grown but at some point, the law-abiding and right-thinking people of Boise had to stand up for themselves and show that the rule of law remained in force. Enough was enough. He marched his men forward with purpose. The shotgun blast in the distance paused them in their tracks, but the two rounds fired in response got them moving again, their speed increasing as the situation was obviously escalating.

The sight of Harry's unmoving body in the dimness of the lantern light, with his old, faithful dog whimpering by his side and licking at his face was all he needed. Gary's resolve was complete.

"Put your gun down!" he commanded, directing his weapon at the man standing by Kate's open door. The man lowered his AR-15 as instructed. Before Gary could move,

Kate's door slammed shut behind their prisoner. It seemed whoever he was, he was expendable.

With their prisoner secured, Gary turned his attention to the house. It remained in complete darkness. He didn't even want to think of what could be going on in there. Three riders had been spotted entering Warm Springs, which meant at least two were inside with Kate and her family. One thing was for certain, they couldn't wait it out. They had to act and act quickly to save Kate, Sophie, and god forbid, even Ava from what would be a life-changing situation.

"Put your guns down and come out!" he commanded with every ounce of authority his anger would allow.

Chapter 30

Trey cracked the door open and emptied a full magazine into the street. The cries of pain brought a smile to his face. He closed the door. That would keep them busy long enough for him to enjoy himself. The way he was feeling, how fired up he was, it wasn't going to take long anyway.

He checked through the spyhole, one lantern was on the ground and its oil had spilled, creating a trail of light that lit up at least two men on the ground, writhing in pain. Others were running to their aid. Trey knew it would be enough to take the fight out of some. It wouldn't stop them all, but whatever number had been there initially he felt sure would halve itself. It was easy being the law when things were going your way. When the tide turned, you began to consider your priorities a little more clearly.

He watched a moment longer as the two other lanterns tracked back towards the injured men. The fight was over.

He turned as the front door burst open. They had played him with the lanterns, using the light to distract him while they'd snuck up on the house. The door propelled him down the hallway. He turned as he fell and pulled the trigger on his AR-15, and it clicked. He hadn't reloaded. Two men rushed towards him. He grabbed for his pistol as he, for the second time in as many minutes, hit the carpet. His pistol had almost cleared his holster when the first man landed on him, and a knee caught him in the stomach, expelling almost every cubic inch of air from his system. His hand fell as did his pistol to the floor as he gasped for oxygen. Whoever was on him knew what they were doing, the knee was continuing to push, making it almost impossible to catch his breath.

Trey bellowed in frustration as he pushed at the man on top of him. His rage gave him the strength to force a breath.

An ear-piercing scream from the basement caught them all by surprise.

Unlike the community volunteers, the stomach-churning scream of a young girl didn't knock Trey off of his stride. He saw his chance and took it, swinging his right fist into the man's side.

***

"Mom!" Danny's tears flooded down his face as he pushed and pulled at his mom's lifeless body.

A scream in her consciousness brought her around. Her body swaying with Danny's efforts, a sudden urge to be sick was quelled as another scream assaulted her swimming mind. She looked around wildly. The attacker, Eddie, that was his name, was moving towards Sophie. There was no doubting his intention.

Sophie was up against the far wall, the man forcing himself on to her. Ava had picked up a piece of lumber and was swinging it. Eddie had Sophie pinned by the throat and turned as Ava swung. He caught the lumber easily in his hand and pushed it away, and with it, Ava. She crashed into the safe a few feet behind them and slumped to the basement floor.

Eddie turned his attention back to Sophie, his hand clasped tightly around her neck to ensure she could do little to stop him from running his free hand down her face and arm. She struggled but with each movement almost choked herself.

Kate tried to get up. Her mind wanted to, but her body failed. She pulled herself across the floor. Ava was just a few yards away and Sophie just a few yards beyond.

Eddie's hand was making its way down Sophie's still dressed torso. Kate wanted to kill him. She pulled herself onwards.

Eddie heard her and turned. She was less than three feet from Ava.

He pulled out a knife and placed it on Sophie's unblemished cheek.

"Ah, ah, mommy. Your fun's coming. Don't go trying to spoil mine! Or your daughter's beautiful face!"

Kate pointed to the unmoving Ava.

Eddie flicked an acceptance, yes, she could see to Ava. He turned his attention back to Sophie as Kate pulled herself to Ava. Kate gasped in horror when she spotted a pool of blood beneath her younger daughter, a large gash on her leg from the corner of the safe. Kate's mind was coming out of its haze. She looked over at Sophie as she waved for Danny to join her and bring the laundry basket.

Eddie checked what Kate was doing. He noticed the blood and the wound on Ava's leg. It would keep her busy. He pulled Sophie towards the far corner of the basement, where the candlelight struggled to reach. A workbench was all the equipment he needed. He lifted the struggling Sophie onto the bench, the knife pressing into her throat, keeping the struggle within his control.

"Twenty-two, twelve, sixteen," whispered Kate to Danny. Danny looked at her, confused. She nodded to the safe's combination panel as she applied pressure to Ava's wound. It was deep, but not too big, she just needed to stop it bleeding. Kate prayed Tim had kept the mechanism and the door well-oiled, she hoped so and fully expected he had.

He'd certainly looked after his guns and could only imagine that extended to where he'd kept them safely locked away. She hated guns and had made him promise their kids would be saved from the same fate as her childhood. Her father had been obsessed with guns, an obsession that ultimately took his life and. she was sure, had led to her mother's death, long before her time.

Danny turned the dial and was rewarded with a subtle click before the safe's door cracked open slightly. Kate signaled for him to hold the cloth she had pressed against Ava's wound.

Kate could hear Sophie's muffled struggling. Each sound drove her on, each sound increasingly clearing her mind. She looked towards the bench. She could barely make out the two figures. She focused. She wasn't too late and Eddie's attention was diverted. She pulled open the door, praying for it to swing back quietly. It did. Its hinges were oiled as well as she knew Tim's guns would be. The candlelight shone against the dull metal of the safe's contents. Three rifles on a rack and four pistols. A number of full magazines for each lay stacked and ready to load.

"You hate guns!" whispered Danny as Kate reached into the safe. "I can help, Dad showed me what to do!"

Kate couldn't help but throw a disproving look at her youngest, despite his innocence in his fathers' betrayal of her express wishes. Her kids should never have been anywhere near the guns. Memories of her father flashed through her mind. She had found him. The image had never dulled, even after twenty years. Fragments of skull and brain matter dripped from the garage ceiling where the majority of his head had been relocated. His death had been instantaneous, her mother's, as a result, was long and drawn out. Ten years of mourning and depression, followed by a slow painful death from a cancer Kate was convinced had been caused as a result.

"I know what to do!" whispered Kate firmly, selecting Tim's Walther PPQ and sliding a magazine into place, pulling the slide back, and chambering a round. She stood and picking up the candle, moved towards the back of the basement, throwing Eddie and Sophie into the light. Eddie spun and Kate breathed a sigh of relief. His pants were still on and Sophie was still fully dressed. She hadn't taken too long.

Eddie pulled Sophie from the bench and thrust her in front of himself. His rifle was out of reach, but his knife was more than adequate as he pressed it against Sophie's neck.

Kate raised the PPQ and leveled it at Eddie.

"Whoa! Be careful there! Wouldn't want your daughter's neck to open up," smiled Eddie.

"I'll be careful!" promised Kate evenly.

"Mom, what the hell are you doing?" panicked Sophie. Her mom pointing a gun in her direction was not something she ever wanted to experience. "You hate guns! Please don't point that over here!"

"Listen to your daughter. You don't want to shoot your daughter by accident, do you? Guns are dangerous things and should only be used by folks that know what they're doing," smiled Eddie, his teeth shining confidently in the candlelight.

"Sophie's right. I do hate guns," confirmed Kate. Eddie's grip on the knife at Sophie's neck relaxed on Kate's confession. She wouldn't dare take the shot.

Kate fired. The bullet struck Eddie perfectly in the center of his forehead. "Just because I hate them, doesn't mean I don't know how to use them!" she said to his corpse.

"You okay?" she asked of Sophie who was standing perfectly still, not daring to move. Eddie's body lay motionless at her feet.

Sophie nodded. Kate turned back to Ava and the open-mouthed Danny.

Ava was coming around. "You two okay?"

Danny nodded firmly, the not-so-with-it Ava nodded half-heartedly, wincing in pain.

Kate raced up the stairs. Their home was under attack and she was damned if she was going to cower and hide. It was her job to protect her family and whoever put them in danger, was going to feel the full force of her duty as a mother to protect her family.

Chapter 31

Trey traded punches with the mass on top of him. He couldn't see much, but he felt the weight and threw every ounce of strength he had into hitting whoever was on top of him. The screams had continued below until a shot ended them. Trey threw an enraged punch as the thought of Eddie shooting Kate filled his mind. It caught the man cleanly on the side of the head. The weight buckled and fell. Trey pushed at the remaining weight and without restraint, it slid to the floor by his side, unconscious. It had been a perfect punch, complete luck as the darkness did not allow for even the slightest inkling of targets.

"Gary? You okay, Gary?" The voice came from further down the hallway. The second man was hanging back. Trey knew his weapon would be trained towards him, but there was no way the man would shoot whilst Gary could be in the firing line. Trey felt around wildly for a weapon, anything to shoot into the voice.

"Gary?" the voice was becoming increasingly concerned.

His hand hit the grip of a pistol. He unconsciously looked to where he knew his hand to be, in a vain attempt to assist in finding the gun. As if by magic, light erupted beneath his hand, faint but eating through the darkness, spreading its weak presence across the floor. Of course, his mind realized that whatever he could see would aid the volunteer at the end of the hallway. He grabbed for what he could identify as a Glock and aimed towards where the voice had emanated. The light was not his friend anymore.

The darkness shrouded the volunteer while the light creeping towards him from the basement below was casting an ever-greater arc through the doorway and across the hallway where he remained.

"Gary, is that you?" the volunteer hesitated. The candlelight was weak and the darkness all encompassing. Its power enough to show a man, but hide his features.

It was all the hesitation Trey needed, he pulled the trigger and sent a bullet hurtling towards where he had heard the latest question.

His hand snapped back in pain. The gun had misfired. He'd heard two shots at once. The pistol lay on the floor once again. The pain in his hand was increasing exponentially with every passing microsecond.

"Don't move!" a voice from his right, a female voice, threatened. He ignored her and turned his head. The candle in her left hand lit up all of her most striking features perfectly. She really was a true beauty.

"Kate," he smiled, ignoring the pain.

"I'm coming out!" shouted Kate. "Is everything okay?"

"Kate, is that you?"

"Yes, can I come out?"

"There were three guys as far as we know. We have one outside. One, you've got in front of you. I don't know about the third."

"The third's no longer a concern," she replied evenly, as much for Trey as anyone. The message was clear. She wouldn't hesitate to kill him.

With Trey tied up and safely secured, attention turned to Gary, following his blind struggle with Trey. He came around quickly and other than a headache and an unnecessary hit to his pride, he appeared to be none the worse for the situation.

"Is Harry okay?"

The silence that followed her question sent tears running down her cheek. Poor, sweet Harry. She wished she had the shot to make again with Trey. She would have aimed for his head and not his hand. But she knew she had done the right thing. The only way to save the man Trey was aiming at was to hit the gun. It'd been a calculated shot and one she had her father to thank for. As a young girl, he'd not only wanted her to operate a gun safely, but he'd wanted her to be proficient. Her competitive nature ensured that was not a concern. Her proficiency was exceptional. Handguns, rifles, whatever you gave her, she'd mastered. She was, as many who'd seen her in action as a teenager claimed, a natural. Where she aimed, she hit. She had saved an innocent life by not taking Trey's.

Kate borrowed a lantern and walked out to Harry's side. Two bullets, center mass, his suffering would have been minimal, if at all. Hank lay by his side, his head resting on his master's chest, looking expectantly for Harry to come to life. Kate's heart broke for Harry and for Hank. He had lost his companion, a man who had loved and cared for him since he was born. An old dog with no memories of a life other than with Harry. Her thoughts went to the terribly sad story of the dog, she couldn't remember his name, that they had heard of on a vacation in Edinburgh, Scotland. When his master had died, he had spent the rest of his life sitting on his grave, mourning his loss.

Kate looked down at Hank, his old eyes sagging pitifully.

"Come on," she said as she grabbed him by the collar. "Say goodbye to Harry. You're staying with us now."

"What are you doing?" asked Gary as she pulled a reluctant Hank by her side, back towards her house.

"Taking Hank home," she said.

"He's another mouth to feed."

"And?"

"Well, things are going to be tough enough –"

"We'll manage," she replied irritably at Gary's less than subtle suggestion that Hank should be euthanized.

"Can you please bury poor Harry and get that piece of shit out of my basement? I'm going to see to my family."

Gary, with two prisoners and two wounded men requiring assistance, had more than enough to keep him busy, but he simply nodded, adding two burials to his 'to do list'. Kate was clearly not a woman you wanted to get on the wrong side of.

Chapter 32

With the first wisps of sunlight breaking over the horizon, Nick was training his binoculars on the housing estate below. The nighttime gunshots and activity from the otherwise safe estate below had not gone unnoticed by he and Alex. Nick had struggled to sleep in any event, the deaths of the teenagers wearing on him, although he knew he'd had no choice. Even the slightest hint that their mission even existed could be catastrophic and endanger everything they had been working for. Every life that had been lost up until that point would have been in vain. Alex had been awakened by the disturbance and both had watched the lanterns moving for a number of hours before finally, a few hours later, darkness once again reigned.

"Well?" Alex yawned as he queried his colleague's findings.

"Nothing obvious yet, all seems calm, Although, there are three horses tied up that weren't there before."

"There's only one place we've seen horses–"

"So, I suppose it's no surprise there was a disturbance last night."

"Oh well. Looks like your little nirvana is about to come crashing to an end," said Alex, turning his attention to his breakfast.

"What the hell…"

Nick's binoculars had caught movement. A number of men had appeared in one of the streets below, two clearly restrained with their hands tied behind their backs. They walked the two men towards the horses. Three men mounted the horses while others helped secure the restrained men behind two of the riders.

"Oh, dear God," sighed Alex, joining Nick, and watching the scene unfold. "They think they can work with the militia?"

"Perhaps they are doing the smart thing?" questioned Nick half-heartedly.

"There are three horses and only two men in restraints!" said Alex, once again turning to his breakfast preparations. "However this ends, it isn't well, certainly not for your 'ray of hope' community."

Nick looked up at the sky. He was sure he'd caught the glint of the drone that circled overhead awaiting their updates. He wondered if they could see him, if they had watched the events unfold throughout the night. If they were getting everything they wanted from the situation. If their actions really did warrant the suffering, destruction, and death.

"Nick," cautioned Alex, watching his colleague's thoughts cloud. "We have our orders!"

Nick nodded as he looked back into the binoculars and followed the three horses making their way down to the main road at the riverside before they dropped out of sight.

"So, what's for breakfast?" he asked as cheerily as his somber mood would allow.

"Random food in a small bag," offered Alex, handing over the MRE pouch he had just heated. It had been another of their purchases on arrival at Boise to ensure their real identity remained unknown should a worst-case scenario arise. A special offer with a selection of MRE meals had been purchased. Unfortunately, the codes on the individual packs identifying the contents were explained on the packaging, and that had been discarded in the interest of weight management. Hence their almost Russian Roulette-style meal selection.

Nick pulled back the top of the bag and was hit with a wave of spices. Chicken curry, a perfect start to anyone's day, he sighed sarcastically to himself.

Chapter 33

Bob, the Duke, was a not a man that anyone wanted to be anywhere near that morning. His temper had frayed beyond reason. The news that his cousin was missing, along with Neil, Eddie and three horses had not been well received. The base had been turned upside down for any clue as to where they could have gone.

The last anyone knew, Trey had given instructions to the four perimeter guards, and ridden off with Neil and Eddie.

They had ridden west into the darkness. Bob looked across to the west and the main city of Boise. Where the hell would they be going in the darkness? Thoughts of the three deserters began to form in Bob's mind, enraging his fractious mood further.

"How many horses do we have?" he asked, already knowing the answer. Over the last few days, they had doubled their number of horses and were adding more each day. They were the future, as far as Bob was concerned. With no other means of transport to ship products, or cover even short distances in good time, the horse and cart once again ruled the west. There was also no doubting their additional power. Five men riding at speed on horseback were a far more intimidating force than five men on foot. Adding their fully automatic rifles to the mix, the militia outgunned and outmanned any other faction in Boise, and had the means to project that power around the city with ease.

Hearing the number, less three, didn't help his mood. Although, had they not discounted the missing three, he'd have been equally as annoyed and likely to punish whoever it was who'd failed to count properly. As it was, he had to go with what he was told.

"Okay, I want twenty men saddled up and ready to leave with me in ten minutes."

His instruction resulted in a flurry of activity, men rushing to meet his ten-minute deadline. Within nine minutes, twenty-one horses sat ready in the center of the militia base. Twenty men were armed and ready to accompany Bob, who strode out of his house on the tenth minute and pulled himself onto the twenty-first horse. He led the way and, rode towards the main gate without so much as a word. Dark thoughts had taken hold in his mind – Trey's betrayal.

"Riders coming in!" came a shout from the sentry post ahead.

Bob threw up his hand and stopped his posse in their tracks.

"How many?" he called.

"Three horses, looks like five men."

The sentry post sat atop the house at the entrance to the estate, the elevated position offering a greater field of vision.

Bob clicked his horse onwards and rode towards the first line of defense, their machine gun nests that sat either side of the entrance to the estate.

The three horses came into view shortly after he, for a second time, had drawn his posse to a stop.

Bob immediately recognized Gary as the lead rider. His mind raced as he tried to work out just what had happened.

"Gary!" he said as cordially as his temper would allow. Gary drew to a halt ten yards from Bob.

"Bob, I'm sorry about this."

"Will you just shoot these guys already!" demanded Trey from the back of the second horse.

"Trey, are you okay?" asked Bob calmly. His temper was settling as his mind over Trey's desertion was eased.

"What do you think? I'm tied up and have a broken finger!" whined Trey.

"That was before he was tied up. He has not been harmed in any way as a prisoner," assured Gary quickly. He'd had no idea just how powerful the militia had become until they had arrived at the base. He thought Bob had twenty or so men. What faced him was a well-armed base and a heavily-armed cavalry troop, with a small army still in reserve.

"Bob–"

"Trey, I think I'll hear what Gary has to say first," said Bob, interrupting his cousin. He turned to his posse and dismissed them. His two machine gun nests and sentries were more than adequate to deal with the threat of Gary and his two men. He also did not want Trey's indiscretion, whatever it was, broadcast across the base.

Bob rode out and stopped next to Gary, allowing their conversation to be undertaken at a more private level. He had to maintain his chain of command and authority, which included ensuring that Trey, his number two, was not the butt of the base's jokes.

Gary took less than five minutes to lay out what had happened. Bob's eyes flickered a number of times to his cousin, only to be met with a defiant, 'so what' look. None of what Gary claimed did Trey dispute.

"So, you have two injured men and one dead?"

Gary nodded. Summing up the night by casualties was not exactly how he would have summed up events. "And one very traumatized family," he added. "Three young kids, one girl who will–"

"Yeah, yeah, I get it," said Bob, seeing where Gary was heading. "Trey, do you want to add anything?" he asked. Trey shook his head.

"Neil?"

"Just that I had no idea why we were going there, Duke. I stayed outside and never went in the house! I was just following Trey's orders."

Gary raised an eyebrow as the name Duke was uttered, while Trey cast a look of derision towards Neil for his spinelessness.

"I don't want any animosity between us. I know you didn't sanction their actions and I brought them back here as a show of good faith, along with the horses," offered Gary, signaling for his men to jump down before joining them. He patted the rear end of his horse, his two men did the same and the three horses, Trey and Neil trotted towards the base entrance. Gary and his two men stood with no more than side arms below Bob, still astride his horse.

"I appreciate you bringing them back and taking care of them." Bob leaned across the horn of the saddle, adding to the sincerity of his words. "I really do, more than you will ever know. Trey, despite his faults, is very special to me."

"We are living in crazy times. I'm sure you appreciate things could have ended very differently."

Bob nodded, "I really do." He turned his horse towards the base and clucked it onwards. "I wish things were different but please understand, I have to maintain the militia's authority." Bob nodded to his sentries as he rode past them on his way back into the base.

Chapter 34

Kate removed the chair that was wedged under her bedroom door handle. If somebody wanted to get in, they'd have had to kick the door down. Danny raced down to let Hank out, although Hank was not in any shape to keep up with Danny. Sophie had hardly moved after they had climbed into bed. She had clamped herself to her mother's side and despite the heat that was generated between them, refused to let go. Sleep had been, at least for Kate, minimal, as the events of the day and night circled wildly. She had killed a man, shot him with a gun. A gun that lay by her bedside, ready to defend her family again if needed. She lifted the gun and slid it into the holster she had affixed to her belt. She looked down at it and the mere sight of it sent a shiver through her. Not because it felt wrong; it felt good. She caught sight of herself in the mirror. She felt powerful, protected.

Kate walked downstairs to the hallway and the scene of the previous night's fracas, fully expecting to see a mess. It was perfect, even their front door appeared to be working properly. Gary and his men had worked through the night to ensure she and her family were safe. She needed to do something to repay their support and kindness. What they had done for her and her family was beyond what she could ever have expected. They'd risked their lives for her and her family. After breakfast, she would make a point of going to visit Gary and personally thank him and his men.

First, she had to go down to the basement. She needed to check that it had been cleaned and secondly, she needed to change the code on the safe. A curious nine-year-old knowing the code to a gun safe was not and never would be her idea of good parenting. She lit the candle and pulled the broken door back from the entranceway. She took two tentative steps, ducking down with the candle and looking towards the far corner. The candlelight offered little help and she had to walk down the stairs. Once at the bottom, she could see where Eddie had fallen. His body had been removed. A dark stain marked the area where his blood had soaked into the floor, but the smell of bleach told her once again that the men had gone above and beyond to help her. Even in the dead of night, they had gone to extraordinary lengths to help her and her family. The sense of gratitude and pride she had for the wonderful community they lived in brought her to the edge of tears. She moved away and back towards the gun safe, wiping her eyes as she walked. She opened the safe and surveyed its contents more thoroughly than she'd had time to the previous night. The revulsion she would have had just a few hours earlier had passed. An epiphany had occurred.

To her, for the last twenty years, guns had been the reason her father had died. Of that she had no doubt, and she hated the sight of them. A brief bout of depression from losing his job had ended instantly and without effort, by one shot to the head. It had been so easy, too easy. There'd been no doubt in either her mind or her mother's. The ease with which he had been able to take his life was the reason he was dead. Had he had to think about his actions, think about how to end his life, they were sure he'd have faltered, sure he would have opened up about his situation, sure he would still be alive. But no. From cleaning his gun to death, in the blink of an eye, one suicidal thought and he was gone.

But everything had changed. The world had changed. Law and order no longer existed. Nothing had made that more evident than the previous night's events. Had it not been for her own actions, her daughter would have been raped, as would she. Trey would have killed Gabe in the corridor and most likely Gary. After being raped, who knew what would have happened. She didn't even want to think like that. Danny. Ava. Still young and innocent. What would have become of them had she and Sophie been taken away to be used? She shuddered at the thought. Guns had saved her. Just as surely as they had killed her father, they had saved her family. She had thought it many times, said it many times over the last few days. They were in a new reality and in that reality, guns were necessary for survival. And if there's one thing Kate was going to ensure, it was that her family was going to make it through whatever was thrown at them.

Without a second thought, Kate began to check the weapons. She knew what to do. Her father had her stripping and cleaning guns from before she could even remember. Her fingers worked the catches and springs as though she had cleaned them every day. It was as the expression went, just like riding a bike, it came straight back. She barely had to think about what she was doing, the muscle memories were so natural from all those years earlier. Once checked, she loaded a magazine in each weapon and after changing the combination, locked the safe. She patted the pistol on her belt, and a sense of reassurance swept over her. A comfort that, despite the previous night's events, she hadn't felt since the lights had gone out. She was in control. She had the power and resolve to protect her family. Never again, would her children be in fear for their lives, not on her watch.

The arrival of Zach who, on hearing what had happened the previous night, had rushed to their aid, meant little was going to happen in the house for the next couple of hours. The events would be relived in great details, details that Kate had no intention of reliving.

With Zach in situ, she felt comfortable leaving the house, at least to venture next door. With a heavy heart, she pushed open Harry's door. He had given detailed instructions over the previous few days that if anything happened to him, she wasn't to hesitate in taking any and every ounce of food he had left. He had stored his supplies in the most unlikely places, in the event of marauding gangs of thieves, which he'd been sure would come. He had advised her to do the same. She worked her way through his hiding spots; empty water tank, toilet cistern, under his sofa, under his bed, in the washing machine, each more obscure than the previous. A small amount remained in the kitchen cupboards, but only to misdirect potential thieves into believing he had little to offer. Harry, like her, had no illusion that whatever had happened wasn't changing anytime soon. Food and clean water were going to be the most important commodities known to man, and worth killing over.

Moving the food via their connected back gardens, she avoided anyone seeing what she was doing, and deliberately left the foodstuffs in his kitchen cupboards. She knew he would be smiling down on her. 'Good on you, girl', he would have said, especially given her U-turn on guns. That, she knew, would have pleased and relieved him.

A final trip took care of Hank's bed, leash, and other items. He was theirs now. Danny was making so much of a fuss, that the old dog barely had time to miss Harry. Kate just hoped Danny gave him some peace. The poor old dog was going to have a heart attack, if he didn't let up.

With breakfast over, it was time to put the previous night's events behind them. Preparations for the winter ahead needed to continue. Kate also wanted to secure the house further. Eddie had come through the back door far too easily for her liking. She also wanted to change the sleeping arrangements. No more sleeping in separate rooms, they would have one sleeping area. All beds in one room that they'd barricade closed each night for added security. She explained what she wanted to do to Zach, and sent him into the garage to fashion what she wanted, using whatever bits of lumber and tools he could find. Meantime, she set about tying numerous knots at regular intervals into a length of rope. Once completed, she placed it beneath the window in her bedroom; it was a last resort escape ladder, should they need it.

By mid-afternoon, Zach was battering and banging with gusto into her door frame, creating cradles for solid wood bars that Kate would drop into place each night. It was just as she had imagined. Perfect.

"Mom?" A shout from below was almost missed, thanks to Zach's banging.

"Hold up, Zach," said Kate, catching Danny's shout.

"Yes, honey?"

"Somebody's here to see you."

"Coming," Kate patted her pistol and walked downstairs, surprising herself at how natural it had become to check that it was there.

Gary's wife was waiting in the hallway, her face streaked in tears. "It's Gary," she exploded as Kate came into view.

Chapter 35

Kate followed Gary's wife out into the street and was met by a number of somber faces. They indicated for her to follow them, but not a word was spoken. Kate followed, not sure what to make of whatever was happening. At the end of the street, she was directed to her right and down the hill towards the river and Boise beyond. She stopped. She didn't need to go any further, a crowd below blocking their way. They all looked up towards the recently obsolete street lights. Three in particular were of interest to the community.

A body was strung from each one. Gary and his two companions who had returned the prisoners to the militia.

With Kate's arrival, the interest moved from the bodies to her. Twenty faces turned to her, still not a word spoken. Kate tried to comfort Gary's wife, but she recoiled to a number of 'tut' sounds. Kate looked around, the realization hitting her. They blamed her. The community felt she had led to Gary's death.

Wherever she looked, the eyes said more than the people had the sense to say. Of course, it wasn't her fault. She had been a victim, her family, victims. Harry was a victim.

"But how? I didn't hear any gunshots," she blurted, seeing the obvious wounds on each of the three men.

"They brought them back. A message to us!' replied Carol, consoling Gary's wife. Kate looked at Carol, a woman who had welcomed them to Warm Springs and made them feel part of the community from day one. Even she blamed Kate.

"Brought them back from where?" asked Kate, struggling to understand what had happened.

"The militia base–"

"Why on earth was Gary at the militia base?"

"To deliver their men and horses back to them–"

"What? You've handed Trey back to the militia?" shouted Kate incredulous.

"We couldn't keep him!"

"What?! He killed Harry and would happily have killed Gabe!" A couple of loud intakes of breath had her looking more closely at the bodies hanging from the street lights. Gabe was there.

"We're not murderers!"

Kate pointed east towards the militia's base, "Wake up, for God's sake, they ARE! Murderers and rapists! My fifteen-year-old was mauled by one of them last night. I killed him! The only reason I didn't kill Trey was to save Gabe's life! As a result, I now have to live in fear for the man coming back to try and rape and kill me and my children all over again, and Gabe's dead anyway. I'm truly sorry they died, but please people, wake up! The world has changed! The militia are not our friends and trust me, we're now in their sights!"

Kate turned and walked back towards her home without another word. A home that until that moment, she had felt comfortable staying in, even after the previous night's events. However, with Trey's release, she had to rethink her strategy. With Gary gone and the look on the crowd's face, the community was as good as dead. Calls for help were clearly not going to be answered anymore. The people crowded around the corpses, not knowing what to do. They had lost a leader who had guided them, given them their strength and courage. As a group, they could be a force, but without Gary that force was spent, and as individuals they were weak, indecisive and clearly, from the way they'd looked at Kate, looking for someone to blame. Warm Springs Mesa had suddenly become a very dangerous place to be.

Chapter 36

The nod to his sentries had sent Gary and his two companions to the grave. Three shots ended their lives before they'd even realized they were in danger. It was a clinical kill, a kill that Bob took no pleasure in, but for him it was necessary. For anyone to think they had any power or ability to imprison or kill his men, for whatever crimes they'd committed, was unacceptable. The militia had to be seen as an untouchable authority. In his Boise, his authority was to be complete, unquestioned and uncompromising. That authority would extend to his men. Anyone taking action against one, would answer to all.

An example had to be made. The bodies of Gary and his men had to be displayed for the Warm Springs Mesa community to understand who was in charge. The militia made the rules; they were the judge, jury, and executioner. They were the new law in Boise, not Gary, not their community effort.

Bob appreciated his cousin Trey, Neil, and his horses being returned. That appreciation would be rewarded, a reward that meant the community would be spared a reprisal attack. Their punishment would be the execution of Gary and his men. They would be spared a posse riding through their streets, shooting their automatic rifles into their homes and their families. Bob could be merciful, but he would not be forgiving. His men had been wronged. If they wanted some action, it was their right to take it. They were going to watch over and keep Boise safe. For that, the community needed to understand and assist with their needs. Whatever those needs were.

"Duke, I'm sorry," Trey said for what seemed like the fiftieth time since his return to the base.

Bob ignored him. His mood was not improving with Trey's apologies. If anyone else had done what Trey had done without his approval, they would've been dead already. Neil had saved himself by admitting he had just followed Trey's orders, although Bob was going to have to keep a close eye on Neil. That same admission was likely to cause Trey to seek some retribution and Neil, given his expertise with horses, was not someone Bob wished to lose. All in all, the whole event had left a bad taste in his mouth. Bob would publicly back his men, of that there was no question. To the outside world, they could do no wrong. To Bob, they could.

"That bitch is going to pay for breaking my finger," winced Trey, as he caught it once again, pushing himself from his seat.

"The bitch who could've killed you? That one? Who instead just shot a gun out of your hand. That bitch?!" fumed Bob.

"Yes, but—"

"But what?" he snapped, "Have you not done enough today? We lost a man and have just sent a troop of men, who by the way, had plenty of work to do here, to hang three bodies from street lights in a community miles away that was no concern of ours!"

"She killed Eddie!"

"I don't blame her! He was about to rape her daughter and thanks to your FUBAR of an operation, was on his own and she had a gun. What the hell did you expect her to do? When will you get it into your thick skull? The reason Eddie is dead and your finger is broken is you! You screwed up!"

"But the men?"

"The men will never know how I feel, of course they won't. You are my number two and as long as you don't pull any more self-gratification stunts without okaying them with me, you will remain so."

"But that bitch needs to pay! I can't have the men think I let a damned woman get the better of me," said Trey, looking at his finger. He had walked Bob into a corner. Back him or sack him.

Bob looked at him with derision. Trey was right. The woman was testament to his failing. She had to be dealt with.

Chapter 37

Kate locked the door behind her and let out a deep breath. Whatever had just taken place had fundamentally altered their chances of riding out whatever was happening. The community blamed her and more importantly, Trey was alive and back with the militia, free to attack them again whenever he wished. She had no illusion that wouldn't be very soon.

"Mom?"

Kate lost the worried look on her face and turned to face Ava.

"What's wrong?"

"Some bad news about Gary." There was no point lying. "How's your leg?" she asked, hoping to change the subject.

Ava looked down at her bandage, covering the three-inch wound she had sustained the night before. "To be honest, sore. But what about Gary?" Her eyes were back on her mother. Ava wasn't a child to easily distract. Danny or Sophie, no problem. Not Ava.

"Can you round up Sophie and Danny, please? We need a family talk." Ava didn't question her; she could see the concern etched on her mother's face.

"Do you want Zach as well?"

Kate had come to see him as part of the family. He and Sophie were all but joined at the hip.

"Yes, Zach as well."

The time for sugarcoating was over. Their lives were all at risk. Kate laid out exactly what had happened. Zach and Ava didn't need any follow-up, they got it. The looks on their faces made that very clear. Sophie and Danny took a few supplementary explanations. Until finally, they both got it. Trey would be back and there was no Harry or community to help them. At least, not as far as Kate was concerned.

"So what do we do?" asked Ava.

Kate looked around her kitchen, her home. It had already been tainted. Eddie's blood stained the basement floor. He and Trey had already breached their sanctuary. Useless appliances and gadgets still littered the room as she finally began to see it for what it was, a husk, a dead husk. Nothing worked, the faucets no longer dispensed water, the sockets no longer created power, the TVs sat dormant. Even the toilets failed to flush. She looked out at the tent in the back garden with some disgust. Up until that moment, the house had offered them a safe place to sleep. Even that was no longer the case.

"We have to move!" she said with determination.

"Where?" asked Sophie, looking at Zach with tears welling in her eyes.

"And how?" asked the much more practical Ava.

"Cool," said Danny. "Can we go somewhere where the TVs are still working?"

Kate opened her arms for Danny to come in for a hug. She hugged him tightly. His mind didn't allow the scarier realities to cloud his world. "We'll try, baby. We'll try," she said, kissing him on the top of his head as he snuggled into his mom.

"Mom, really, how?" asked Ava again. "We have no car, no transport, and there's nowhere to go."

"I'm not leaving Zach," blurted Sophie, holding his hand tightly.

Kate should have seen that one coming. Sophie was fifteen, she'd do what she was told.

"You need to stay with your family, honey," she said calmly.

"Zach is my family!" shouted Sophie.

"Your mom's right," said Zach, trying to calm everyone down.

"Do you love me, or don't you?"

Zach's face exploded into a deep red as four faces awaited his answer. He'd never said those words out loud to anyone but Sophie.

"That's not fair, Sophie. Zach's only trying to do what's best for you," offered Kate, trying to save Zach from the firing line.

"Well, do you, or don't you?" asked Sophie, ignoring her mother.

"You know I do." said Zach quietly. His world was in just as much turmoil over the thought of losing her.

"If you had just killed that Trey guy…" Sophie stopped herself from saying any more. She knew Kate had done the right thing and was proud of her for it.

Kate looked around at the husk. Damn it, it was still their home. She thought about what Tim would do. He'd never run from anything in his life. When needed, he'd stood up for what he believed. It had cost him his life and taken him from her, but she couldn't fault the man for who he had been, nor would she have wanted him to have been any different. He was a man she would forever be proud of.

Kate stood. "You're right!" she announced and left the table. The four faces followed her as she walked down the hallway before taking a right and heading down into the basement.

"What have you done?" asked Ava of Sophie.

Sophie shrugged. She had no idea.

Kate appeared a few minutes later, carrying two rifles and a bag full of ammunition. One rifle was adorned with a scope. The other looked more like an automatic rifle.

"What are you doing?" asked Ava warily, concerned she already knew.

"I'm going to practice some shooting and then I'm going to make us safe again."

"But the only way you're safe is if…" began Zach.

"Trey is dead!" finished Kate.

Chapter 38

Nick and Alex watched the events unfold in the community below, the riders tying the bodies to the streetlights. Then the community circling the bodies, nobody appearing to know what to do. The summoning of the woman whose child had been attacked, and from the location of her house, the person they believed to have been attacked the night before. They wished they could hear the conversation, which appeared heated, and resulted in the woman marching back to her house. The crowd hung around awhile longer before dispersing, and the bodies remained in place.

"Told you," said Alex as the last member of the community shut their door and the streets emptied, despite only being mid-afternoon. "Coffee?" he asked brightly.

Nick shook his head as he looked down at the community he had felt sure were going to prove Alex wrong. His hope for a future had rested with the hundred or so homes that lay below. He focused his binoculars on the three bodies. Nobody had come back to cut them down, bury them, do anything for them. They had just been left to swing gently as the afternoon breeze picked up. It was a sad and depressing sight.

"I think we'll give it one more night and then move around the hillside," said Alex. "I want us to get a feel for what's happened in downtown after a week."

Nick nodded somberly. He wasn't in the mood for talking and quite frankly, not having to watch the destruction of the community he'd had so much hope for wouldn't be a bad thing. He felt as though he'd been invested in their futures. He'd built up backstories in his mind over the last couple of days as he had watched their lives transpire. They'd saved that boy from an unimaginable fate. He didn't even want to think what would've become of him, or his mother. Under other circumstances, he most definitely would've liked to get to know her. Whether the father wasn't around out of choice, or by accident because of the power outage, he didn't know but he'd certainly noticed that a father wasn't around.

A movement on the street caught his attention. It was the boy's house. The family were coming out. The older boy, who'd been hanging out with the older daughter, was leading the children away with him, while the mother stood by herself by her door. He could sense her despair as her kids walked away, each turning and waving frequently. Once again, he wished he could hear what was happening.

With the kids out of sight, she walked back into the house. He was just about to follow the kids when he noticed the garage door come to life. Once opened, she wheeled out her bike and with some effort, lifted a bag. The strain in her movements made it clear that the bag was heavy. Her clothes were unlike any she had worn previously. Trousers, boots, and a long-sleeve top, all in black. It was almost like a tactical outfit. He focused more closely on the bag, long and slim, a lot of weight. It was a gun bag.

He scanned back to the kids and the older boy was leading them to his house. A few streets away.

She hoisted the bag over her shoulder and cycled off.

"And where the hell is our little redhead off to?" asked Alex. He had noted Nick's sudden increase in interest.

"No idea, but I don't think she's planning to have a coffee!"

They followed her movements as far as they could before losing sight of her. She was heading east towards the militia base. Nick looked at Alex. He shrugged, what the hell, he was just as intrigued. They quickly covered their camp, grabbed their kit bags and jogged east along the hillside.

***

Waving her kids off was one of the hardest moments of her life. Every single thought that passed through her mind was screaming at her not to do what she was about to do. Yet one thought overrode them all. It was their only option. She cycled a mile from the community and stopped. She laid out a bunch of targets, old bottles and cans, and picking up her kit and bike, measured out three hundred yards.

She pulled out Tim's Remington 700. It was a beautiful piece, she thought, surprising herself. The hatred she'd had for guns had evaporated in an instant. She appreciated them for the finely manufactured functional tools they were. She had killed a man with one, no remorse, none. He had meant her daughter harm. It'd been either him or Sophie who would have died and perhaps, even the whole family. She wanted Sophie alive. Therefore, his death meant she lived. That simple thought almost brought a smile to her face. She stopped herself. Smiling about killing someone was perhaps a step too far. Even recognizing that fact comforted her.

She knew the weapon. Tim had talked about it in her presence. Not with her, but while she was in the room. Chambered in .338 Lapua Magnum with a twenty-six-inch barrel. She thought of her father as she nestled the rifle into her shoulder. The last time she had been in that position, he'd been there guiding her every movement. She remembered his instructions as though he were standing over her, twenty years later. He had taught her how to respect and use guns from a young age. She moved through her setup as though reacting to his exact instructions. She lined up her first shot. She knew her distance and conditions and factored them all into the shot. It was only three hundred yards. The target fell.

She walked back another two hundred yards. Tim had told all his friends how it easily handled a thousand yards. She repeated her preparations and breathed just how her daddy taught her. Her finger pressed gently, increasing the pressure on the trigger. The rifle kicked, she followed the bullet, the target fell but only just, she had caught it on the corner. It wouldn't have been a kill shot. She lined the shot again, talking through all of her father's instructions, ingrained in her memory. Once aimed, she focused on her breathing and pulled the trigger. Dead center.

Kate rose and walked back another two hundred and fifty yards. A total of seven hundred and fifty yards. It took her five shots before she felt ready to stretch the rifle to its limits. A thousand-yard shot.

Kate lay down, exactly as her daddy instructed. Every movement had come back to her, the preciseness and intricacy of how she set up her position, crucial to how well she performed. The more mechanical and robotic she could be, the better the result. She had to clear her mind of every other thought. She and the weapon had to become one, one purpose, to hit the target from wherever you were.

***

"You have got to be kidding me! I'm in love!" exclaimed Nick, watching Kate's shooting. "That has got to be a thousand yards she's shooting down there, and she's hitting the target, one after the other. Did you see her first few shots? It was like she hadn't even used the rifle before, like it was her first time, and now, she's pinging targets from a thousand yards! Holy shit!"

Alex couldn't disagree, it was seriously impressive shooting. "But what do you think she's practicing for?" He looked off to the distance and the militia base.

"We should stop her," said Nick, following Alex's gaze. Whatever the woman was planning, going up against the militia was nothing more than suicide.

"We cannot expose ourselves to the populace. You know that."

"She has no idea what she's going up against. She can't have. She's a mother with kids!"

"Maybe she's doing it to save the kids? You hear about that sort of thing, mothers sacrificing themselves for their children."

"Maybe, but I'd bet a lot of cash none of them could shoot like her!"

"She's moving. Come on, we'd better get going or we might miss what she's planning," said Nick, as he packed away his binoculars. Alex was just as caught up in the story as he was. He just didn't want to show it. They both tracked along the hillside continuing east. Being on foot, they would struggle to keep up with her and needed to get moving fast.

***

With the bag repacked, Kate climbed back aboard the bike. She couldn't believe how well she had remembered everything her father had taught her. She felt a closeness to him she hadn't felt since the day he had killed himself. It was as though she had re-found him. He had become a disappointment, a failure in her mind. The hours he had spent each weekend with her had been erased with one cowardly bullet. He had been a wonderful father, doted on her, and loved her above all else. He spent every moment he could with her, answered her most inane childish questions. He had never once complained about taking her to any gymnastics practice or competition, no matter what time they needed to get up or how far they had to travel. Up until that one bullet, she didn't think there could have been a more perfect father.

Her world had ended, a part of her had died, and now a part of her was coming back to life. She had kept his memories and him at bay for all these years. Shooting, hunting, camping, they had done it all when she was young. He had taught her how to be a strong, independent woman. The more she cycled, the more she realized just how much he had shaped the woman she had become. A warmth passed through her as tears began to flow for the only other man she had loved and a man who she had never mourned the loss of. She had only ever hated him for what he had done to her and her mother.

***

Nick and Alex walked quickly and soon started to jog. Before they knew it, they were running to reach their vantage point over the militia base before the woman arrived. When Nick stopped to check on her progress and scanned the riverside road, he couldn't find her. She couldn't, he thought, have gotten that far ahead. Nick and Alex were fast runners and with her heavy bag, she couldn't have been cycling so fast that they would have lost her. Other than a few blind spots, where houses and buildings blocked their view, they had a clear view of the road.

"Whoa!" exclaimed Alex loudly, catching Nick's attention instantly.

"What?" Nick scanned to where Alex was focusing his binoculars. He didn't need Alex to explain any further. "Holy shit!"

Chapter 39

Kate dropped to the ground as the first explosion rocked the ground beneath her. Her bike wobbled onwards for a few yards before joining her on the ground. She reached for her bag, but it had been caught on the handlebars of her bike and lay out of her reach. She pulled the Walther PPQ from her hip holster, and kneeling for a better view, tracked the area for targets. She was all alone, not a soul within her field of vision. The road was empty ahead and behind. A second explosion shuddered through the tarmac beneath her, and heavy and prolonged gunfire followed. A deep boom, boom; Kate guessed it was a heavy machine gun. The individual booms were quickly joined by others. Somewhere to her east, a battle was underway. She hadn't been there, but from where the sounds were emanating, it sounded like the militia base was under attack.

***

Nick watched as the rocket-propelled grenades signaled the commencement of the attack. He recognized some of the uniforms as police and the rest, from their military uniformity, looked like National Guardsmen. They definitely weren't regular US forces. It seemed the people of Boise hadn't rolled over quite as easily as everyone had thought.

"I count at least two hundred in the attacking force," said Alex, scanning the area as the attackers launched their offensive against the militia's stronghold. The attackers' heads rose as the rockets hit the machine gun nests, and they charged. They had encircled the base, working their way through the undergrowth, and had positioned themselves without being noticed within striking distance, but still a few hundred yards of open ground to cover.

Alex and Nick were over a mile away when the attack had begun. Their bird's eye view from the hilltop allowed a perfect vista from which to survey the outcome. There was no doubt the militia had been caught off guard. They had clearly believed they had already gained and asserted control to the point that complacency over their security had set in. A mere six days and they believed they had beaten the fight out of a city of over three quarters of a million people. It was either extreme arrogance or stupidity. But to be fair, from what Nick had witnessed, it was a justified arrogance. Whoever had pulled off the surprise attack had obviously worked exceptionally hard over the previous few days. With no communications or transport, getting that size of force together and mounting a counterassault had been no mean feat, particularly as they had managed to keep it under wraps.

***

In the corner of his eye, Bob caught sight of the flash of a high explosive round being fired, He watched almost in disbelief as the subsequent flashes followed, almost instantaneously as the world appeared to slow. His base was being attacked. The hillside above them had come to life. He looked to his outposts stationed above the hill. Explosive shells flashed down from them also. His lookouts had failed, but had no doubt already paid the price.

His machine gun nests took the brunt of the explosive attack, the ground rocking beneath him as each explosive landed, spraying a cloud of sand within its fiery mix. Screams erupted around him as the men manning the posts bore the brunt of the initial assault. With the first phase over, the hillside and the land around came to life, men rose and ran towards the base. Small arms fire led the way. Bullets were pinged and whizzed around him as men dressed in police tactical and army fatigues charged at his base.

***

Colonel Wyatt Gratchik, retired, had barely slept the previous few days. The militia's quick action on the first day of the outage had taken the city by complete surprise. The news of the militia's destruction of the local police force had spread slowly but steadily across the city. The setting up of the militia's base of operations and the scale of its success followed shortly afterwards. On reaching the Colonel, he had immediately reached out to the Mayor and Chief of Police to offer his services and that of the National Guard, or at least what was left of it. A significant number had already been federalized and shipped out to the Middle East to the Iran crisis.

Over the following days, they had tracked down and located as many of the Guard and tactically-trained police officers as they could. It had been a monumental task. With all records stored electronically, they'd had to rely on each of the men knowing where others lived. With no communications, it'd been a slow, laborious process reaching out to each man and coordinating a meeting point, whilst maintaining a level of secrecy from the militia. The power the militia had managed to exert during those first few hours had paved its way to becoming the most powerful force in Boise. And from the Colonel's perspective, it was a force he had no intention of tackling until he had the men and resources in place to ensure success.

With each day passing, the numbers that arrived at the meeting point had grown. The Colonel assumed command and welcomed the tactically-trained police officers into his fold. By the fifth day, they had over two hundred highly-trained men ready to fight and take back control of the city. The Colonel had, with a couple of his men, surveyed the base and had come up with a plan of attack. With the Mayor and Chief of Police's approval, he had begun the operation that morning. Their first task was to take out the militia's hilltop watch points.

From their surveillance, they had ascertained that there were two points in the day when the militia was the most exposed: when darkness, and around four p.m. at the shift change. Darkness was quickly ruled out, for lack of night vision equipment, or even a working flashlight between them. The likelihood of friendly-fire was too big a risk. Darkness was no one's friend. This left the 4.00 p.m. option. After a long day, it was clear from the previous few days' observations, that the militia men's enthusiasm waned as the day progressed. The late afternoon shift change was a downsizing of the guard on duty. The feeling appeared to be that another day was over and a level of complacency and relaxation took over. Food was prepared and the sentries on duty seemed to be exhausted, even before they started. With three hours of light still left, the Colonel was going to take full advantage of that complacency.

His guard was made up of reservists and retirees like himself, a number of whom had served in various branches of the regular military. It was those more experienced men he called upon to take the hilltop sentry points, the most crucial part of the plan. His men had to get in position and strike without alerting the militia below. Over the course of the day, three men had worked their way slowly into position, using camouflaged ghillie suits. A sniper and two Marines had the experience required and offered to undertake the task. They had excelled and as the new shift settled in, they struck. Their silenced weapons took out the four sentries in the two hilltop nests without raising the alarm.

With the hilltop watch points under control, the Colonel was free to move his main force into position. A signal had the force moving, crawling through the undergrowth and as near to the base perimeter as they dared, which unfortunately, thanks to Bob's paranoid planning, meant they were still a few hundred yards from the base. The Colonel knew this was the most crucial part of their attack. The heavy machine guns were his biggest concern. Taking them out was crucial to their success and the commencement of their assault. Unfortunately, their only weapon capable of that task was the older Carl Gustaf M3 anti-tank weapon. The majority of their equipment had, as with everything else within Boise, been fried during the power outage, rendering useless every projectile with electronic guidance. Unfortunately, that equated to everything except for bullets, a handful of grenades, and the very limited resource of old M3 high explosive rounds for the all but defunct launcher, which should have been decommissioned years earlier.

***

Bob remained calm as the last explosive round landed. He looked to his machine gun posts and directed fresh men towards them. Injured and dead militia men were tossed aside as the posts were re-manned. The sandbags had done their job. He had doubled and then trebled the number of bags around them. He knew how important they were to his security. The deep boom of the powerful .50 caliber M2 rounds being expelled began to surround him as his men rushed to take up their pre-arranged posts. Training had been extensive over the previous months for his core militia and intensive for their new intake over the previous few days. Everyone knew exactly what was expected of them without any orders being issued.

Only one of the six M2s that protected the base failed to fire. It appeared the attackers had expended their arsenal of explosives in their initial assault, hoping it would give them the upper hand. The M2 that failed was quickly replaced with two M249 light machine guns, easily replacing the additional power the M2 offered them over their attackers. With his men taking up reinforced positions around the base, the attackers' assault was already faltering. Yes, they had caught them unawares, had overrun their outer defenses, but they had failed to deliver a killer first blow and for that, they were going to pay. The houses offered exceptional lines of sights from the upstairs windows, and with sandbags lining the inside of each of the houses' walls, his men easily had the upper hand and protection from which to direct their fire at the defenseless attackers. What could have been a glorious attack soon became a duck shoot as his men picked off the attacking force with ease.

***

Colonel Gratchick looked on in despair. He had taken up a hillside vantage point and wished there were some way he could have called off the attack. The moment they failed to neutralize the M2s, the battle had been lost. But with no means of communication, everything had to be pre-planned and the main force had been directed to attack from the moment the explosives had landed. It was entirely his failure. He had not foreseen the strength of the machine gun nests and simply assumed their high explosive rounds would have done their job.

Over half his men were cut down within the first few minutes while the rest, realizing the futility of the attack, tried in vain to escape the kill zone that encircled the base. It was a complete and total disaster. Of his two hundred men, he looked on as barely a quarter made it out of the kill zone.

The bullets continued to fire, even after the kill zone stopped moving. Corpses flinched as the militia made it clear that no prisoners were going to be taken.

***

The Boise authorities had tried to retake their city. Tried and failed catastrophically. Bob 'the Duke' Jackson looked out at the sea of men his militia had repelled. He knew he should have been pleased at how well his men had performed. He wasn't. He was pissed, seriously pissed. How dare they challenge his authority? It was *his* Boise, and the city was going to find out exactly what that meant.

Chapter 40

Kate needed to get back to her family. Whatever was happening, it was happening out near the militia base. The gunfire was unrelenting, and unlike anything she had heard since that first day. She looked up the hill towards home, she wasn't far away. Her target practice had gone better than expected and her return home would be earlier than anticipated. The more she had considered running, the more she realized how futile it was. Winter was around the corner. They had enough food to last them at least a few weeks, thanks to Harry, but running with no transport really wasn't an option. They'd barely be able to carry a few days' worth of food and they had nowhere to go in any event.

She had a plan. They'd keep a watch during the day. They'd see them coming and with her rifle, she'd do her best to hold them off while the kids got to safety. After that, her plan sort of fizzled out, but she'd do whatever she had to. That's what a mother did. If they did the same as before and attacked at night, she had a plan for that too. Ultimately, one man was the problem, Trey. If she could just manage to take him out, she felt sure things would settle back to normal, at least for her and her family

Kate pushed on up the hill towards the estate. She came around the final bend and was horrified to see the three bodies still swinging from the street lights. Those were men that had given their lives for the community. No matter how that had transpired, they had done what they'd thought was best. She cycled on to the first street, but it remained empty. Doors were firmly closed. The next street and every other street she passed on her way to Zach's house was the same. She may be able to save her family, she thought. The community was a different story. It was an 'every man for himself' scenario, and Kate had never in her life felt she couldn't do at least the same as any man. By the time she reached Zach's house and collected her family, the shooting had stopped. Silence had once again descended over the city. An eerie uneasy silence that nobody had gotten used to. The hustle and bustle of daily life had created far more noise than any of them had ever realized, until it was gone. With the shooting stopped, Kate had only one thing she wanted to do before it was too late. It was the least they could do. Gary and his men had come to their aid and saved them. Zach and Sophie, fully understanding what the men had done for them, didn't hesitate to offer their assistance. It was an unpleasant job and Kate couldn't have been more proud of the two of them understanding just how important it was, and putting their fears and revulsions aside to do what was right.

"What are we going to do with them? It's almost dark," asked Sophie as they laid the last of the three men on the sidewalk.

"We'll just have to get some lanterns or something. We can't leave them here, the coyotes or bears will take them," said Kate, casting her eyes towards the fading sunlight.

The three of them had been so engrossed in what they were doing, racing to beat the darkness, that the voice from behind startled them all.

Chapter 41

With two hours left before darkness, Bob had no intention of letting anyone retreat.

"I want every man who can ride, on a horse now!" he commanded. He wanted to hunt down every last man who had dared to attack his base. He wanted to know who had instigated, directed and ultimately led the attack. He wanted revenge and the revenge wasn't going to be restricted to the soldiers and policemen who had taken part in the assault. He wanted anyone and everyone who had played even the smallest part in the assault.

The defeat had been overwhelming and humiliating for the attackers, but for Bob that wasn't enough. He wanted to crush thoughts of future attempts. He wanted the people of Boise to understand the power and control he had over them. He wanted to crush thoughts of revolt, before they began to form in people's minds. To do that, he had to break them, and that meant every person involved would be swinging from street lights throughout the city.

Four posses left the base, each heading in a different direction, each with the same instruction: no prisoners. Bob led the posse that headed into the hillside. It was the best vantage point, a point where anyone leading an attack would want to be. He wanted the leader. More than anyone, he wanted the leader on his knees, begging for a forgiveness Bob would never give.

***

"Shit!" said Nick as the horses were being led from their corrals. The militia were going on the hunt. "I think maybe we should get out of here."

Alex swung his binoculars to see what Nick was worried about. He had been watching the assault's retreat. A tight group was about a mile along the hilltop from Nick and Alex's current location.

"I think you may be right," agreed Alex. "What should we do about them?"

Nick looked to where Alex was pointing. He recognized the uniform of a Colonel, a captain, and a lieutenant, accompanied by a sergeant and two corporals.

Nick swung his binoculars back to the base, the horses and riders were already heading out. One set was heading up the hill towards the group.

"You're the boss," he said.

"Yeah." Alex looked at the group heading towards them, unaware of their presence. "Our orders are clear. We cannot and must not compromise our orders. They are far more important than a single colonel, or even this entire city."

"I agree," said Nick, supporting Alex's thought process.

Both packed away their things and slipped back into the undergrowth and on towards the tree line that lay just behind them. Once in there, no one would ever find them unless they wanted them to. Alex and Nick had been very carefully selected for the mission. They were among the best the military had to offer, and it had been made very clear by the President himself, that their mission was one of the single most important undertaken in the history of their country, if not the world.

***

"Colonel!" shouted the sergeant, bringing up the rear of the small group.

Colonel Gratchick turned to face the sergeant he had known for over fifteen years. He didn't need to ask him why he'd shouted. The situation more than explained itself. It was nearly a mile until they reached the tree line that would lead them into the woods at the back of Boise. Woods that stretched off into the wilderness for hundreds of miles. Their location atop the barren hillside offered little or no cover, other than the knee-high undergrowth. Useless against horse riders, who were barreling towards them and who were easily going to catch them before they reached cover.

"Stand and fight?"

Five nods were returned. Nobody was willing to surrender, given what they had just witnessed.

They kneeled and readied themselves for the militia. Three semi-automatic rifles and three pistols pitted against twenty heavily-armed men on horseback, traveling at speed. They lined up their weapons,

"Hold it," steadied the Colonel.

"Hold it,"

"Fire!"

***

As much as Bob wanted to be at the head of his posse, he knew that's where he should have been. Leading the charge, the Duke leading his men on into battle. The reality of the situation was a little less cinematic. Bob was not the best of riders. At slow speeds, he was fine, but when the horses picked up the pace, he was unsteady and visibly nervous. It was for that reason and that reason alone that

Bob survived the first volley of fire from the Colonel and his men.

The front three riders fell as the first hail bullets were fired. The posse spread out across the hillside and barreled on relentlessly, the more accomplished riders firing back at the group of men, who against all sense, remained together. Shots were traded, Bob losing another three men while the Colonel lost four, leaving only the Colonel and a corporal out of ammo and facing Bob and thirteen of his men.

Bob sloped off of his horse and walked towards the two men. The corporal threw himself at Bob with his rifle raised as a club. One of Bob's men's rifles kicked as a bullet tore through the corporal's head. The corporal's body slumped to the ground five feet from Bob.

The Colonel raised his pistol and pointed it towards Bob.

Bob ducked wildly. "Don't shoot him!" he cautioned his men. "We want to know what he knows!"

The Colonel smiled, turning the gun on himself.

Bob raced to the Colonel, shouting at his men. "Stop him!"

But it was too late. The Colonel's pistol fired, his final round leaving Bob in a fury. He looked at the men lying before him, they were the brains, the knowledge behind what had transpired. His other posses were chasing the brawn. He had failed to capture the brains. He fired wildly into the bodies, emptying a magazine in total futility.

Sporadic gunfire rang out across the city below. His men were doing their job, chasing down the survivors while he had failed in his; uncovering those behind the attack. Of course, the Colonel would have been key, but there were police officers and others involved. He wanted names, addresses, people he could drag into the street and make an example of and families that would suffer because of the actions of their husbands and fathers.

He wanted revenge.

Chapter 42

Kate spun, her hand reaching for her holster as she reacted to the voice. Her hand dropped as she caught sight of the source of the voice. It wasn't as she had feared, Trey and the militia. It was a group of her neighbors, shovels in hand.

"We want to help," said one man who Kate recognized, but did not know his name. She had seen him as she had driven through the estate, one of many people she knew to say 'hi' to when she'd seen him at the supermarket, but nothing more.

"Thank you," she said, genuinely surprised at the appearance of the men.

"It's been a trying few days," the man offered by way of apology, or at least that was how Kate interpreted it. Perhaps their community wasn't dead quite yet.

The group assured Kate they would take it from there. The three men were to be taken to each of their respective homes and buried in their gardens, at least until things got back to normal. Not one person said that with any sense of feeling. It was clear, just as they approached one week in, the belief that the federal government, Army, or whoever, would ride into the rescue was becoming less and less likely.

As the evening turned to night, the sporadic gunfire ended. Once again, the self-imposed nighttime curfew fell across Boise. Kate hunkered down with her kids, pulling the barricade across the door as planned. Sophie had begged for her to let Zach stay, but Zach's parents wouldn't be happy with the idea, despite the new sleeping arrangements, which ensured it would be a very innocent affair. She couldn't blame them. Kate had a target on her back. Why would they allow their son to be in danger? In their favor, they had offered for Sophie to stay with them, even extending that to Ava and Danny but not, understandably given her current wanted status, to Kate.

To their credit, including Sophie, they all wanted to stay with their mom. For once, they agreed. She was far more badass than Zach's father who was a lovely man, but not a man you'd run to for help. Unlike their mom, she had kicked ass the night before and clearly, would do whatever it took to keep them all safe.

***

Nick and Alex broke out of the woods and worked their way back towards their base above Warm Springs Mesa. They had made good time and managed to beat the sunset. Arriving just in time for Nick to witness Kate walking back into her house.

"She must have just been practicing, she's okay," he said cheerfully to Alex.

Alex raised his eyebrows to the sky. "We've just watched up to two hundred men being slaughtered, but you're happy because your little woman made it home safe?"

"Well, when you put it like that, I suppose it sounds a bit..." began Nick. Stopping mid-sentence. "What was that?"

Alex didn't answer. Nick tore himself away from the view below and turned to Alex. It was no surprise he couldn't speak, a blade rested uneasily across his neck. An arm wrapped around his head, ensuring Alex didn't make any stupid movements. Nick reached for his pistol, but stopped when Alex's beaming smile lit up in the last wisps of sunlight.

"Son of a bitch!" said Alex carefully. The edge of the razor-sharp blade cutting into his skin with every movement of his Adam's apple. "Sean, is that you?"

The blade was removed instantly in answer.

Chapter 43

DAY 14

Kate was worried. She'd dressed Ava's wound for the fifth time in as many days, but the redness was getting worse and there was some heat in the wound itself. Even more concerning was the fluid that seeped from the wound, its yellowish hue was getting stronger as was its pungency. It was definitely infected. She had tried the previous day to find antibiotics in the neighborhood, but whether there weren't any or no one was willing to give up what they had, she wasn't sure. Whatever the case, she needed to find some and quickly. She had hoped she was being overcautious the previous day but twenty-four hours later, her concerns were definitely well founded.

The previous week had been quiet in the community, not something she could say about Boise itself. Gunfire had reverberated throughout the city furiously and by far more frequently than in the first week. The militia, it was rumored, was exerting its authority over what they had labeled 'an attempted coup'. Of course, few failed to see the irony in their seizing power in exactly that way. A coup against the elected and legal authority in Boise on the first day of the outage.

She couldn't even remember which day it had been that she had given up hope of anyone coming to their rescue. Initially, she'd had her doubts but she had kept watching the highway at points throughout the day, willing something to move. But sometime over the last week, that had stopped. She couldn't remember exactly when in the last few days she had stopped watching the road, but she had. Help wasn't coming. They were on their own.

"What's wrong? asked Ava, as Kate seemed to drift off while changing her dressing.

"Nothing, just thinking."

"It's getting worse, isn't it?" asked Ava. "It's not feeling any better."

"It'll be fine, honey. Just need to keep changing the dressing," she smiled. Of course, Sophie or Danny would have bought it, Ava definitely not. She was the smart one, the one you couldn't bullshit, and unfortunately in this circumstance, the know-all. She was a walking medical encyclopedia and knew exactly the consequences from infections and sepsis.

"We need antibiotics, don't we?"

Kate nodded. There was no point lying. Ava would just undress her wound and see clearly for herself. With a limited number of dressings, even that was a concern. She wouldn't be able to keep dressing it each day.

Zach's arrival was Kate's signal to undertake what she knew was going to be a dangerous journey, visiting the hospital. If anyone still had antibiotics, surely they would. She had heard how bad it was, but she had no option. She had to at least try.

"Zach, would you mind if everyone went to your mom and dad's?"

Kate wasn't ever going to leave the kids in the house alone. She knew the day would come when Trey would try again. When that day did come, she was ready and prepared. but her kids weren't.

"Of course, but is it okay to leave Hank here? My mom's not a fan."

"Yeah, that's fine," agreed Kate, much to Danny's disappointment. He had kept Hank by his side almost every second of the day since Harry's death. He was a lovely old dog and his attachment to Danny was obviously helping with his loss of Harry, but Kate fully understood Zach's mom. Hank stank.

"Mom, what are you doing?" asked Ava.

"I just need to go and check on an old friend."

Before Ava could argue, Kate was heading out of the door and climbing onto her bike. Her Walther PPQ was holstered on her hip and two spare magazines tucked into her belt. Her water bottle was half full. Her next concern, after getting antibiotics for Ava, was going to be finding fresh water, or at least drinkable water. They had rationed the bottled water they had as far as they could, but they really were getting down to their last reserves. She had heard from the few neighbors she had seen, that there was a stream just above the estate that flowed down to the river, but the biggest problem was transport. Water was heavy and the terrain to the stream only allowed access by foot.

It had been over a week since Kate had left the estate. The gunfire and violence that had erupted after the attack on the militia had stopped all but vital excursions. She had considered taking a rifle with her, but the weight and conspicuousness felt wrong. Getting in and out under the radar was more important. Speed versus power.

The cycle across the bridge and into Boise itself was a shocking transition. With the transformation from expansive suburb living to tight city living came the realities of large volumes of people living in a constrained environment. Trash lined the streets, and as the bags were split, they were ravaged by vermin and scavengers leaving remnants strewn across the street. The stench of old and rotting food mixed with what she could only imagine was human waste filled the air. She tried not to breathe as the smell of death began to overpower even the trash smell. She turned a bend in the road and the reason was strung up for her to see. Numerous bodies had been strung up. It was a truly hideous sight and clearly a warning from the militia of their power. Each of the bodies wore a uniform of some description, either military or law enforcement. The shootings over the last few days were explained in an instant. The militia was hunting down and killing anyone they perceived to be a threat.

Kate pedaled on. The streets were empty, blinds and curtains twitched, but nobody dared come out of their homes. The stench of death pervaded the air. Boise was clearly in fear for its life. The family clinic was just beyond the shopping center where she had first encountered Bob, Trey, and their militia, two weeks earlier. She refused to look as she cycled past. It was just too sad.

She reached the clinic, but it had been ransacked, its doors hanging uselessly from one hinge. She paused long enough to see a number of people, like her, making their way there, looking for help. Although, it was clear from the state of those trying to get there, they were in a far worse state of health than anybody she had seen up until that point. Young and old, they were struggling to walk, their bodies ravaged. They were like the people she'd watched on those charity ads in war-torn or drought-ridden countries that made your stomach churn, painfully thin and almost unable to support their own weight.

Kate cycled on. A mother and young child were walking towards the clinic.

"The clinic's gone," she offered, slowing as she passed them.

Neither seemed able to lift their heads, they just turned and shuffled back the way they had come. Kate stopped and cycled back, but kept out of their reach. There was something very wrong with how they were moving.

"Are you okay?"

The mother used what seemed a huge amount of effort to stop and look at Kate. Her lips were painfully cracked. The daughter's head lifted even slower, the lack of energy almost unable to lift her own head. Her lips too, were painfully cracked.

"Water?" the mother said, the pain of the effort clear. She was looking at Kate's bottle on her bike frame.

Kate didn't hesitate as she pulled it out of its holster and handed it over, careful not to touch or come in contact with the mother.

The mother put the bottle to her daughter's lips and let her sip some before taking some herself. Kate's heart sank. The two of them were desperately ill.

"What's happened?"

"We think it's the water, so many people ill, dying. The river, it was the only source after the first few days."

"Oh, dear God," replied Kate. She had passed over the river, but she hadn't dared look down. The smell of the river was bad enough. She had heard that dead bodies were floating in there, but the smell itself had stopped her looking. It'd smelled like an open sewer. The people in the city had been drinking it. She had heard people would drink anything if thirsty enough. Surely they would have taken precautions, boil it, something.

The woman offered more water to her daughter, and she took a bigger sip before her mother took more. She offered the bottle back to Kate. She held up her hand, "No, please keep it."

It wasn't just that whatever disease was afflicting them would be all over the bottle, she genuinely wanted to help them and wished she could do more.

"Thank you," she said, shuffling away.

"Where are you going to go?"

"Home, nowhere else to go."

"What about the main hospital?"

"Too far," she said, shuffling away with her daughter.

Kate watched them walk away, wishing she could do more. However, without knowing what was wrong with them, contact was not something she could risk, not just for her but for her family. Like the mother, she would have given her children the first drink and like the mother, she was sure, would not knowingly expose her children to illness.

She watched them struggle for a minute, wishing there was something she could do. She cycled after them.

"What's your address?" she called from behind them.

"Why?"

"If I can get you anything at the hospital, I'll bring it on my way back."

"And for daddy, too?" said the daughter. The first words she had uttered.

The mother looked at Kate as her daughter spoke, the pain in her eyes and the short shake of her head were more than words could have ever portrayed. The father was dead, and from the pain, it was obviously very recently. Kate could only assume he, like the mother, had given what he could to save his wife and child and succumbed to the illness to save them, or the militia. However, the worry in the mother's face suggested it was the illness, an illness that had killed her husband and she fully expected to kill her and her daughter. She gave Kate the address. Kate wouldn't forget it. She'd do whatever she could to help. She turned and cycled away, praying to a god she had never forgiven since taking her husband from her.

The smell of death and worse continued through the city. The signs of the militia also prevailed. Every so often, another street corner bore the brunt of their anger at the city's attempt to overthrow them. The sight of more wasted souls shuffling began to build as she neared the hospital. The street signs directed her towards the main hospital. She turned the corner and was met by chaos. Hundreds, if not thousands of people sat hopelessly in a line that stretched off towards where the hospital signs directed. Young, old, babies, they all sat quietly, waiting, hoping that the line would move. The fact that the line even existed was testament more to the seriousness of their illnesses than to good manners. Most looked as though they wouldn't make it the few hundred yards around the block. Kate stood out amongst them all. The city had been ravaged while the suburbs had persevered. She cycled on, assuring people as she went, that she wasn't staying. She just needed to ask a question. When that upset a few of those in the line, she advised that she was just looking for someone to take them home and out of the line. That appeased everyone, one less in the line was good news.

The sight that faced her as she turned the final corner was one she should have expected, but she was in America. A first-world country. A country that had everything. A country that could look after its people when in need. What faced her was bedlam. Tents and canopies covered a few beds, but mostly just mattresses on the wet ground. The stench was unbearable. The smell in the city had been bad but here, it was concentrated to the point that her eyes burnt from the strength of the odious smell. Medical staff wore biohazard suits, the few that were there, and clearly not enough to cope with the sea of patients that covered every inch of open space in front of the numerous hospital buildings. The area easily covered two football fields. Kate looked more closely at the ground. It hadn't rained for days and it wasn't wet anywhere else. She suddenly realized what it was and backed up. The entire area was swimming in it, the mattresses on the floor had no protection from it and soaked it up. The patients that lay on the beds barely moved, moans and groans and screams of pain filled the area. She hoped she would never see anything like it again in her lifetime. A lifetime. If this was what their new world was going to be like, she hoped it would end soon.

"Where are you from?" shouted a doctor, or at least Kate assumed he was a doctor, but under the bio-suit he was wearing, it was hard to tell.

The doctor abandoned the patient he was dealing with and walked quickly towards Kate.

"Suburbs," replied Kate quietly not wanting anyone else to hear her, nor was she going to be more specific. Certainly not when this was what happened when too many people lived in close proximity.

"You're about the healthiest person I've seen outside of the militia in a week!"

"What's wrong with them?" asked Kate, her mouth hanging open as she stared at the scene in horror.

"Dysentery, Cholera, Botulism, a mix of them all probably, and God knows what else. We've no way to test, but we're talking old world waterborne diseases. We're so used to clean water that our bodies have little or no natural protection from contaminated water. The slightest bacteria and we're here," he said, waving his hand across the forecourt.

"Oh, my God," breathed Kate in disbelief, covering her mouth.

"You should be okay. I don't think any of it is contagious, just whatever you do, don't drink any water that's not from a sealed bottle or been properly boiled."

"Surely most people would have boiled water first, the river…"

"Appeared to be perfectly fine for a few days. The problem was, it was a week before this took hold, this has all happened in the last few days. Before that, it was just violence-related problems. That, we could just about cope with, although not much we can do. No power stops us doing a lot of things."

"And now?"

"We're out of everything. No pain meds, no antibiotics, no clean bedding, no nothing. We're having to boil river water to hydrate people, but the volumes are just impossible. To be honest, most people here will die. We just can't cope. They are too ill and we don't have the food or fluids to help them. We are fighting a losing battle. The strongest have a chance…"

Kate looked again at the fluid running towards the gutter from the sea of patients. It was their life, pouring from them. Had it been a darker color, it would have been more evident that it was human waste. It was almost clear, a sign of how little remained in the patients and how little nutrition and chance of a survival they had.

"How can you do it?" she asked, when a section of young children caught her eye.

"It's what we do," he shrugged. "So, why are you here? You obviously don't need any help, as I said, I've not seen anyone as healthy as you for a few days."

Kate felt embarrassed, seeing the despair, pain, and suffering in front of her. "My daughter," she brushed it away as nothing. "Cut herself and needs antibiotics."

"Describe it?"

Kate gave a detailed description.

"And she's healthy otherwise?"

Kate nodded. "Like me. We've got enough provisions, probably for a couple of weeks and I think we have a source for fairly clean water."

"Don't tell me where!" he advised. "People would kill you for what you have and probably kill me to find out."

"Okay, I won't," she said with a heavy heart. It felt wrong not to offer the doctor the information when he was helping her.

"You're right about your daughter and she would have been a candidate for antibiotics here. Most of these people are too far gone, we wouldn't waste it on them. But we ran out a couple of days ago. So, I'm afraid I can't help."

"Anywhere else I can try?"

The doctor thought, "There is a rumor about the Capitol building. The tunnels beneath that double as a shelter in a crisis. I'd imagine they'd have thought of the basics and I'd certainly make sure that was in any kit I had in a shelter."

"Thank you," said Kate. "Is there anything I can do for you?"

"Just make it out of this alive. Some of us have to," he said, meaning every word.

Kate wanted to hug him and thank him but whatever he'd said about contagion, she wasn't taking any chances.

She began to cycle away and he shouted after her. "And you really need to get her started on them within the next seventy-two hours!"

Kate waved a thank you over her head, turned the corner and was stopped almost instantly, by a wall of people blocking her path.

Chapter 44

The arrival of Sean and his partner Lonnie, had been a surprise to Alex and Nick. They didn't realized their reports would or could result in additional resource being allocated. However, the militia's almost instantaneous rise to power had caught everybody by surprise and more information on exactly how it had come about was wanted. Sean and Lonnie had been parachuted in over twenty miles away from Boise during the previous night and had trekked all day through the woods to Alex and Nick's location, catching them by surprise that evening.

It had been a quick and short-lived reunion. Sean and Lonnie had one mission, to infiltrate the militia and understand more about it, how it had come to be and its setup. After one night with Alex and Nick, they had offered their services the following day. Both had been chosen for their knowledge of the city and previous ties, unlike Alex and Nick, who had been chosen for the opposite reason, to ensure their reports were free of emotion and were objective. It was understood that to be able to join the militia, Sean and Lonnie would need to know the area and have a reason for being there. It also helped that both had been adorned with prison-style tattoos, suggesting they had a less than stellar past. A reference to the number of prison tattoos on members had been noted in previous reports. Although not permanent, they would at least last a couple of months to ensure their cover remained intact.

Although they could only travel with what they could carry, they had managed to bring at least a few supplies to supplement Alex and Nick's ability to fulfill their mission. Most importantly, a satellite phone, a solar charger and night vision equipment, including binoculars and scopes for their rifles. They were items they'd had initially, but had been destroyed despite their best efforts. The night vision equipment opened up their ability to travel and report without exposing themselves, using the cover of darkness. While Boise slept, Alex and Nick explored unobstructed and unobserved.

They had watched and reported the growing health crisis that had swept through the city over the previous few days, being reassured by satellite phone that they were in no danger, as long as they boiled or sterilized their water.

They had also watched over and reported on the increasing violence by the militia. Thanks to a couple of secret night meetings with Sean and Lonnie, they had been made aware of the scale and capability of the militia, which was far greater than they had envisaged. The brutality of its members, which had stunned even Sean who had seen plenty throughout his military career, included some of the worst terrorist atrocities. The militia was as bad as any jihadist terrorist he had experienced. He and Lonnie had witnessed entire families being killed by the militia, including children, to deter the populace from further uprisings against them. Sean and Lonnie had both managed to avoid the actual killings, as there was always someone keen amongst the group to pull the trigger. However, watching the killings was becoming harder and harder to stomach. Both had requested to be pulled out. Alex had to tell them their request was denied, the information they were gathering was far too important.

They maintained their base above Warm Springs Mesa. A couple of bikes that had been acquired during one of their night-time excursions into the city had transformed their travel time and opened the entire city up to them over the course of the night. They managed to stash the bikes above the community, just off the trail that led them closest to their hide. Despite their new hours, Nick had maintained his interest in the tight-knit community and in particular, his interest in the woman and her family.

There was no doubt that the community was faring far better than the wider city, but there was a definite reduction in contact and movement throughout the day. In fact, over the previous two days, barely a soul had ventured out of their house. Resources were running low, of that Nick had no doubt. Less and less trash was being deposited each day. Alex warned him to lower his expectations. When hunger set in, the community would, as he'd always predicted, fall apart. It was just a matter of time. Nick prayed the community spirit would live on, but the lack of interaction between families was leading him towards Alex's way of thinking. It wouldn't take long.

"They just need to follow the trash," observed Alex. Replacing 'money' with 'trash' in the well-known phrase.

It was true. While some houses in the community had not deposited trash for a few days, others added daily. It wasn't hard to detect who still had food. He, through pure interest and for no particular reason, had noted the woman was still depositing trash. However, she was smart, it'd been at night and not outside of her own house. While their trash pile remained unchanged, others' grew. He had also noted something else about her at night, having spotted her a couple of times as he and Alex had prepared to leave. He couldn't help but think it was a very smart move, given all that had transpired.

Watching her cycle off that morning, he couldn't help but worry. He knew it was crazy and had absolutely no attachment to her, other than the voyeuristic oversight he had maintained over her and her family over the previous ten days. When he followed her cycling towards the city and not towards her target range, his concern grew. He looked at Alex, but he was sound asleep. They had only just returned from another night of exploration and reporting. She crossed the bridge, and he could taste the stench that would be assaulting her as she disappeared from sight. He looked back towards the trail and where they had stashed their bikes and then back at Alex. Their orders ran through his mind, 'avoid contact at all costs'. Keeping watch over a lone woman in a city overrun by a militia hell bent on killing any and all signs of authority would probably be construed as disobeying that order.

He checked the pistol on his holster and slipped out of their hide. Alex stirred as he moved.

Chapter 45

Kate rested her hand on her pistol grip as the group that were blocking her path refused to move. They were a pitiful sight. They could barely hold their own weight, but it wasn't stopping them brandishing a variety of weapons. Kate looked around desperately for help. Nobody who waited in the line looked as though they were fit to care, never mind help.

"We're wondering where you live?" asked one of the men in the group. The group stepped forward threateningly as he spoke. They were just a few yards from Kate with a number of pistols aimed at her. There were twelve men against one woman while hundreds watched. What the hell had become of the city?

"Back up, guys," she said in as an authoritative a voice as she could muster, pulling her PPQ to bear and aiming squarely at the talker.

"Lady, look at me," advised the man. "Do you think a quick death is really something I'm worried about?"

Kate lowered her aim to his genitals. Earning a laugh from a number of the group.

The men held steady, not retreating but not moving forward. Kate hoped the pause would have some of her fellow Boise citizens coming to her aid, but few even raised their heads to see what was happening. A week of killings by the militia and illness had all but knocked any fight out of them.

"So which is it?" asked Kate, wanting to take control of the situation.

"We don't want you. We just want some food and clean water!" offered another man, his voice more pleading than demanding. A number of nods from the group echoed his sentiment.

Kate couldn't help but wonder if things had become so bad in the city, why they hadn't already been overrun in Warm Springs Mesa by city dwellers moving out to the suburbs to take whatever they could get. It didn't make any sense until she realized why; it was the militia. They were based in a suburb and had wreaked havoc over the city for the last week or more. The doctor had mentioned that things hadn't really gotten bad until the last few days, certainly from an illness perspective. The reason they hadn't been overrun was because of the militia.

"I'm with the militia," she replied confidently.

"On a bike and on your own?" scoffed one of the men.

"I don't like horses."

"Whatever. It's also a reason we should just kill you!"

She had no choice but to double down and go with it. She had only one option, to talk her way out of the situation. It was clear that no help was coming.

"Let's just say, if anything were to happen to me here, I hope none of you have any children or family you care about."

"They're never going to know who we are."

Kate glanced over to the line. "What, all those people are going to risk their lives and their families lives to save you bunch?" she sneered. Inside, she was shaking. If her bluff didn't work she was in serious trouble.

She could see doubt beginning to enter at least some of the men's faces, but others remained resolute, it was touch and go.

"I call bullshit. They'd let a good-looking woman like you wander around on her own, when they ride about in posses to ensure they are safe?"

"Hey, leave her alone," came a shout, strong and commanding.

***

Alex stirred, and Nick stopped moving. Alex settled, and Nick moved again, getting out of the hide without waking him. He picked up his backpack.

"Hey, where you going?" asked Alex. The movement had woken him after all.

"Just going for a pee," replied Nick.

Alex sat up, fully awake, the lie hadn't fooled him. "With your backpack and rifle?"

Nick couldn't tell a blatant lie. No matter how small their operation was. Alex was his senior and therefore, commander, and despite the small size of the team, the importance of the operation had not been missed on them. The weight of the importance bore down on them every day. The operation had been one of the tightest kept secrets in the history of the country. Only a handful of people were trusted with the truth. Alex and Nick were two of those people and the reason they, and they alone, were trusted to oversee and report on the city of Boise. The drones overhead, flying high and out of sight of the people below, were monitored by fewer than a handful of the country's most trusted men and women.

"The woman. She's going into the city on her own."

"Nick, please, you know the situation, we cannot compromise our position or our mission."

Nick nodded, he wasn't sure he'd have gone further than the bike. The moment he had stepped out of the hide, before Alex had spoken, he'd already been regretting his foolhardy decision.

"You're right. I was being stupid."

"So I can go back to sleep?"

Nick nodded and climbed back into the hide. He prayed for the woman's safe return and knew, under any other circumstance, he would have helped her.

***

Kate turned. It was the doctor.

"She says she's with the militia!"

"She's frightened and scared, just like you are. Come down to the hospital and I'll make sure we sort you guys out!" he offered.

The line mumbled dissent, but the doctor stared them down. He was saving a woman's life.

Kate mouthed "thank you" out of sight of the men.

She turned back to the men in front of her, three had already stepped aside. Although the leader of the group remained resolute.

"You'll help us and our families?"

"I'll give you everything I can to help them," said the doctor truthfully.

Kate winced silently, she knew the doctor had nothing. His promise was worthless. He was going to pay for his deceit. She just prayed, not with his life.

The leader stepped aside. Kate didn't hesitate as she pushed on her pedals and left as quickly as she could. Despite her interaction, she had no intention of heading home just yet. She had to get to the Capitol building and find some antibiotics. The doctor hadn't said as much, but the look of concern on his face and his seventy-two-hour deadline were as clear a warning that Ava's life depended on them as he was going to issue, not wanting to panic Kate.

Gunshots echoed behind her, she guessed from the hospital. She looked straight ahead, she couldn't think about the doctor and what may or may not have happened to him. She had to think about her daughter. She also wondered who she had become. She wasn't the type to turn her back on people in need, but times had changed. She had to think of her children and how best she could protect them. To do that, she had to survive. As cold as it sounded and felt, she had no choice. She prayed the doctor was okay and pedaled on regardless.

Her heart sank as she turned the corner and the sight of the Capitol building in all its grandeur stood before her. Its stunning façade was bullet-ridden, hardly a window had escaped a brutal assault. Its doors, like those of many other public buildings, hung open. The idea that the tunnels remained intact despite the assault soon evaporated as she neared the bottom of the grand staircase that led to the entrance. Two bodies were tied, bullet-ridden and clearly dead, to the central two pillars. The Governor of Idaho and the Mayor of Boise. Whatever lay inside, Kate already knew it would have been pillaged, including the tunnels, where these two men would have sought refuge, just like every other resource the militia had pillaged in Boise.

She turned to leave. And stopped. She couldn't leave without checking. She'd forever wonder if they had missed it. If they had caught the men before they'd had a chance to seek shelter. She dismounted, picked up her bike, held her pistol in her hand, and made her way up the staircase. The scene inside painted a picture. A trail of officers and guards lay in a line across the grand foyer towards a door at the back of the building, a door that had been blown open. Stairs led downwards into darkness. She looked around for a candle, lantern, or anything to help her search downstairs. She secured a lantern and a lighter from a guard, 'God bless his soul', she thought quickly, feeling as though she were robbing the dead.

The doctor was right. The tunnels were there, including a first aid room and just as she had predicted, the militia had taken everything of any use. It was stripped bare.

A shiver ran through her. She knew who had the drugs that could save her daughter's life. The question was, what was she willing to do to get them?

Chapter 46

Taking a circuitous route home not only avoided any further dangers, but also gave Kate time to think through her options and consider the consequences of any potential outcome. Whatever way she cut it, going to the militia was not only endangering her and Sophie sexually but in all reality, all of their lives. There was no way she could trust them and in particular, Trey. She had seen the evil in his eyes on two occasions and she had no intention of seeing it again.

Of course, none of that solved her problem. Ava desperately needed antibiotics. She could spend the day cycling around every pharmacy or drug store in Boise, but she knew that would prove fruitless. Every store would've been stripped of anything of any value within hours. Two weeks later, she'd be lucky if there was so much as a brick left. She thought back to how often she had thrown old drugs away. Half empty packets of unused items, including courses of antibiotics that had been started and never finished, despite the doctors telling you to always finish the course. What she'd have given for just a few of those old packets.

She cycled on with a greater purpose. She had it. She'd once again be asking for the community's help, but surely amongst all those houses they'd be able to scrounge together enough pills to help Ava. She wasn't asking for much, just some forgotten pills that may be lurking at the back of their medicine cabinets or drawers.

"Come in, Kate," offered Zach's dad, stepping back to let her in.

"Thanks."

"How'd it go?" he asked.

Kate described the scene, restarting as Zach's mother joined the conversation. Both their faces fell as Kate described first, the mother and daughter and then, the situation at the hospital. She left out her altercation with the group. Zach's dad was already behaving differently with her after her shooting Eddie. Danny joked that he thought it was because she was 'badass'. Kate didn't think so. He was a religious man. He more likely did not approve or condone her taking a life. An action she had relived many times in her head and every time without hesitation, she would have done the same thing. Eddie had to die to save her family.

"So," she concluded. "I'm left with the task of going door to door to see if we can find any old meds that will help. Basically, anything that's an antibiotic of some description. Anything's better than nothing."

Zach's dad turned to put on his coat, as did his wife.

"What are you doing?"

"You'll never make it to all the homes before dark on your own."

Three hours later and with the last wisps of sunlight ebbing into the night sky, Kate led Sophie, Ava, and Danny home. Her mind barely able to concentrate on putting one foot in front of the other as she tried desperately to think of a way to save her daughter's life. She had to remain strong and not let on how desperately worried she was. There was a clock ticking. Each minute and second that went past ate into the seventy-two hours. She corrected herself, that'd been eight hours earlier, sixty-four hours. She wouldn't have minded if half of the people she had asked had even pretended to go and look just to see, but the answer was a simple 'no' before she'd even had a chance to explain what it was she wanted. It wasn't that she wasn't offering something in return. She'd offered to share whatever they had, her daughter's life was on the line.

As darkness fell, there was little else to do but worry. Another twelve hours. Twelve hours to do nothing but deduct every minute from the doctor's countdown. She had twelve hours to think of a solution and when the sun rose, there would only be fifty-two hours left to save Ava's life. Less, if sepsis set in. A condition she was all too aware of, following a friend's shocking and tragic death aged just twenty-eight, after a seemingly innocuous Urinary Tract Infection went untreated for too long.

Of course, there was a chance Ava's young body would fight it off, but from Kate's experience they were beyond that point. The infection had taken hold, and without meds, her daughter's leg and life were in danger.

Chapter 47

Trey sat upright on the back of his horse, excitement coursing through his body. Bob 'the Duke' Jackson led the way, fulfilling the promise he had made to his cousin a week earlier. A posse of thirty men followed them, heavily-armed and ready to follow any orders to the letter. Just as they had done over the previous week.

Retribution for the attack on his base had been brutal. Anyone with any authority had been a target, and they had swept through Boise with a fine-tooth comb, squirreling them out. State Senators, Representatives, Councilors were amongst those targeted beyond any remaining law enforcement or military veterans, each tortured to give up anyone else they may be aware of. If torture failed, their family members were executed one by one until they did give up others. When they ran out of family members, the individual was killed and strung up for all to see.

Bob had known from day one of the operation where the Governor and Mayor were, hiding in their secret bunker below the Capitol building. He had left them until last. They were the crowning glory in Bob's victory. Proof that he alone was in complete control over the wider Boise-Nampa Metropolitan area. With the removal of the Governor and the Lieutenant Governor the previous week, he was in effect the de facto governor. He had toyed with changing his title, but that was the old world. In his world, a 'Duke' ruled the States and a 'King' ruled the country.

Trey had been at his side throughout, he had never strayed, although his mind, Bob noted, wandered often. There was no doubting where. Bob would catch Trey looking longingly at the Warm Springs Mesa area looking down over Boise.

"Soon," he would promise. He had already promised Trey they would teach the community a lesson, but Boise had to be tamed first.

Not only had it been tamed, it was under his constant watch. Strategic outposts had been secured throughout the city. Garrisons of men were ready to quell any uprising and with fire stacks atop their outposts, they were ready to issue plumes of smoke during the day or beacons of fire at night that would send reinforcements to wherever was required urgently.

He held an iron grip over three quarters of a million people. He corrected himself, *previously* three quarters of a million. As Bob had expected, that number was reducing fast as the apocalypse transpired. The lack of clean water and sanitation were wreaking havoc amongst the coddled masses. They had no clue how to look after themselves. No comprehension as to how dangerous water could be. Of course, he hadn't helped matters by dumping the bodies into the river but in all reality, he had simply accelerated the inevitable.

The population reduction was a necessary component of the ongoing survival of the city. He'd rather have a hundred thousand well-fed, able-bodied citizens than three quarters of a million permanently starving, useless bodies. Food production would be a fraction of what it used to be and with no external food source, the city of Boise would have to produce whatever it needed for itself. The first wave of disease would eradicate the weak and infirm. Only the strongest would survive, able to work and provide food for Boise. He'd build up his forces and over time expand his power base, extending out beyond the city to the wider state and ultimately beyond.

Before that, he had a promise to keep. Even with darkness falling, he could see Trey's white teeth shining, his face unable to break the smile that had erupted when Bob had told him it was time.

Bob was no fool. He had a number two whose loyalty would remain unquestioned - a ruthless, callous killer with no ability or power base to usurp him. Even though they were family, Bob knew that meant little to Trey. Trey was not a man to dwell on such trivialities. He'd as soon kill family as a stranger, if it helped him get what he wanted. The man was an emotionless void and perfect as his number two and enforcer. Trey was nothing without Bob. With him, he had the pick of the women across the city to quench his sexual urges and an army of men at his side to aid his penchant for violence. Bob knew he had a man by his side who would kill anyone who dared question him. Quite simply, Trey's life depended on Bob's rule.

It was a perfect partnership and Bob knew Trey was straining at the leash. He had put his quest on hold for a week. A quest that Bob had agreed was necessary a week earlier, for the sake of the militia's authority. An authority that, a week later, was quite frankly unquestioned and in no likelihood to be questioned any time soon, certainly not from the people of Boise. As far as Bob was concerned, their only concern now lay beyond Boise and the potential that the federal government got its act together and sent help. However, as each day passed, Bob couldn't help but surmise that there was no federal government to ride to the rescue. That world was gone. His was the new world. It was time for people like Bob to step up and take control, an opportunity Bob had every intention of making the most of. First though, they needed to blow off some steam.

He clucked his horse and sped the posse up. Trey's smile grew as the speed increased. Bob was beginning to enjoy riding. The previous week had doubled his experience and made a huge difference in his confidence. He clucked again.

"Yeehah!" screamed Trey as the speed picked up even more. The last fragments of light ducked behind the horizon as they swept up the hill towards Warm Springs Mesa, their lanterns leading their way.

The clip of the hooves cascaded through the estate as the posse raced towards Kate's home. There was no subtlety about their entrance. These were rulers coming to reap their spoils.

""That one!" pointed Trey, jumping down from his horse. Like the rest of the street, it was in darkness. Bob remained seated, but motioned for six men to accompany Trey. Three headed around back while three joined him as he walked towards the door.

Trey tried the handle, the door was locked. He stepped back and with one mighty step, kicked the door open, using every ounce of his weight behind his boot. Trey listened as the door clattered back and forth before finally coming to rest. Silence.

"Trey!" instructed Bob from the road. "Let the boys clear the way for you!"

Trey stepped reluctantly back as the three men rushed forward, their weapons drawn and ready. Trey grabbed the first man.

"Do not harm a hair on her head!" he warned icily before letting him go.

A crash at the rear signaled the rear team's entry.

Trey drummed the doorframe with his large fingers as he heard the teams crash from room to room, shouts of "clear" emanating after each crash.

A sustained banging ensued with no shout of clear. "It's barricaded!" came a call, finally explaining the problem.

Trey rushed in before Bob could stop him.

***

Kate's heart raced as the first sounds of the horses' hooves began to sound. It wasn't the first time they had heard them that week. But it was the first time they had heard them that loudly and noted the volume was increasing. Finally, they were coming. She looked around at her preparations. Not that there were many, it was simply going to work or it wasn't.

The moment she had heard them, she'd known they were coming for her. The volume increasing by the minute until finally, they stopped outside. The number of hooves and the sheer volume were beyond any force she could possibly contend with. She had expected Trey with a couple of friends, not anything like the amount of men they had brought. She had planned everything. Nothing had been overlooked. Or at least Kate thought she had thought of every eventuality. The sound of a struggle in the darkness was the first sign that she had made a mistake. The whimper escaping from Danny's hand that was desperately trying to stifle Hank's warning barks. He meant well, alerting them to danger, a danger that unfortunately would be all too evident, were he able to bark. Kate had no choice, she had to stop him. She withdrew the hunting knife from its sheath and dived across the room. Hank had to be silenced.

***

Trey raced up the stairs towards the end of the hallway where his men were trying to break through a door. Their lanterns sat on the hallway floor while they took turns, trying to kick their way through.

"Out of the way!" shouted Trey as he picked up his pace, racing down the corridor. As the last man cleared his way, Trey jumped and threw his right leg forward. He was a big guy and as he hit the door, the momentum of his body weight and speed were enough to break through the top half of the door. Trey sat atop the wardrobe that had stopped the bottom half of the door moving. He was in. He gestured wildly for a lantern to look for Kate, but already knew something was wrong. There was no way if she were there, that he'd still be alive. She wasn't afraid to shoot. The lantern was handed to him and shone its light across the collection of empty beds that filled the room. Kate and her family weren't there.

"Tear this place apart!" he screamed.

***

Kate winced as she heard Trey's scream. She couldn't see Hank and Danny in front of her, but Hank was not at all happy with the length of sheeting that had been cut and tied around his muzzle. Fortunately, it was retaining 95% of his bark, barely a whimper was registering from him, certainly not enough to alert anyone to their location. Kate winced as Trey's desperate cry to tear her house apart echoed around the street.

***

Trey looked at the open window, the homemade rope ladder leading out and down into the night. He sent a team of men to look for them, just in case they had escaped but he wasn't fully buying it. Ten minutes later, he was beginning to believe they had escaped. They had torn the house apart, not a crawl space had been left untouched. They were not in the house.

"Search the neighbors!" barked Trey.

Bob sat atop his horse. He had fulfilled his promise. Whether Trey found the woman or not wasn't really a concern. He, of course, would prefer his cousin got what he wanted, but there was always a danger that the reality wouldn't meet the expectation. If nothing else, Warm Springs Mesa would appreciate the power and authority of the militia.

The neighbors were hauled unceremoniously into the street. Many wearing only their nightwear. On a clear and starless night in November, it didn't take long for someone to suggest that Zach's house, a few streets over, might be a good place to start looking.

"What about those houses?!" pointed Trey. One house was Harry's and the other, Mrs. Somerville's. Nobody had come out of either.

A neighbor explained that both were dead, and nobody had been seen in them recently. They left out the fact that one had died at Trey's hands.

"And you searched them?" he asked of his men.

"Yes," came the response.

"Wait here, in case they come back," he instructed six of the men before leading the rest towards Zach's house.

***

Kate had to hold on to Sophie with every ounce of strength she possessed. Their night-time sleeping location had been Harry's loft space for the last week. Once darkness fell, they would sneak across to the safety of the attic. None of them could sleep in their home following the previous attack. Each night, they went through a routine to fool the neighbors. Kate had no illusions that if were they aware, the neighbors would give them up in a heartbeat. To the community, they were still living in their home, which was true during the day to keep up the appearance. However, Kate lived an almost unending vigil, watching for the day that Trey came back. Her rifle was permanently at the ready to take them out from a distance, long before they became a risk to her family. Unfortunately, at night, the darkness ruled out that option, hence the subterfuge over their sleeping situation.

Trey's men hadn't lied. They had searched Harry's house. They just hadn't spotted the hatch in the ceiling of the main bathroom. Not that she blamed them, the smell of the blocked drains had them retching for the first few minutes every night.

Through the roof tiles, there was little they couldn't hear from outside and on hearing Zach's name, Sophie had understandably begun to panic. She had to warn her boyfriend and his family. Something Kate could not let her do. Zach knew where they were. He was the only person, outside of the four of them, who knew about their sleeping arrangements.

Zach would break. Kate had read enough novels, and watched enough movies to know that everyone broke. No matter the outcome for Sophie, he wouldn't be able to stop himself. The times of interrogation, and enhanced interrogation were gone. These men could do whatever they needed to discover whatever they wanted. Kate knew they just had minutes to get out.

"We need to get to Zach!" said Sophie angrily, but keeping her voice low.

Zach was dead, he just didn't know it yet, nor did Sophie. "I'll see what I can do," she lied. She needed Sophie to move.

"Mom, you need to save him!" demanded Sophie. "We're not just going to let them kill him and his family, are we?"

"I'm not sure how that saves us," replied Kate, unable to bite her tongue.

"If that's all we're worried about, perhaps we're not worth saving!" cut Sophie.

Kate paused, her daughter was right. She almost couldn't believe it had come from Sophie's mouth and not Ava's. She turned towards Ava. Not a sound had come from her area of the attic for a while.

"Ava?"

Silence.

Kate felt her way across the attic space, feeling for Ava as she walked, making sure she didn't fall over her. Finally, her hand felt skin. Burning hot skin.

"Ava?" Kate gently swayed her daughter to try and wake her.

"Yeah," she replied after a few seconds, her voice weak and sleepy.

"How do you feel?" asked Kate.

"My head hurts and I'm really cold."

Kate wanted to scream. The doctor's timeline was way off. There was no way she had two days to get her daughter the help she needed. She had a day if she was lucky.

"Mom, what about Zach?!" insisted Sophie.

Kate turned and flung the hatch open in frustration, and a pair of eyes stared back at her, almost as startled as hers must have looked. She grabbed her pistol.

***

Trey didn't waste any time with niceties, he jumped off of his horse, strode to the front door and with his boot connecting with it, kicked it open and came face to face with Zach's parents.

"Where is she?" he demanded.

"Who?" asked Zach's father.

"Kate!"

"I'd assume she's in her home," he answered stoically, placing his body in front of his wife.

Trey responded, throwing a crushing fist into Zach's father's face. His nose exploded in a sea of red before he crashed to the floor. He looked up and caught sight of Zach. He was behind the intruder, but the lantern Trey carried lit up the room enough for the two to share a final goodbye. Zach had been sliding the patio door open as quietly and carefully as he could. Zach had stopped and was about to come back to his father's aid. His father smiled and coughed to cover any noise Zach made, shaking his head almost indiscernibly but enough for Zach to know he wasn't to come back. Zach blew a kiss to his father and was gone. He climbed over the fence, just before the rest of Trey's men flooded the house and gardens in search of Kate and her family.

Screams of pain followed Zach's footsteps as he made his way towards Harry's house, avoiding any of the militia. Tears blinded him and on more than one occasion, he turned to go back but deep down, he knew he'd only add to the death toll. He'd not only get himself killed, but he'd give away Sophie's secret sleeping place and get the Wolfes killed as well. The sound of two gunshots sent him to the ground, emptying his stomach before him. His mom and dad had most likely just ceased to exist. He was all alone in a new and very violent world.

He picked himself up. Sophie needed him. He reached Sophie's street and stopped. He could see at least four men milling around the front of the house and had to assume there were some out the back of the house too. Fortunately, he had grown up on the estate and had spent his childhood negotiating most of the back gardens at some point in his earlier years. He ducked back into the nearest back yard and felt his way through to the next. It was slow-going and he was shredding his hands on the bushes and trees, but he had only one person left in the world, and she needed him.

Chapter 48

Nick grabbed his rifle at the sound of the horses below, its night vision scope offering him a view of what was happening in the darkness.

"Are they heading here?" asked Alex, grabbing his own rifle, also fitted with a night vision scope, courtesy of Sean and Lonnie.

"No," replied Nick, following their route to the woman's house. "They're back for the woman, it seems," he relayed, as he watched the men rampage through her house. He flicked to thermal imaging and smiled at the five heat spots as he scanned to the next-door property's roof.

"That's one hell of a lot of muscle for one woman and her kids," exclaimed Alex, counting the number of men and horses. There'd always been the concern that Sean and Lonnie had been exposed and had given away their location. On hearing the horses, he had instantly regretted not moving after meeting Sean and Lonnie, but it was such an excellent location. He had balanced their ability to extricate themselves quickly versus finding a location anywhere near as good. Their hide was almost invisible and their view across Boise unobstructed and of course, Nick had his pet project below that kept him amused.

The rousing of the neighbors was an unexpected turn. The militia hadn't been content with just checking her house and assuming she had moved on. Nick hoped none of the neighbors had spotted the family's night-time dash to the next-door house. Otherwise, things were going to go south very quickly. His fears were soon allayed as the majority of the riders made off shortly afterwards. Six remained.

"Where is she?" asked Alex, his curiosity peaking.

"Thought you weren't interested?" teased Nick. He had taken a pounding from Alex over his interest in the Warn Springs Mesa community and in particular, the woman and her family. "What was it you said, corny daytime soap opera?"

"Something like that," said Alex. "So, do you know where they are?"

Had the situation not been as dire, Nick would have teased him longer. He had been there himself, his wife watching some corny nonsense with a storyline you were half-aware of and something big happens. Your curiosity gets the better, you get intrigued as to how the situation ended.

"Flick to thermal and then scan left to the house next-door."

"Ahh, clever girl," said Alex, watching the five blooms of heat in the attic space appear.

"Did they not search it?"

"Yes but luckily, everything but the attic."

"So where have the other riders gone?"

"Looks like the older daughter's boyfriend's house." Nick looked at where the posse had stopped.

"And he knows where they are?" concern creeped into Alex's voice. Nick was already asking himself the same question and getting a very worrying answer. He noted the concern in Alex's voice, but thought better of picking up on it. Alex was engaged or at least intrigued.

"I don't know," replied Nick, looking cautiously below. A flare of warmth appeared at the back of the house and hopped over the fence. Just one, fast and agile, disappearing, just as four men entered the back garden. The boyfriend had escaped.

"The boyfriend?" asked Alex, following the same drama with increasing interest.

"I guess," replied Nick, following the boyfriend's heat signature as he weaved his way through the estate, using the cover of the bushes and shrubbery expertly.

Two gunshots ended his running. Nick watched as a plume of heat erupted in front of the boyfriend.

"Oh, shit!"

Alex scanned to where Nick was focusing. The boy was bent over a lump of heat in front of him.

"He's fine! He threw up!" said Alex, relief in his voice. He was getting dragged in more and more by the second. "The shots were from his house."

"His parents?" asked Nick.

"I think so," said Alex.

"What was that?" asked Nick, he scanned to his left, movement catching his eye from the other side of the estate. No riders had gone anywhere near that area. Two plumes of heat were making their way from one house to another. The gunshots had alerted the community and they were once again, going to stand up for one another. Nick got his bearings, and his heart sank. He knew where he was watching, Alex had been right all along.

"What?" asked Alex, having waited for Nick to tell him what was happening.

"Nothing," replied Nick, looking back to the boyfriend. The house the two plumes had left had been one of the homes not depositing any trash for some time, while the other had been increasing their trash pile daily. Gunshots rang from where he had been watching. Alex looked and to his credit, didn't gloat as the two plumes ran out of a house, their arms full as the heat plumes inside the house faded.

Both watched silently, that one act had changed everything. Of course, it may have been an isolated incident.

One bad apple. But it was symptomatic of what had transpired across the wider city. It really was everyone for themselves.

"Where is he now?" asked Alex. He needed to focus Nick's mind. He was one of the best soldiers he had ever served with, a man who, when things got tough, you would want by your side. A stone-cold killer, one of the best shots, and certainly better than himself, but he was also a man with a heart and sometimes it got in the way. Alex was worried. He had seen it before, and he should have closed down the whole soap opera straight away. However, this wasn't Afghanistan in the middle of a war and it had until that moment, been a welcome distraction to an otherwise boring oversight role.

"He must know where they are. He's heading towards the neighbor's house," replied Nick, his voice almost vacant. The impact of what he had just witnessed between neighbors had shaken him to his core.

Chapter 49

Kate pulled her PPQ to bear and pulled on the trigger. Her finger stopped just short of the pressure required to fire.

"It's me," mumbled Zach from the darkness, his voice cracking.

Sophie shoved past her mother and rushed down the steps and into his arms. Kate heard deep sobs and knew they weren't Sophie's.

"What's happened?" she managed, realizing how close she had come to shooting her daughter's first love.

Between the sobs, she just about discerned that Zach's parents were likely dead. More blood on her hands, she thought, although immediately pushed that from her mind. None of what was happening was her fault. She was protecting her family. As a mother, that was her first and foremost role in life. If she was doing that, nobody had any right to criticize her.

"I'm so sorry," offered Kate.

"Thanks," replied Zach, pulling himself together. "But we need to get out of here, or they died for nothing!"

"Did they know about this place?"

"I don't think so. I didn't tell them. But they saw you this evening. So, they'll know you're somewhere here!" concluded Zach.

"Quick," ushered Kate to Danny and Ava. "Let's go!" She turned to where Ava was. There was little sound of movement as Danny and the still muzzled Hank slipped past her. Kate worked her way back to Ava and helped her up. She was in no state to go anywhere.

"Zach!" whispered Kate as loudly as she dared.

Between the two of them, they maneuvered Ava into the bathroom below the attic. The sounds of the posse once again invaded the silence. They were coming back.

"What are we going to do?" asked Sophie, saying what everyone else was thinking.

"First things first. Get out of here and into the hills." Zach and Kate each grabbed one of Ava's arms and walked her down to the back door, her feet dragging behind, her body unable to support her own weight. The cascade of hooves stopped in the street out front.

"Fan out! They're here somewhere!" shouted Trey.

They could hear footsteps beginning to walk down the side of the house. Kate held her pistol in one hand and Ava in the other, while her rifle was strapped across her back.

"Sophie, take Ava from me," she said, freeing herself to take out whoever was coming their way.

"When I start shooting, you run for the fence, get over, and run into the hills. We'll meet tomorrow at our picnic spot if not before," she ordered. Tears were flowing from her eyes which fortunately none of them could see. She doubted she would see them again once the shooting started. With a lump in her throat, she said "Now, get ready!"

She felt for the handle and opened it gently. The door creaked as she pulled it back gingerly. The footsteps paused at the sound before increasing in pace at the side of the house. The front door opened behind them. The militia was about to re-search the house. Any doubts about making a break for it disappeared. She pulled the door open and with her pistol at the ready rushed out into the darkness, pulling Sophie behind her. Kate stepped to the side, keeping her body between the oncoming militia and her family as they piled out behind her. Danny last, with Hank being dragged behind him on as short a leash as he could use.

The darkness gave way to the faintest of light as the militia man racing down the side of the house neared with his lantern. Kate raised her pistol as her family dashed towards the fence. There was no way they'd make it before the militia cleared the side of the house and caught sight of them. Kate was going to have to take the shot and give her family the few seconds they needed. A shot that would alert every militia member and Trey to her location. She just prayed she had enough bullets, to hold them back long enough to let her kids escape.

The angle of the light increased across the garden as the militia man neared. Although tucked tight against the wall, the beam was almost upon her. He was nearly there. Kate glanced to the kids. Zach was on top and pulling Danny over, having already pulled Ava over while Sophie was pushing at Hank's rear to help him over. They needed another few seconds, seconds she wasn't going to have once she pulled the trigger. The men in the house, when they heard the shot, would be on her in a second.

The militia man cleared the corner. His mouth opened to speak as he caught sight of first Sophie and Zach and then Kate, pointing her pistol directly at him. The first semblance of a word formed as he raised his AR-15 in unison with his shout.

"Ov—"

His head disappeared before he could form the rest of the word. One second it was atop his shoulders, the next, gone, a spray of droplets replacing it. The body faltered, long enough for Kate not to see it fall. She was already moving, rushing towards Sophie and pushing her unceremoniously over the fence before Zach pulled her up.

***

"What the hell?" exhaled Nick in disbelief, watching the militia man's head explode after the kick of the rifle immediately to his right. He turned to Alex, who was already packing up his kit.

"I think I may have just compromised our mission!"

Nick didn't need to check. Bullets were already heading in their direction as the militia trained their gunfire in the approximate direction from which they had seen the flash of Alex's rifle. Fortunately, the AR-15s were struggling to reach them, nor were the militia able to see in the dark like Nick and Alex could.

Nick raised his rifle. With the mission compromised, he may as well take out the boss. He was easy to spot. He was the only one who'd remained calm, while everyone else around him was panicking.

Alex's shot was no mean feat. The distance and turbulence in the wind as it swirled down the hillside made it all the more remarkable that he'd scored a direct headshot. Nick centered on the man's body. He was moving too much for a headshot. He squeezed the trigger gently, feeling the break, controlling his breathing. He was in the zone.

He was on a hair trigger, the slightest of movements by his trigger finger, and the bullet would be sent on its way.

***

The gunshot from above echoed across the estate. The militia men scattered for cover in all directions, as they were unsure of where the shot had come from.

"Up there," shouted one of the men, having seen the flash from the corner of his eye. "Near the crest of the hill."

The militia emptied most of their magazines as they fired off in the general direction of where they were directed, while trying to get to cover.

"Anyone hit?" shouted Bob. He'd remained calm amongst the chaos. "And stop wasting bullets! They're too far away!" He rode up and down the street, calming his men.

"One man down, head's gone," came a reply.

Bob changed course and rode towards the body, it was at the side of the neighbor's house. Why expose yourself and take out a man walking down the side of a house? he wondered.

"Trey, take ten men and get around the back of that house. There's every chance they were protecting the family!"

"The rest of you, saddle up. We're going to see who's up in those hills," he said out loud while thinking 'how they can shoot a headshot in the dark from almost a mile away...' Whoever was there had working electronics, they had to, to have taken that shot. Only a night vision or a thermal scope could have given them that ability. He dug his heels into his horse's side and clucked loudly. He wanted to get up there as soon as he could. His horse bucked under his forceful kick and sent him unceremoniously off of its back. Bob didn't even hear the crack of the rifle that had killed his horse, taking the bullet that would have ended his life.

A militia man dove across the street and pulled Bob behind the horse's carcass.

***

The area around them lit up again with gunfire as Nick killed the unsuspecting and innocent horse.

"We need to get out of here!" instructed Alex as Nick failed to hit the militia leader. Nick took one last look at where the woman and her children were. They had cleared the fence and were on the trail, just about to head off of it and into the surrounding woods. It looked at least in the short term, they were going to make it. The militia men weren't going to get to them before they left the trail.

"Okay, let's go," said Nick, grabbing his kit. They would be deep in the woods within five minutes, long before the militia would be near them and in the darkness, Nick and Alex most definitely had the upper hand.

***

"What now?" asked Ava weakly as they rested against a tree. The sound of the militia thundering past on the nearby trail had them all holding their breaths.

Kate waited until the riders were gone before speaking. "We wait here until the coast is clear and then head back to get our bikes."

"Our bikes?" they echoed in unison.

"I've got an idea!"

Chapter 50

Kate barely slept, the sound of the militia combing the hillside carried on for hours. She guessed it was at least three in the morning before they called it a night and headed back to base. Daylight was going to be a whole different story. She had no illusion that Bob would be back with a far larger force. Not only did they want her, she realized, but whoever had taken that shot had equipment way beyond the capability of anything in Boise. Whether a loner or an advance party for a larger force, she didn't know. Whatever the case, she had little time to wait and find out. Ava's fever was worsening by the hour.

Thirty minutes after she had heard the last sounds of the militia, she roused her family, a family that had grown in the last two weeks and hours. Her heart had broken as Zach had told of the last vision of his father, waving him away. Knowing they would never see each other again. The vision of Tim waving goodbye to them before leaving on his deployment rushed before her. It was as clear as though it had been that morning. She would never forget it, forever hold on to it, the love for her and his children, clear in his eyes. He hadn't wanted to leave them, but he was a man of honor, a man of duty. A hero, her hero. She stood up as the thoughts rushed through her head. She had to save the kids, for Tim, if nothing else. He'd given his life for their future, just as Zach's parents had for him, and she was damned well sure it wasn't going to be in vain.

"Okay, we've got three hours until sun up. Let's go."

"Where?"

"Home for whatever we can carry, and then as far from here as we can manage."

"And Ava?" asked Sophie.

"What about Ava?"

"Where is she going to go?"

"With us of course!"

"Mom, she can't even walk, never mind cycle."

"We'll work something out," said Kate, not really sure what yet, but knew they had to do something. There was no way she would leave her daughter behind.

They worked their way back to the estate. Kate in front, her weapon at the ready while Sophie and Zach supported Ava as best they could. Danny and Hank brought up the rear. Kate halted them at the edge of the trail.

"Wait here, I'll check it's clear."

Kate left them hidden at the side of the trail and worked her way north. She wanted to make a slight detour on the way back to their house. It was hard to work out where she was exactly, but finally found what she was after. She circled around back and entered through the back door. She stumbled over the lounge furniture before tripping over an item in the hallway. She fell and landed in a wet pool. She knew what it was without having to look. The blood of Zach's parents. She felt their bodies beneath her, discarded in the hallway. She thanked God she had come here on her own. It was no place for a son to be, or a sight for him to witness, even if the darkness did spare her the gory details. The amount of blood was telling her more than she needed to know. It had not been a quick and painless death. Both hearts had pumped until there was no blood left to pump.

Kate stood and stumbled her way towards the kitchen. Listening for even the slightest sound to suggest she wasn't alone. She pulled the curtains closed and flicked her lighter, closing her eyes and opening them carefully to accustom her eyes to the brightness after the dark. She stopped herself looking back and walked towards the door that led from the kitchen to the garage. The lighter burned at her finger as she held the flame alight far longer than it had ever been engineered for. She spotted the bike and released the flame, much to her finger's relief.

Five minutes later she was back at the trail, handing Zach his bike.

"My parents…" he asked as she approached them.

She took him in her arms in answer. "It was quick, very quick," she lied.

Sophie stepped forward and took him from her mother, rocking him gently. From his reaction, he had clearly hung on to the hope they were still alive.

"Wait here," instructed Kate once again. Disappearing into the night. Danny was having none of it. He wanted to be with his mom, and with Sophie and Zach distracted and Ava all but unconscious had his opportunity and took it, following quietly after her with Hank in tow.

Kate edged her way along the street. She could just make out the outline of their house. She ducked behind a bush, as a shadow passed behind the window of the house opposite. Just as she had expected, they were waiting for her.

The question was how many and how long did she have before the main force returned. She worked her way quietly into the neighbor's back garden, the one adjacent to that where she had seen the shadow. Six horses chewed on the grass in the next garden. Six men, too many. She didn't stand a chance against six. She turned to leave before being spotted.

A rustle had her rolling and drawing her pistol.

"Mom," came a panicked whisper.

It was Danny. She relaxed and tensed at the same time. She needed to get him away from the danger.

"Where are we going?" asked Danny as his mother led him and Hank back towards the trail.

"There are too many," she said.

"Why not just take the five we need?"

Kate couldn't see the quizzical look on his face, but she certainly felt the stupidity on her own. She didn't need the bikes, they were no use in any event for Ava. But the horses, they were perfect, better than anything they could have found in the house. Would they guard their horses, or were they so confident in themselves that they wouldn't concern themselves with the horses and what happened just across the road at her house? From what she had experienced, they hadn't lacked confidence. They weren't concerned about anyone daring to steal their horses.

"Wait here!" she instructed. "And I mean it, wait here!"

Kate worked her way along the back of the house, keeping her body as tight to the property as she could. Just in case anyone was looking out over the back gardens. A gate between the gardens allowed easy access for the neighbors and on this instance, Kate to get to the horses. Unfortunately, the gate was human-size and not built for the horses. There was not going to be an easy way to sneak them away. Her presence caused more than a few whinnies and neighs from the horses and it seemed too many for one of the militia men. The door of the house opened. Kate froze against the wall as the militia man hushed the horses. Ironically, he was worried they would frighten Kate away. The door closed as the horses settled despite Kate's presence. She worked her way back to the gate and back into the other garden. She had to widen the gap, but could make no noise doing it.

A hand clamped over her mouth, stifling her scream.

Chapter 51

Alex and Nick worked their way through the woods. They had a plan. A plan they had already worked out many days earlier for just such an eventuality. Alex had messaged that they were extracting. There was little left for them to report on in any event. Boise was lost both to disease and a tyrannical ruler with an iron grip and an endless supply of food and clean water. There was only so much they could stomach as soldiers. Their job was to protect and defend, not watch the slow and tragic death of innocent people while doing nothing.

The biggest surprise was that it had been Alex that broke. He had been the stronger of the two, or at least Nick had always thought so. It seemed he had just been better at suppressing his despair at what they were witnessing. The soap opera of Warm Springs Mesa had been a needed distraction for them both and the fall of that, the one shining example of goodness, was just too much. Nick should have realized when Alex didn't move after Sean And Lonnie's visit that Alex was wavering, but Alex had managed to bullshit a reason to stay beyond the fact he needed to.

Their plan was simple. Night was their friend. They would make their way to the militia base and under cover of darkness, take two horses and ride the hell out of town. If they could take Sean and Lonnie with them all the better but if not, so be it. They had information and equipment that would compromise everything they had spent the last two weeks suffering for.

"They keep trying to call us!" said Alex, the satellite phone vibrating in his pack.

"Should we just switch it off?" asked Nick.

"Or we could just drop it and leave it here?"

"We might need it for an extraction should the shit hit the fan though."

They stopped walking. "I should answer it."

"They'll order us to stay!"

"Maybe not, we know too much and we're being hunted." The phone stopped buzzing. "Damn, missed it," smiled Alex.

The phone began to buzz again. He ripped his pack off of his back and extracted the phone, its screen lighting up their faces.

Alex hit accept and put the phone to his ear. He immediately knelt, pulling Nick with him and looked behind, flicking to thermal image. Ten faint blobs glowed off in the distance. They were being tracked.

He ended the call and replaced the phone in his pack.

"We've got a drone tracking us. They spotted the tracking party and wanted to alert us. Whoever they are, they're good, they're tracking us through woods in the pitch dark. We are most definitely blown, so the extraction is approved. Even though we're on our own, since obviously, no intervention can be offered without exposing capabilities."

"What about the trackers?"

"We're free to engage or outrun as we see appropriate."

"What, are they… a half mile behind?" guessed Nick. "We have three miles to the target. Any shots may spoil our escape plan."

Alex checked his watch. They had at least three hours before the first hint of daylight. "Speed up and hopefully lose them, or play with them."

"Bit of both?"

"Like it," replied Alex and both spun away into the woods. They'd double back and start causing mayhem with their trackers, using their night vision equipment to its full advantage. They hadn't thought for a second anyone would have been tracking them and had made no attempt to cover their tracks. With knowledge came advantage, they went stealthy, and their trackers weren't going to know what hit them.

***

Bob had taken half the men back to base. A small contingent had been left to watch the woman's house in case she returned. Another was sent into the hills to try and find the shooter. A Native American who was said to know the hills better than any man alive led the hunt for the shooter. Patwin, 'Pat' to all who knew him, was a member of the local Shoshoni tribe, born and raised in the hills. He could, they said, track a man blindfolded through the woods in a storm. He had been raised as his father before him, and many, many fathers before his, to be at home in the wilds. At one with the nature surrounding them, appreciating the wonder that the spirit gods had created. The slightest inconsistency in his woods stood out to him like an inappropriate apostrophe would to a an English professor.

Bob had heard tales of the legendary ability of the Indians to track, but in the dead of night through woods, he was not so sure. He planned to return at first light with an army of men and hunt down whoever it was who had killed his man and his horse, for which they would hang.

"There are two," announced Patwin as he found the shooters' hide. The men around him mumbled their skepticism. They could barely see their hands in front of their faces, and yet Pat was following a trail left by two men at least an hour or so earlier.

As they reached the woods and Pat sensed they were gaining ground, he ordered all lights to be doused and chatter to end. The men, he assured them, were only a half mile or so ahead. With no light and nothing like Pat's ability, the nine men behind him had to put one arm on the shoulder of the man in front, hoping that the man in the lead could not only keep up with Pat, but ensure that any obstacles in their way were avoided.

Pat stopped abruptly. The man behind him stopped in time but the others, concertinaed into one another barely keeping their feet. The last man in the line coughed as he stopped, a spray of liquid hitting the man in front of him on the back of the head.

"Hey!" he whispered loudly in annoyance. "That's disgusting!" The last man didn't respond, his body just fell against the annoyed man, liquid pulsing from his cut throat.

Pat, at the front, grinned as the knife buried itself in his stomach and cut upward, gutting him from navel to throat. There was little else he could do, other than appreciate the skill of the men they were tracking who had proven they were more than worthy of him. His last breath would be in the woods that he loved so dearly, a fitting end to a life he had grown tired of since the rise of the militia. He had never liked the militia, nor he was sure did they like him. Racists, rapists, and killers, they had press-ganged him into service the previous week with little choice, when a drinking acquaintance had mentioned his tracking abilities. Their behavior was unworthy of him and the thought that the men he had so little respect for were about to die a terrifying death left him some comfort, but none more so than knowing he would soon join his wife's spirit in the land of the wolf and coyote.

***

Alex slit the second to last man's throat and ducked back behind a tree. Two men down. He knew Nick would take out the man at the front His stealth skills were legendary and with the benefit of vision versus those without, it was as unfair a fight as you would ever see.

As predicted, the men panicked, the woods alit with a blaze of gunfire. The men shooting wildly into the dark and each other, whilst Nick and Alex took shelter behind the trees. Screams of pain followed the shooting. Screams that Nick and Alex were only too happy to quell. They had wanted and needed to issue some payback for the atrocities they had witnessed over the previous two weeks. They darted in and out of the trackers, slicing and cutting silently. Those that lived until the final blows almost died of fright before being mercifully slain by their invisible attackers.

"We need to get a move on," said Alex, realizing how much time had passed. Their plan required darkness to cover their tracks.

Chapter 52

"Don't move!" said the voice behind her.

Kate did exactly that, trying desperately to see that Danny was not in any danger. There was no way she could have seen him in the darkness, but it didn't stop her trying. An irregular dark shape filled her field of vision, and a muffled snarl accompanied it. Hank. He crashed into them both. Old and overweight, it was his only real move, particularly as Danny had been clever enough to leave the tie around his muzzle to keep him quiet. Kate and the man crashed to the ground under his onslaught as he took them both by surprise. Whimpering as he landed, he stood unsteadily, ready to pounce once again, or at least try, should the need arise.

Kate rolled first, her agility beating the larger man. She pressed her pistol into the base of the man's neck.

"Don't shoot," he said quietly. "I'm not militia!"

"So who the hell are you?"

"That I can't say, but let's just say it was my colleagues that saved your life earlier."

"Army?"

"I really can't say and you don't have time to keep asking. You need to get those horses and get the hell out of here before daybreak."

Before she could respond, the fence began to creak and through the darkness she could have sworn pieces of wooden boarding were moving.

"That's Lonnie, I'm Sean. We're going to help you, so please take that pistol out of my neck."

The rapid fire of weapons from the hills above could not have come at a worse time.

"Lonnie?" a shout came from the house before all hell broke loose. Lanterns lit up the scene and exposed Lonnie mid-removal of a fence board. Fortunately, they had not spotted Kate, Sean, and Hank on the other side of the fence.

The militia men were apparently not the most trusting and didn't wait for the relatively new recruit, Lonnie, to respond. Whatever he was doing, they didn't like it. A three short burst ended Lonnie's fence dismantling and had Sean spinning out from under Kate and swinging his AR-15 into action. There was no doubt from his move that he knew what he was doing. Kate grabbed Hank by the collar and yanked him towards her and out of harm's way, or at least from view.

Sean fired off a burst before racing into the next garden. An 'oomph' suggested he had hit what he had shot at. More bursts of gunfire followed.

"Mom?"

"Danny, stay where you are," called Kate, her pistol leveled at the gate. The lantern that the first man had held was still lighting up next door's garden. The horses barely flinched, such was their familiarization with gunshots over the previous two weeks.

Kate heard footsteps behind the fence, someone had come back out of the house. Heavy and clumsy, they were not Sean's footsteps. Kate readied herself.

"It's me, Sean," called Sean before coming into view.

He stumbled unsteadily, checking Lonnie for a pulse, as he came through the gate. There clearly was none as he stumbled on towards Kate. She caught him as he fell, cradling his fall, unable to bear his weight. Her hand was soaked where she held him, blood flowing from a wound in his back.

"It's safe…" he managed before his eyes closed.

Kate held him for a few more seconds as his final breath came and went. She had no idea who the man was, but he had just given his life, as had his friend, to save her and her family. She called Danny to her and hugged him so tight he winced.

"Right. Let's get the hell out of here!" she said, steel in her voice. Now, she was pissed.

Chapter 53

The panicked shooting from above reverberated through the stillness of the night. Sounds that before the outage would have been lost in the white noise of the city, lingered on, the sound waves bouncing from hill to hill, building to building, their volume reducing with each bounce, but still greater than the almost negligible background noise of the deadened night.

Bob knew it was his men. The rapid fire of the automatic weapons was unmistakable, even amongst its own echoes. The silence after the violence felt quieter than before, although he knew it wasn't. He listened for more but none came. His men had either taken out the shooter or fallen to him. Whatever the case, there was little he could do before sun up. He wasn't going to fall foul of a man with a massive advantage.

"What d'you think?" asked Trey, breaking the silence the shooting had created.

More gunfire, even further away than previously, but yet again, automatic fire reverberated, causing Bob to pause.

"I think we need some daylight to get out there and sort things out," said Bob angrily.

"You think the shooter got our guys?"

Bob nodded.

"And the woman?" asked Trey, looking across to Warm Springs Mesa. He had not wanted to leave, but Bob insisted he stayed by his side.

"You'll get to taste that fruit later today!" he promised wryly. "Now sleep, we have a busy day ahead!"

Bob passed the reins of his horse to Neil who had waited for them as they entered the corral back at the base. The faint light of a dozen lanterns lit the entrance to what had become the home to every able-bodied horse within the Boise area.

Neil took Trey's horse reins as Bob walked away. Trey eyed Neil warily, he had not forgiven him for his betrayal.

"I'll see to them, have them ready for you in the morning," said Neil, turning to leave.

Trey grabbed Neil's arm in a vice-like grip. "We have unfinished business. Rest assured, I will repay you for your betrayal," promised Trey, winking.

Neil had kept a deliberately low profile, keeping out of Trey's way in the hopes that the situation from the previous week would just blow over. Neil walked away, knowing without a doubt that Trey would never let it go. Trey was going to kill Neil the first chance he got, whether the next day, week, or year. The man was certifiable and grudges, rather than fade, festered, growing into something far bigger than they were. All he had done was say he had followed Trey's orders. What Trey had read into that he didn't know, but he obviously wasn't going to let it go.

As much as Bob was like a father to Neil, he had no illusion that with Bob, blood was most definitely going to win the day. Neil's days were numbered, at least while Trey lived. Neil walked the horses back to the corral and pulled off their saddles. He contemplated his options. Kill Trey or leave? Killing Trey was a risk. There was every chance Bob would kill him, no matter how good he was with the horses. Trey was Bob's most trusted protector and not somebody he would likely fail to avenge. Leaving was the easy option. He had the transport, but to where? The militia was his family, the first place he could call home, all until Trey and his craziness had spoiled it. Trey's obsession with Kate was driving him mad, and driving Neil out of his home.

There was one other solution. Kate. Deliver Kate to Trey. He'd definitely forgive him, if he did that for Trey. He could still have his home, his horses, and his family. He just needed to get Kate.

Neil saddled up a fresh horse and grabbed a lantern and weapons.

***

They had picked up their pace after dispatching their trackers. Even with all their kit, they could easily cover the three miles in less than half an hour. With just over two hours of darkness left, they slipped into the militia base's corral, past a number of guard stations, and selected two horses from the back paddock which homed the freshest-looking bunch of horses. They saddled them up in silence and quietly walked them out into the darkness between the extremities of the guard positions which, thanks to their night vision, they could see, where others couldn't.

They paused as movement at the other end of the corral caught their attention. They weren't the only people mounting up in darkness. A lone figure appeared atop a horse, clearly visible above the hundreds of horses that filled the area. Whoever he was, he had access to an area that was as secure as any they had seen on the base. Whoever he was, he was leaving alone and obviously had some authority.

"What do you think?" asked Alex.

"I think taking one of the militia's bosses with us, just might minimize any fallout of our earlier than expected extraction."

"Funny, I was thinking the same." Alex clapped Nick on the back and once out of line of sight of the guards, mounted their horses and followed after the militia man at a distance.

Chapter 54

"Has anyone got any idea how we are going to do this?" asked Kate, looking at the pile of equipment, food and clothes they had assembled in the garage. The candles were offering their final wisps of light, adding to the urgency for decisions to be made.

"We have six horses," said Zach. "One each and then one for supplies."

"Ava can't ride on her own, that means two for supplies," corrected Kate.

"What about Hank?" asked Danny.

"He can run alongside," said Zach, looking at Hank and re-considering. "Or you'll have to have him up with you."

"Where are we going?" everyone turned to Ava. Her eyes were struggling to open, but she was still thinking beyond them.

"Our old home, the Air Force base, it has a small hospital," replied Kate, going to Ava's side. She could feel the heat radiating from her, the fever was worsening.

"Start loading with the most important things first and stop when you can't take any more," she suggested, wincing.

Kate dabbed Ava's brow. She had started complaining of stomach pains, and the pain seemed to be increasing. Kate had no idea what it meant, other than she had to get her meds as soon as possible. Time was running out. If it hadn't already.

"Zach, open the garage door," instructed Kate urgently. They were wasting too much time and Ava, as ever, was right. Carry what they could with the important items loaded first.

Sophie was waiting as the garage door opened. The six horses were ready and waiting to be loaded. Ten minutes later, with Kate and Ava on the same horse, and the others trailing behind, they moved out of the estate. Each horse connected by rope to the one in front, forming a train of sorts with Kate leading the way. Kate wasn't even tempted to look back. She had spent so little time with Tim in the home, the memories were far more negative than positive. For all the happiness they had shared, the sorrow weighed far heavier.

"Are you sure you're okay?" asked Danny for the fifth time in as many minutes.

Sophie sniggered as Zach replied. "Yes, fine!" he insisted, although clearly he wasn't, with the amount of shuffling he was doing. Hank wasn't the lightest or nimblest of Labradors and given Danny's size, it was evident there was no way he could hope to have him on his horse with him. Zach had had to step in and save Hank from being left behind.

Kate followed the darkness of the tarmac, as it cut down the hillside. She had two objectives, avoid the militia base and be clear of Boise before sunrise. Both sounded easy enough but unfortunately, the route past the militia base was by far the quickest, while avoiding it meant a long trek through the center of Boise which came with its own troubles, as she was well aware. A woman and four kids on horses were going to be a significant target, but not until sunrise. Riding past the militia made them a target every minute of the day or night.

She turned right at the bottom of the hill and led her family in the opposite direction of the Air Base and towards the center of Boise. As counterintuitive as it felt, avoiding the militia had to be paramount. The noise of the horses' hooves clattered against the tarmac. Each clip alerted whoever was in their path of their approach. It was high risk despite the hour, but she had to weigh it against the other option that took them within yards of the militia's home base.

***

Neil had been around horses most of his life and as a result, was an expert and confident rider. He wasted no time on leaving the base and clucked his horse up to a fast canter. It was five miles to Warm Springs Mesa and he wanted to get there and back if possible within the next two hours, before Trey and Bob woke. With luck, he'd have over an hour to try and find Kate before having to head back to beat the sunrise. He had no idea how he would find her where others had failed, but he had to try. Otherwise, he would have no option but to go on the run, and spend the rest of his forever looking over his shoulder. There was only one way to leave the militia and it did not come with a breathing option.

***

Alex and Nick had both been on horses before, but neither were anywhere near as skilled as the man they were following. They tried in vain to keep him within range of their scopes, but it was not to be. However, it didn't take long for either of them to work out where they were going, or at least hazard an educated guess, Warm Springs Mesa. With that revelation, they slowed slightly in an attempt to survive the ride. They just had to hope they didn't arrive too far behind their target.

***

Neil barely slowed as he reached the base of the hill below Warm Springs Mesa, egging his horse on up the road. Why the horse chose to stop there, Neil didn't really know. Whether he'd sensed danger, something wrong, he didn't know, but he brought his horse to a stop. The world silenced around him as the crashing hooves let up. Two sounds soon filled the void he had left. Horses ahead and behind him.

Behind were fast-paced, somebody was following him. He had no clearance to leave the base, in theory he was AWOL, a deserter, although nothing could be further from the truth, at least until he failed to find Kate.

The horses ahead of him were slower, more of them but a slow steady pace. The only horses out that night were the horses with the men watching Kate's house and the riders in the hills. None he was aware of should have been heading downtown. Surely not, he thought, the shooting earlier that had stopped Bob in his tracks, it couldn't have been Kate. There were six men.

Perhaps they had found her trail, he thought more logically, they were doing what he was doing, being proactive in an attempt to impress Bob, or in his case, get Trey off his back.

The riders behind were gaining fast, he had to make a choice. He turned to follow downtown, but stopped as his heels raised to kick his horse on. Kate had outwitted them before. Finding her as part of the posse would do him no favors, finding her after outwitting them, would. She would want what she could salvage from her house, leading the posse a merry dance to create a diversion was just her way of thinking. All or nothing, he thought. He kicked on and headed up the hill. It was a gamble, but one he had to take.

***

Kate had hushed them all as she heard the horses cantering behind. They couldn't have been more than a few hundred yards to their rear but in the darkness, it was as good as a mile such was the lack of visibility. Beyond the sharp edges of the buildings and the roads, there was little else to make out. The cantering stopped. She toyed with stopping, but that would just suggest they were trying to hide. There was no way they hadn't been heard already. She just had to hope they wouldn't assume it was her and her family on the horses, but just a regular patrol out doing checks. Of course, that was tenuous; nobody went out in the dark unless they really had to.

Kate kicked on as the sound of the hooves fell away. She needed to speed things up. Clearing the city before sunrise was not their only concern. Whoever had ridden up to the estate was about to realize they had made a mistake. They had underestimated Kate.

People had always underestimated Kate, whether her size or her friendly and pleasant manner. They had never seen her inner strength, until it was too late. Whether as a gymnast or as a mother fighting her kids' corner at PTA. They had all come to appreciate Kate was a formidable force. Previously underestimating Kate didn't mean much. In the new world, it was a life and death mistake.

Chapter 55

Alex and Nick pulled their horses to a stop. A lone horse stood in the driveway of the woman's house. Its rider was nowhere to be seen but from the noise inside the house, whoever they were, were less than happy about whatever they had found.

"You two!" the man shouted as he exited the woman's house.

"Check the neighbors, find out where they went!"

The man looked at them more closely, his eyes beginning to see the faintest of outlines in the darkness.

Nick sped things up for the man. He flicked his goggles from thermal to night vision and a small green light shone above his goggles.

The man stumbled back. It was the first sign of power he had seen in two weeks and was no doubt what helped him see the two rifles pointing at him.

"Who the hell are you?" he stammered as Alex jumped down and took the man's hands behind his back, tying them tightly. He removed the man's weapons, making them safe before uttering a word.

"What's your name?" he asked, pushing him towards his horse.

"Neil," replied their captive.

"And you're a member of the militia?"

"You're not?" asked Neil, relief in his voice, surprising both Nick and Alex.

"Are you?" repeated Alex.

"I suppose," replied Neil.

Alex looked at Nick. He really wasn't wanting to get into a long chat with the guy.

"There are six militia men in that house over there," whispered Neil out of the side of his mouth. Alex and Nick both turned, flicking their goggles back to thermal. One heat spot shone, not six. They scanned up and down the street. Other than a few heat spots in bedrooms, there were no heat spots consistent with the man's claim.

"Is that supposed to scare us?"

"No, definitely not, warn you," he replied defensively.

"What position do you have in the militia?"

"I'm a lieutenant, one of the Duke's right-hand men.

"The Duke?" asked Alex. They had never had the chance to speak to a militia man before.

"That's Bob's preferred title. You know, like a ruler? He says Dukes run states and one day we'll have a King, maybe him."

"Sounds like you like this guy, Bob, so why you warning us?" asked Alex.

"Bob's great, like a dad to me, it's his crazy-as-shit cousin, Trey. He's got it in his head that I betrayed him. He's gonna kill me if I don't haul ass out of here."

Nick leaned forward on his horse. "So how does that explain you being here?"

"Last gasp effort. Trey's got a thing for the woman who lives here…"

"Not the only one," smirked Alex under his breath.

"…I figured if I could get her for him, I might save myself. But she's gone and I guess the posse I heard going into the city are chasing after her."

Alex's eyes flashed to Nick's, unsurprisingly his head had swiveled on hearing Neil's revelation, towards the city below.

"So, you're happy to come with us?" asked Alex.

"If you keep me away from that crazy Trey, I'm all yours."

"One wrong move and we shoot you, understand? No warnings, no second chances, one wrong move!"

Neil nodded in the darkness. Fortunately, their goggles helped them see it and saved asking for clarification. Alex helped the hand-tied Neil up onto his horse.

"I can't ride very well with my hands behind my back!" he moaned.

"And that's exactly why they're behind you, you ride too damn well," offered Alex, pulling himself up onto his horse.

"So where was that posse?" asked Nick, itching to get moving but not wanting to sound too eager.

Neil led the way, his speed significantly slower than previously as he tried to get used to riding without hands.

Alex sidled up to Nick. "It's not really part of the plan. We're supposed to be hightailing it out of here. There'll be a small army hunting us come sun up."

"You scared of a few cowboys?" chided Nick. He knew how to push Alex's buttons.

"Which way?" barked Alex to Neil.

Chapter 56

Kate rode as fast as she dared. Twice she'd had to speed up as people tried to catch them. Fortunately, the size and power of the horses buffeted them away each time. Zach was by far the worst off. Hank was not in the least happy about his confinement, but Danny had made it clear where Hank went, he went. Kate was in no position to fight with Danny, her focus had to be on Ava, her life hung by a thread. Kate could feel the strength ebbing from her. With every mile, Kate was having to offer her more and more support to sit upright in the saddle in front of her.

At present, she was riding as fast as she felt comfortable to. If at any point Hank's presence caused them to slow for any reason, she would deal with it swiftly and deal with the resulting consequences of Danny's hatred. In the meantime, she focused on moving forward.

"Sun's coming up!" called Sophie, spotting the first hint of light on the horizon.

The sunlight wasted no time in spreading its light across the vast plain that lay before them, stretching off into an endless distance. Kate looked back. They had cleared the southern side of the airport. Other than a few homes dotted along the road here and there, they were out of the city. They had made it. And with time to spare. Surely it was an omen, they were going to make it. Between them and the base there was nothing, particularly as she had cut south and picked up the back roads. Although neither offered any cover to speak of, she felt the interstate, if anyone was looking for them, would be their first port of call.

"Mom?"

"Yes," she said with more bite than she wanted, she could sense it was going to be Hank related. She turned and threw him a warm smile of apology. He wasn't looking at her, he too was looking back.

Kate didn't need to ask what he was looking at. There was a fire burning atop the air traffic control tower, black smoke billowing up high into the sky for all of Boise to see. There was no way it hadn't been set deliberately. With a pair of binoculars, there was no doubt that whoever was in the tower was more than likely looking straight at them. And if they were using the scope on a hunting rifle, had them in their sights.

"Everyone get down!" ordered Kate. "Keep the horses between us and them!"

Kate pulled the Remington 700 out of its holder and as the kids kept the horses as calm as they could, she lined up the shot. She was guessing it was at least a mile. She made the alterations to her scope, there was not a breath of wind. She zoomed in. There were two men in the tower, the flames above them were beginning to drop down into the tower. The tires, or whatever they had used to create the smoke, were melting and sending hot burning droplets of rubber down on to the gangway that circled the top of the tower. The men had nothing more powerful than AR-15s, they were no threat at that distance. She wasn't even sure they had spotted them until one raised binoculars and looked straight at her.

She pulled the trigger and waited. He flinched at the flash and started to move, but the bullet beat him. His body was propelled across the tower and disappeared out of sight. Kate had already sent another shot on its way as the second man rushed for cover. Kate's snap shot missed. She lined up another. She had to stop whoever they were signaling from telling them which road they were on. The Tower had a perfect view of both the back roads and the interstate. With the man out of sight, she had little to go on other than what she would do in his shoes. She aimed and fired. She would never know whether she was right, but they had to get moving and quickly.

***

The billowing smoke had the militia base rushing to action. Men raced from their barracks to the corral, saddling horses and preparing for action. Bob barked orders as he raced to join and grabbed the first saddled horse he came to, racing towards the smoke. Trey wasted no time and like Bob, pushed a militia man aside who had saddled his horse and chased after his cousin. The men who had been awaiting orders and were ready to ride followed suit. A steady stream following thereafter. Within ten minutes, more than fifty men were racing to the tower, just over six miles from the base. Within thirty minutes, that number had swollen to over a hundred. Bob had his army and was on the hunt.

The sound of the high-powered rifle rounds had Bob kicking his horse onwards. Those were not the sound of shots from his men. With no sound of return fire, he feared the worst. His men had died and with them, who they had seen and where they were going.

***

Alex and Nick had struggled to catch either sound or sight of the posse that Neil had heard. With sunlight imminent Alex had been about to call it a night and suggest reverting to plan A, getting out of Boise for good, when the air traffic control tower, just a few hundred yards ahead of them started billowing smoke from its roof.

The subsequent sound of the rifle being fired off in the distance, a noise that brought a smile to Nick's face, had them picking up speed and heading towards the shooter.

"I see that smile," laughed Alex.

"You recognize the sound of the rifle, too?"

Alex nodded. They had heard the woman fire that exact same rifle the previous week. "You think she's on the horses?"

"I wouldn't put it past her, somehow she just might have."

"You know that's a watch tower for the militia," advised Neil, looking at the plume of smoke. "They'll see where we're going."

Alex changed direction and headed for the tower.

"How long until the militia get here?" asked Nick, hopping off his horse as they arrived at the tower.

"I'd say it's about seven miles or so. Best case from the base, I'd say twenty-five to thirty minutes on a fit horse."

"So we need to get the hell out of here, quick as we can," advised Alex as Nick raced into the tower. The burning roof was looking precarious.

Nick wasted less than a minute. "Two dead," he announced on his return. "One through the wall, catching him in the neck. Quite a mess up there."

"Did you see them?"

Nick nodded. "I'd guess just over two miles that way. Six horses,. Couldn't make out who was riding them, but didn't look like a posse," he winked at Alex.

"Pleasant Valley Road," advised Neil.

"Where does it go?" asked Nick, jumping back onto his horse and leading the way.

"Nowhere really. Although, you could use it as a back road to Mountain Home."

"The Air Force Base?" asked Alex.

"Yeah, you guys Air Force?"

"No!" said Alex, ending the conversation and speeding his horse up.

"Guys, I've got no hands!" shouted Neil as they took off at a pace, he was most definitely not comfortable with hands free.

"Well, we aren't untying your hands and we aren't slowing down, so I suggest you just grip harder with your legs!"

***

"Mom!"

Kate turned. "What, Danny?" she called to him three horses back.

"I'm scared!"

"We'll be fine, honey. The Air Force will protect us."

"If we make it to them!" mumbled Sophie loud enough for all to hear. Nobody disagreed.

Chapter 57

By the time they reached the air traffic tower, the top was gutted by fire. With no sign of any militia men, he had to assume they had been shot, which left him no further forward. Just twenty-four hours earlier, he had celebrated his control over Boise and Idaho by killing the Governor. He was the law; he was in control. Nothing could have run smoother over the last two weeks, everything had run exactly or better than planned. Had he dared dream he'd be in control of Boise and Idaho in just two weeks, he'd never have believed it. Yet, every time his men had anything to do with that woman, something went wrong. Sixteen men had remained last night and not one had been heard of since, despite the gun battle that had ensued. He had a feeling deep down, he wasn't going to see them again. Sixteen men for one damned woman. He looked at Trey by his side. He could have throttled him. His obsession with the woman was costing him men and more importantly, his reputation.

"Get up there and see what you can see," he barked, throwing binoculars to the man nearest the tower door.

"But there's nothing there!" replied the man, looking to the smoldering stub at the top of the tower where the office had once sat.

Bob aimed his AR-15 and shot him.

"You," he pointed. "Get up there!"

The second man grabbed the binoculars and entered the building without hesitation. He appeared at the top, coughing and choking from the fumes he'd had to endure on the staircase to the top. He could be seen walking gingerly. "Not much floor left up here, Duke!" he shouted down.

"Just tell me what you can see."

The man had an unobstructed view across the plain to the south of Boise. He focused on the interstate, following it down as far as the binoculars would allow him to see. Nothing moved. The few cars that had been on the road two weeks earlier when the power stopped remained abandoned. Their drivers long having given up on them ever starting again.

"Nothing on the interstate!" he called down.

He turned his attention to the myriad of country and back roads that crisscrossed the plain.

Bob was off his horse and pacing, trying to control his spiraling out of control temper. "Well??" he shouted up in frustration as the lookout went quiet.

"I've got something, looks like three horses moving fast down Pleasant Valley Road."

"How far?"

"Past the prison, but not as far as the gun club," he replied, two of the only buildings he knew in the area.

"Four five miles, shit, how'd we catch them…Where's Neil?" shouted Bob.

Neil didn't come forward.

"Anyone seen Neil?"

"He went out just after you got back this morning," said a voice from amongst the men. He was one of Neil's stablemen. The man guided his horse through the growing crowd of militia towards Bob.

"Out where?"

"I don't know. He had words with Trey after you left, saddled up, and rode out. Seemed to be in a hurry!"

Bob's head swung to his cousin, fury spouting from his eyes. "What the hell did you do?"

Trey threw a stare of hatred at the speaker before pleading his innocence with Bob.

Bob batted away his protestations. "So, how do we make up five miles?" he called to his men.

"Duke, there're more ahead as well! I think, half the distance again!" the lookout shouted down.

"How many?"

"Too far to tell, but I'd say more than four horses."

Bob swung back to his men.

"Fewer men, more horses," replied the stableman, having thought through the options.

Bob looked at him quizzically.

"Each rider has three or four horses. Horses tire less with no one on them and can run much faster. You simply stop and change horses every so often and they can maintain a much faster pace. You should catch up the five miles in a few hours."

Bob looked across his swelling army. Almost a hundred men and their horses had assembled at the tower. He started pointing to some of his best men. "If I point to you, take another three horses from the men around you and move over there!" he shouted.

He then pointed to the stableman, "You get over there and get them ready to move out, any other stablemen here?"

Two more men moved towards the stableman and assisted.

Within fifteen minutes, Bob had his fast response posse ready to move out, twenty-one of his hardened militia, assisted by the stableman, himself and Trey, giving a grand total of twenty-four men and ninety-six horses.

Bob turned to the stableman. "Okay, lead on. You set the pace, we want to catch them as soon as we can!"

***

Kate looked over her shoulder, a cloud of dust was visible behind them. It was still a long way off, but it was there. She wanted to speed up but with Ava on her saddle with her, she really was going as fast as she dared. How she'd even conceived they'd have managed this by bike she had no idea. They had already covered, she guessed, over ten miles with another thirty at least to go. She'd planned to cover it in a day, but she had no intention of going as fast as they were. Although the forced speed had one major benefit, they'd get Ava help sooner. If they made it, that was. She focused on the road ahead. If they got any closer, she always had the Remington to keep them at bay.

It could be worse, she thought as she caught sight of Zach. Hank was wrapped around his upper torso, his two front paws and head resting on Zach's shoulder. It seemed they had found their comfortable spot, at least Hank had. Zach looked decidedly pissed off with the situation.

"You okay, Zach?" called Kate with a smile.

"Yes," he mumbled in response.

Kate couldn't help but think the situation with Hank was a godsend. Zach's mind was being kept occupied and not dwelling on the death of his parents.

She gently nudged her horse on.

"Mom?"

"Yes, honey," she called back to Danny.

"We nearly there yet?"

Chapter 58

Operation Center
Secure Location
Pacific Ocean

Scott picked up the photo and stared at it, his wife and newborn baby daughter. He had no idea when he'd see them again. He switched off the bedside lamp and slipped the precious photo back into his wallet. He could only pray they were okay. It had been four weeks since his orders to report to the airbase, and as long since he'd had any contact with his family, or anyone he knew.

His orders had taken him to an office where he had been instructed to board the transport aircraft. Six hours later, after one of the bumpiest and most uncomfortable flights he had ever had, he had the pleasure of experiencing a night-time landing on an aircraft carrier in the middle of a storm. The single scariest thing he could ever imagine. The following morning, he had been introduced briefly to seven other operators like himself, none of whom knew or had ever served with one another previously. It was as if they had scoured the four corners of the country to find eight complete strangers.

His room was like a cell. Once off duty, he'd had no interaction with his colleagues, no opportunity to get to know them. Other than work, he had nothing. Even the main body of the ship and the crew were kept from them. It was them, one commander, and four nameless civilian contractors who appeared to be running the show. None of it had many any sense, not even when they were put to work, which was nothing more than familiarizing themselves with an area and understanding the routines of the populace. It was by far, the dullest work he had ever undertaken, and as far as he was concerned, a scandalous waste of not only the equipment but their ability as operators. For two weeks, he had watched as cars ferried precious little darlings as little as a few hundred yards to school. Garbage trucks picked up and deposited waste. Police chased criminals, schools put on football games, firemen fought fires, planes took off and landed. Basically, anything and everything you'd expect to happen in a town or city, they watched. At the end of each shift, he was taken back to his secure room and deposited, before being picked up for his next shift with only a TV to amuse himself. At no point or nowhere available to them was there any possible device with which to communicate with anyone. Other than being drone operators, the only information he had been able to ascertain about them all was that, like him, all had been vetted in recent months for additional security clearance.

He rose from his bed. He had five minutes until his door would once again be opened and his temporary reprieve from captivity lifted for him to get to work. Another sleepless night, another night struggling to cope with the devastation he had witnessed and the destruction of a beautiful city in just two weeks. He had no idea what had become of his wife, he just had to pray she was safe. All he knew was what he had witnessed in Boise, a city, until four weeks earlier, he had only ever heard good things about. He would struggle to ever have anything good to say about Boise in the future, if he even had one. Nobody spoke to them, or told them what was happening. There had been no increase in operations over the previous two weeks from the aircraft carrier. He'd have expected something, certainly after seeing what he had witnessed.

He arrived on station. He had a five-minute handover, their shifts rotating and therefore seldom seeing the same operator twice within a few days.

"Holding steady at 25,000 feet south of Boise, we have an incident underway…" the operator explained what had transpired over the previous few hours, their bird's eye view from 25,000 feet with every technology available to man allowed them almost daylight clarity twenty-four hours a day. Scott listened as the operator relayed the two firefights that had happened and subsequent escape of a number of individuals, which was still underway.

"Enjoy!" he offered as a parting gesture.

"Thanks," said Scott half-heartedly, taking the seat and the controls. He daren't raise his hopes. Some of the most upsetting scenes he had witnessed over the previous two weeks were when he had been stupid enough to hope that somebody would help, somebody would step in or stand up for their fellow citizens. Each time, his hopes had been dashed.

The previous operator had circled the area of interest with a virtual highlighter. Scott made himself comfortable, shuffled himself into position and pushed forward on the small zoom control with his thumb at the top of his right joystick. The view on his screen moved seamlessly from an expanse of brown dirt viewed at no zoom from 25,000 feet to being able to look at the individual strands of hair on a person's head from the same distance.

Scott zoomed back slightly and focused on the front group. The dust they were kicking up obscured most of their features, but he counted six horses. A thermal check suggested six horses, two without riders, two horses had two people. He corrected, five people and a dog. He recounted as instructed everything into his headset.

He zoomed out before zooming back in to the group behind, much simpler, three horses, three riders.

A final zoom out and in wasn't as simple. The final group more than filled his screen. He let the system do the work for him this time. It wouldn't accidently recount as he would be likely to do with such a large mass of bodies filling the screen. The dust made it impossible to see any detail without switching to thermal. Twenty-four riders and ninety-six horses.

Scott zoomed and selected each of the three groups, marking them for the system to automatically track. Details immediately appeared in front of him. He read them into his head set.

"Group One, speed 12.3 mile per hour. Group Two, 2.7 miles behind Group One, speed 13.7 miles per hour. Group Three moving faster than both One and Two and 6.2 miles behind Group Two and 8.9 miles behind Group One."

A second screen instantly computed the time to meet if nothing altered. Group Two would catch Group One in one hour, fifty-nine minutes and thirty-three seconds and Group Three would catch Groups One and Two in two hours, fifty-three minutes and fifty-five seconds, assuming Groups One and Two moved at Group One's pace once Group Two had caught them. Whatever the case, he had a six-hour shift. He was going to know the outcome.

"You're Scott?" asked one of the civilians. They said little, but watched everything.

'Yes."

"We're waiting for confirmation, but believe Group Two are two of our own."

"Our own?" quizzed Scott, not entirely understanding what the civilian meant.

"Operatives working for us."

Scott stopped there. The civilians weren't the most friendly and pressing the 'us' was bordering on showing too much interest. Something that had been frowned upon previously.

"Okay, am I cleared to engage weapons to protect?"

"Not authorized at present. We're monitoring the situation. Should it change, you will be advised. Otherwise, no, weapons are not authorized," he added for clarity.

"Well, just make sure you decide within the next couple of hours or so," advised Scott, pointing to the computation on his screen.

The civilian scurried away. They obviously hadn't done the same check and had probably assumed the groups would stay evenly apart, as they were all riding horses.

"Amateurs," mumbled Scott into his mic.

Chapter 59

Alex kept watch as much behind as in front. They were going as fast as their horses would allow them to, but the group they always knew would be coming from behind had finally come into view.

"How many do you think there are?" shouted Nick above the sound of their horses.

He didn't know, but one thing was certain. "Too many!" he replied.

"How can they be gaining on us?" asked Nick to Neil.

Neil looked back. His life was just as threatened as the two men he was with. Two men who had still told him nothing.

"Chances are, they're using multiple horses. They'll probably stop and change every so often. It may cost them a few minutes, but they can ride much faster overall."

"So they'll catch up with us?!"

Neil felt the ties on his hand, it was his one chance of explaining his desertion. He had been kidnapped. "Yes, so I hope you've got a plan to get us out of here beyond riding as fast as we can, because that isn't going to work."

Alex rode next to Neil, took out his knife and shakily reached over, severing the cord binding Neil's hands. "Can we go a bit faster now?"

Neil watched the only excuse that would have saved his life drop away to the dirt beneath. "Yes," he said with a new vigor in his resolve to get away.

"Not too fast that we have to shoot…" Alex was interrupted by a buzzing in his backpack.

***

Kate couldn't stop looking back, the group behind were getting closer. Not by much, but they were definitely gaining, and with a long way to go, it wasn't boding well. Their horses were tiring, more than likely needed water and at least a few minutes' rest. Much like herself. Running the horses into the ground wasn't the answer and certainly wasn't going to save them. As she neared the top of a small summit, her view back was as good as she would get and looking ahead, the land dipped. She was about to lose sight of their pursuers.

"Let's take a quick break and water the horses," she called, slowing her horse and receiving an audible sigh of relief.

"Sophie, Zach, can you look after the horses? Danny, you look after Ava," ordered Kate, removing the Remington from its holster.

She knelt and rested her elbow on her knee, steadying the rifle for her to get a clear view down the plain to their pursuers. She tried to gauge the distance, it was more than a mile she was sure of that, but less than two. Three men. She tried to hold as steady as she could to recognize any features but as steady as she was, the men weren't. They bounced up and down with each stride of their horses. The rider at the front seemed awkward, his hands behind his back. Another rider rode next to him and pulled out something, slashing behind the man's back. He had just freed his hands. He was, or at least had been, their captive.

The man who had cut the man's ties suddenly started fighting with his own pack. It was an almost comical sight, until it wasn't. Kate almost dropped her rifle, her breath caught as the man retrieved what he had been fighting to achieve. He held it to the side of his face, just like you used to hold a phone.

She watched in astonishment. The ramifications of what she was seeing, not fully formulating as she watched. He looked up before ending the call. She wished she could hear, as what appeared to be a heated argument ensued, before finally they turned a sharp ninety degrees and headed back towards the interstate and away from them.

Kate lowered her rifle and looked up at the sky. Was someone up there looking down?

"Mom? You okay?" asked Ava, her voice growing weaker.

"Yes, fine," she snapped a little too quickly. Her mind was racing, trying to think through everything she had just witnessed.

"Mom!" snapped Sophie, chastising her mother.

"Sorry, but…" began Kate, stopping, not sure what to say or whether she was just seeing things.

"What's up?" asked Zach, joining the discussion.

Sophie put her fingers to her lip to stop him talking and indicated that they were waiting on Kate to talk.

"I don't really know what to say. They've turned away. They're not chasing us anymore," said Kate, watching them race away.

"Does that mean we made it?" asked Danny excitedly.

"Well, we've still got to get to the Base," said Kate, looking at Ava. the tiniest of smiles forming on her face, something Kate hadn't seen for days.

"Any idea why they've stopped chasing us?"

Kate looked up at the sky. "I think they were ordered to," she replied wistfully.

"By who?"

"Whoever called them." She watched their faces as she spoke. Their mouths dropped just as much as hers had, Sophie's just a fraction later than Zach and Ava's.

"Who called them?" asked Danny innocently.

***

Nick fumed as they rode. He glanced back constantly, willing the family to start riding again. They were obviously unaware there was an even greater threat to them than they had thought there was.

"Surely we could at least warn them!" shouted Nick in frustration.

"Our orders are to get as far from that family as possible!"

"They'll die!"

"And according to the powers that be, so will we if we stay with them. According to the intelligence, they're the target, not us."

"We can't…"

"We can't compromise the mission…what we know….C'mon, you know we can't take any unnecessary risks. If we were the target, fair enough. But we're being told we're not."

"Who the hell *are* you guys?" burst Neil. He had held his tongue as long as he could, left speechless when Alex had answered a working phone.

Both Alex and Nick ignored him.

"We must be able to do something?" vented Nick.

Alex looked skywards. "They're watching our every move. Don't forget, they'll do anything to avoid the mission being compromised. Anything!"

Nick followed Alex's eyes, he understood. The missiles on the drones above were just as deadly when fired against friendly targets, and extremely effective at ensuring secrets weren't discovered.

Nick looked back, relieved to see the family were on the move again. He looked the other way, the larger cloud moved relentlessly onwards, gaining ground by the minute. At ground level, the visible horizon was around three miles away. He reckoned they were just over two miles back. It wouldn't be long before the family realized there was a far larger group bearing down on them.

"How far to the Air Force Base?"

"This isn't the way to the Air Force Base," replied Nick.

"I know that!"

"Another fifteen miles I'd guess, give or take."

Nick's heart sank, they'd be overrun within the hour. There was no possible way they could make it, and they couldn't lift a finger to help.

Chapter 60

"Duke!"

"What?"

"It looks like they're turning towards the interstate," advised Trey. "Should we cut across to intercept?"

"Any sign of the first group?"

"Not yet."

"You can't see them ahead of the other group?"

"Nope, looks clear ahead of them."

"Why turn sharp left? They know we're behind them, we can see them. If we cut across the angle, we'll catch them quicker. It makes no sense."

"Maybe they're just following the other group that can't see us?"

Bob shook his head. "No, they'd have cut across, just like we would. They should be able to see the first group."

"So what do we do?"

"Let me think!"

Everyone remained silent as Bob considered their options. The first group ahead, he knew, contained three horses. The group further ahead had, according to their lookout, at least four horses. Three horses ruled out the woman, she had three kids, so four horses minimum. There was at least one shooter and Neil in the mix. Maybe there were two shooters and Neil was mixed up with them. Or perhaps, Neil had nothing to do with any of it. He had ruled out the three horses ahead being militia, they'd have slowed when they had seen the larger force. Whoever they were, they were running. And nobody ran from him and lived to tell the tale.

"Trey, you take six men and keep heading towards the Air Force Base, We have to assume that's where the woman's headed." Although he hadn't confirmed who it was, every ounce of intuition was screaming at him, telling him it was that damned woman.

"I'll take the rest of the men and head towards the other group. There's a chance the other group are ahead but even if not, I think those three are our shooters from last night and if they are, they'll put up more of a fight than a woman and her kids. Once we've dealt with them, we'll head back to support you."

Trey couldn't have asked for a better outcome. He'd have her to himself. With Bob out the way, he could enjoy himself at least for a few hours before Bob rode in and took control.

"Sounds like a good plan," he grinned, signaling for six men to follow him as he kicked his horse onwards, accelerating away with his men from Bob, who directed his group to cut across the plain and chase down the three men.

Chapter 61

Scott raised his hand to attract the civilian's attention.

A flick of the head was the nearest he got to the man asking him, 'What?'

"I think we may have a problem. The large group just split. The larger of the split is chasing down your men. The smaller group is continuing on their original course after Group One."

If Scott expected a response, he was disappointed, the man just walked away, pushing a phone to his ear.

Scott shook his head. They had forgotten the one major factor missing in Boise. There was no information available to people in Boise, other than what was put in front of them. There was every chance the groups had no idea who was chasing them or who they were chasing.

***

"You're telling me something I can see!" screamed Alex in frustration. All their little diversion had done was lose them ground.

Nick waited to hear whatever had been relayed.

"It didn't work! A bigger group is following us than is following the family! And don't look so happy – you realize there are two groups out here that will happily kill us if needed." He looked skyward.

"What do you keep looking up there for?" asked Neil, looking up and seeing nothing. "And who else will kill you?"

"You don't need to know!"

"So what then?" asked Nick.

"Strength in numbers, I suppose," he said, turning back towards the direction of the family.

"What about them?" asked Nick, motioning back to their pursuers.

"At some point, we're going to have to slow them down, but they're still too far back. We just need to beat them to the Air Base."

***

Kate watched as the three horsemen appeared once again behind them. She looked off into the distance. She knew the Base was less than an hour away. She just had to keep the men at bay until they reached the Base.

***

Scott zoomed out and highlighted the separate groups again. The computations were done in an instant. The Air Base was too far away. They'd never make it. The chasing group was going to overrun the smaller groups long before they reached the safety of the Base.

He wondered if there was anything he could do to help, alert Base security. Anything. He changed the angle of the camera and scanned ahead, zooming into the Base. It was amazing how detailed the image was, 25,000 feet up and over ten miles away, yet he could still have identified the color of a person's eyes. Of course, for that to be the case, he'd have had to find a person to see their eyeballs. Nobody, not one living soul was anywhere to be seen. He flicked to thermal, it may have been they were all indoors. Nothing, not even a hint of warmth from a decomposing body.

The Base was empty and by all accounts of what he could see, it had been emptied in a hurry. People, equipment, everything that wasn't screwed down, was gone.

If the people that were racing to the Base thought they were going to find safety, they were sorely mistaken.

Chapter 62

"We're not making up any ground on them anymore," said Nick. They had just caught sight of the Air Traffic Control tower rising out of the horizon, but no sign of the buildings.

"That stop they made, watering their horses, it made all the difference," advised Neil.

"Now you're telling us?!"

Alex was focusing on behind. The militia had dramatically closed the gap between them in the last half hour.

"It's time!" announced Alex.

Nick pulled his horse to a stop abruptly. Neil slowed, not sure what was happening.

"Neil, water the horses, or whatever you do. Make a move and we kill you, understand?"

Neil nodded, Nick couldn't have been more clear. Although he wasn't entirely sure where he was materializing the water from, but thought better of asking as the two men slipped two very serious rifles from their bags.

"You know a horse can run a mile in about ninety seconds," advised Neil as he watched the militia get nearer and nearer. "That's a lot of men with a lot of guns!"

Alex and Nick were in the zone. Neither was interested in Neil. They were focusing on the targets moving on horseback, most definitely not the easiest of targets to aim at.

***

Bob had noticed the top of the tower. They were nearing the Base. He'd have to keep an eye out. It may well be his first showdown with federal forces. Forces which he no longer recognized as having any authority within his State.

"It looks like they've stopped!" came a shout from ahead.

"When?"

"Not sure, but they're definitely not moving."

"Get your heads down, hug your horses, and attack!" screamed Bob.

The man who had warned of them stopping, took the first bullet. The rest were already moving when the second whizzed past, narrowly missing another militia man.

***

"Get the hell out of here!" shouted Alex. They weren't slowing the militia down, they had just sped them up. With their heads down and over ninety horses to choose from, it was almost impossible to hit anyone.

The three jumped on their horses, they barely had a mile advantage. They were never going to make it.

***

Scott watched intently, he was more than aware of the atrocities the militia had committed over the previous two weeks and like many of the operators, he was sure they were desperate to wreak some payback.

He raised his hand.

The soundless nod told him he had been seen.

"Am I free to release weapons?"

"No, we cannot expose our capabilities."

Scott looked at his screen in frustration. He had a myriad of weapons at his fingertips and he was about to witness the death of their own men, or worse, rape, torture, and murder of a young family when he could so easily stop it.

He raised his hand again. He was running out of time. He answered once again to the nod.

"What if we don't expose our capabilities?"

"Be quick." He had piqued the civilian's interest.

He explained.

***

Bob and Trey were, like the rest of their men, hanging on for dear life as their horses reacted to their repeated kicking to make them run as fast as they could. With so many different horses, strung in teams of four and varying capabilities of rider, what had been a tight formation spread dramatically as the horses accelerated to their maximum speeds. Bob and Trey, although far more experienced than they had been, were still some of the poorer amongst the riders.

Whatever the case, they were catching them. They had covered half a mile before the men had managed to get their horses moving and were still gaining ground even after the men were mounted, which allowed Bob and his men to once again ride properly, free from risk of being shot.

They had covered the mile by the time the men had moved less than half a mile. They weren't even eight hundred yards away. Bob ushered his horse on. He hated not being at the front.

***

Kate checked behind her as the gunshot echoed off the hills that framed the valley they were riding through. The large militia group that had appeared in the distance in the last hour was charging the smaller group behind. She looked ahead, the Base was still at least two miles away. The speed of the larger militia group was too fast. Her groups' horses had nothing left in the tank. They'd be lucky if they *even* made it the final two miles never mind outrun their pursuers. She couldn't believe it, after riding most of the day, covering nearly fifty miles, they were going to fail in the last mile. Ava was wrapped in her arms. She had barely gained consciousness in the last two hours. If she was lucky, she would stay as she was and not witness the hell that was certain to befall them.

Kate looked up at the sky, looked for her Tim and begged his forgiveness for failing his children. She had tried, given everything she had, but it just hadn't been enough.

She looked back towards the Base. It was in view, she had to at least try. Maybe some of them would make it.

"Kids, ride as fast as you can, or as fast as your horse will take you! Don't stay together, just go!"

She clucked at her horse and was surprised at the burst of speed that was her reward. She was less surprised when a sound wave hit her, explaining the sudden burst of speed. The massive sound of an explosion sent their horses into a frenzy and fortunately in a forward direction.

***

"What if I drop a bomb exactly where our men stopped to take a shot? They'll just assume they rigged a charge?"

The civilian looked around and lost his voice again and almost his ability to move his head, but Scott noted the tiny nod. It was as much as a 'go for it' as he was going to get.

Scott hit the release button, having already set the laser guidance and sent the bomb on its way. It was going to be close. Not being able to use missiles had limited his capabilities and it was going to be down to blind luck as to when the bomb hit the target and how long the militia took to reach the same target.

He didn't have long to wait. The bomb hit just ahead of the first militia rider and filled his screen with plumes of red billowing smoke, dust, and fire.

Chapter 63

Kate had stopped looking behind and kept her eyes on the prize, the Base ahead. Danny and Sophie, the lightest riders were just clearing the perimeter whilst she still had a few hundred yards to go, but so far so good. Zach was alongside her. They were going to make it. She knew exactly where the small hospital was, and with the belief that she was actually going to make it there, changed her direction towards it. She even plucked up the courage to look back.

Nobody. The coast was clear. No riders were bearing down on her. Nobody was about to snatch her away from Ava, just as she was nearing the hospital. She knew there were people still out there. One explosion couldn't have killed them all. But all she needed was the time to get the meds and they could move on. Or if the Base were able and willing to protect them, stay. Whatever the case, she needed the meds before deciding what they'd do next.

Kate hadn't even noticed the lack of people as she rushed towards the medical facility. Her only thought was getting antibiotics into Ava's system as quickly as physically possible. She almost leapt from her horse with Ava in her arms as she reached the door. It was unlocked, she pushed on it, it flapped wildly on one hinge. Her heart sank. That was most definitely not normal. She entered. The facility was bare, nothing. She dropped to the floor and wept. Ava, despite all of the motion, remained unconscious.

She laid her down gently, and needlessly checked every cupboard and crevice of the building. What had been a ward with various rooms and storage areas, was nothing more than an empty shell. She slumped against the wall and slid to the floor, Ava laying before her. Sophie, Danny, Zach, and Hank rushed in to help and stopped in their tracks when they saw the empty shell.

"What now?" asked Sophie.

Kate shrugged her shoulders. She was out of ideas and time, as Ava's breathing began to labor. She had failed.

Chapter 64

Nick shook his head to clear his thoughts. Nothing really made sense. One second he'd been riding as fast as his horse would carry him and the next, he was lying on the ground with his horse nowhere to be seen. He looked around. Alex was looking as bewildered as he was, while Neil was nowhere to be seen.

"What the hell happened?"

"Best guess, they just dropped a five-hundred-pound bomb on our asses!"

Nick suddenly remembered the militia that had been chasing them down. He looked back. Carnage, lumps of meat littered the plain behind them. Further back he could see some movement, but it was not coordinated. Whoever had survived was as shaky, if not more than they were.

"Where's Neil?"

"He probably managed to stay on his horse."

Nick spotted the Base ahead, about a mile or so away. He stood, his legs managing to hold him upright. He pulled Alex up and the two made off shakily at first before building up to a slow jog as they found their balance after the shockwave.

***

Neil galloped into the Base. His horse, like all the others, had bucked wildly as the explosion rocked the immediate vicinity of the blast. Fortunately, where others fell, he had managed to hang on and control his horse. He had chased after Alex's horse and grabbing its harness, calmed it down, enabling him to retrieve Alex's rifle from its holder.

He still had a chance to return home to the militia, but needed to get Kate. He just had to hope that Bob and Trey, or at least Bob, hadn't been caught in the blast.

Deserted was the first word that came to his mind as he galloped across the runway. Not an aircraft in sight. Tumbleweed drifted slowly in the wind, where the once pristine tarmac had been home to thundering and powerful jets. It had an eeriness to it that had Neil reconsidering his plan. He could just keep riding. But where was he going to go? If everywhere was like the Air Base or Boise, it was either nothing or a slow pitiful death in a festering hellhole. The militia was his home and whether Trey was alive or dead, Kate solved his problems, explaining his absence to Bob or appeasing Trey.

He pulled his horse to a stop and listened. They had to be there somewhere. The Mountain Home Air Force Base sign welcomed him to what could only be described as a small town. A Burger King sign beckoned him onwards. Everything else was gone, only the bare structures stood where he once imagined the powerful fighter jets would have awaited their calling. Not one person reacted to his presence. He rode on and turned towards the Burger King sign. Empty parking lot after empty parking lot. Even the Burger King had been stripped bare, only a few chairs and tables remained. Where the server and kitchen once sat, there was nothing, just an empty void. Everything of value was gone.

He rode on, a housing estate sat off at the opposite end of the Base, between him and the estate, empty shop after empty building lined the streets. Not a car to be seen. Mountain Home Air Force Base was no more. The realization of how long it was going to take to search for Kate hit him. It was no small task.

He looked around wildly. The survivors of the blast would be heading towards him. He had limited time. Where would they have gone? One sign pointed towards the exit, the far side of the Base and wherever it led to beyond. He looked around again. Standing in his stirrups to maximize his range, but nothing stood out. There were hundreds of places they could be, even one of the homes way at the back. Too much time was passing. It hadn't looked anywhere near as big when he'd ridden in. He clucked his horse onward. He had tried. He rode towards the exit, almost skidding to a stop. To his right sat a Pizza Hut, it too was empty like the Burger King, but that wasn't what had stopped him. Behind the restaurant sat another building, and out front were six horses.

***

Trey picked himself up and looked around him, barely four men were wandering aimlessly around him. Bob was to his right, slightly ahead. He remained motionless. Beyond that, he didn't particularly want to look. Body parts, human and equine, littered the area around him. The horses lucky enough to survive had scattered in almost every direction. None remained. He and whoever was able to would have to walk.

"On me!" he shouted, receiving little response. He barely heard his own shout, his ear drums ringing from the blast.

He waved his hands and caught the attention of those on their feet and using signs, managed to get what turned out to be six able-bodied men by his side.

"What do we do?" asked one, looking at Bob's motionless body.

"We complete our mission!" said Trey bluntly. "It's what the Duke would expect. And I don't know about you guys, but I want some payback!"

With six nods, Trey led the way, taking a slightly more circuitous route to avoid the worst of the carnage. Off in the distance, he spotted two men jogging into the Base. They were too far ahead to be any of the militia. He grabbed his AR-15 from its shoulder sling and aimed. They were well beyond its range, but that didn't stop him trying.

Chapter 65

Nick fell to the ground, as chunks of tarmac began to spit around them. Alex was bemused for a moment before the realization hit him. Somebody was shooting at them, but they couldn't hear because of the distance and the explosion.

"Son of a bitch!" screamed Nick. "I've been shot in the ass!"

Alex grabbed him and dragged him unceremoniously as fast as he could to cover. They were just fifty yards from the first hangar. Safely behind cover, he removed his sidearm and tentatively looked to see where the shooters were.

Seven men were walking towards them. Still a good way off, but each was armed with an AR-15. Both of their rifles had been strapped to their horses. Between him and Nick, they had two pistols and two knives and a man with a bullet in his ass. Bullets pinged against the fabric of the hangar, forcing him back inside.

"Seven guys with AR-15s," he relayed to Nick, who was removing a medipack from his kit. He injected the wound with what they had been told was the latest advancement in battlefield wound management. His ass cheek numbed and the faint whiff of glue filled the area. "I've just shot myself up with coke and superglue, haven't I?"

"Does it feel better?"

"I don't feel anything!" he said, looking over his shoulder at the site of the wound.

"And it's stopped bleeding, result! Now, I think we should get the hell out of here," suggested Alex. As he pulled Nick up, Nick buckled as he struggled to cope with one side being numb. Alex held him for a second.

"Okay?"

"Bit strange, but let's go." Nick hobbled as fast as he could after Alex. They burst out of a door at the back of the hangar and on into the Base proper, out of sight of the militia.

***

As the debris subsided, Scott could make out the outcome of his strike. He felt sorry for the horses, but not the militia, some of whom were clearly going to take a little longer to die. As the survivors began to surface, his finger hovered over the trigger ready to finish the job. Their two men had made it, but were still in danger. He counted seven militia up and moving.

"Take your finger off of that trigger!" ordered the civilian who had given the approval to drop the bomb.

"Our guys are in trouble."

"I've just had my ass chewed off for dropping the bomb. We are, and I repeat verbatim, 'not authorized to drop so much as a fart'. Our guys can look after themselves and if they can't, they know what they have to do."

"What they have to do, what does that..." Scott stopped himself. He understood what it meant. Scott looked back at the screen just as one of the men took a bullet and went down. His hand moved to his joystick and the trigger.

The civilian drew his side arm. "Don't!" he warned. "You have no idea how important what we are doing here is. It is far bigger than any of us and those men understood when they signed up for the mission. I will not hesitate to put you down."

Scott thought of his wife and daughter and relaxed his hand. "Understood."

"Do I need to relieve you of your duties for the rest of the day?"

Scott shook his head. "No, I understand. I am not authorized to fire weapons."

The civilian replaced his pistol, but remained at Scott's shoulder.

***

Trey reached the hangar and swore loudly as only a patch of blood remained. They followed the men out the only way they could have gone, and were faced by a town ahead.

"They could be anywhere!" moaned one of his men.

"Shit!" exclaimed Trey, thinking the same. If they went to ground, they'd never find them before dark and if Bob's concerns were true, his superior numbers and firepower would be meaningless.

"Where first?" asked one of his men.

A gunshot beat him to his answer. "There!" said Trey confidently, pointing to where the sound of the shot had come from.

Chapter 66

Kate cradled Ava in her arms, rocking her gently. She was having to fight back the tears, not wanting to show Ava how worried she was. She couldn't help but stare at Ava's leg, and her cut, a cut that had never healed, the redness spreading from the wound despite how clean they had fought to keep it. Whilst still in her leg, they had time, but when the infection spread to her blood, that clock had accelerated dramatically as the blood pulsed the infection through her, through her organs. Her body was fighting, but it was fighting a battle it had little or no chance of winning without help.

Sophie and Zach were across the room. Sophie wasn't able to hold her tears back and was hiding them as best she could, burying her head in Zach's chest. Her heaving shoulders, rising and falling with each intake of breath as she struggled to keep her tears silent.

"Danny, could you feed Hank please?" asked Kate. She wanted to keep him busy. He was still not fully aware of how bad things were. The longer that lasted the better. Deep down, he was a deeply emotional boy who had still not fully come to terms with his father's death. Ava was closer to him than anyone. Her passing was going to be devastating for him.

"Come on Hank," called Danny. The food was on one of the two pack horses outside, something Kate had failed to consider before asking.

"Zach, could you keep an eye on him please?" asked Kate, throwing an apologetic look and reaching her arm out for Sophie to join her and Ava.

Zach followed Danny out, the sight and sound of Hank growling at him as he stepped outside the door taking him by surprise, especially after having carried him for the best part of fifty miles.

"Turn around real slow, kid!"

Zach realized it wasn't him Hank was growling at. It was the man behind him with Danny in his arms and his hand over Danny's mouth. Danny was struggling against the man's vice-like grip, but the rifle pointing at Zach stopped him from offering any help.

Zach put his hand on Hank's back to try to settle him. He wasn't going to be appeased. His growl increased the more Zach tried to calm him.

"Shut that dog up or I will!" The rifle moved from pointing at Zach to Hank. Hank's teeth, old and yellowed came into view as his growl moved to a snarl in response. Zach felt the old muscles begin to flex under his hand. Hank was getting ready to attack. Zach looked at the man, his finger was tightening on the trigger. He was as frightened as they were.

Zach was no weapons expert, but he knew a bolt-action rifle needed two hands to chamber another round. The man had one bullet available to him and two targets. Hank and Zach. With Danny in his other arm, he was in no position to reload. His finger tightened further, and his arm began to shake slightly. It was a heavy gun to be pointing and holding with his left arm.

Zach began to prepare himself. He held Hank in place. The old dog was straining.

"Don't even think it!" warned the man. "I'll shoot you both!"

"I don't think so," said Zach confidently, the rifle swung from pointing at Hank to Zach as he spoke. Zach released the pressure he was using to hold Hank in place. He shot like a young pup, covering the distance to the man and Danny like a greyhound, lunging at the man who was holding his Danny.

The rifle barrel flew skywards as the man pulled the trigger, its bullet following its intended path while the rifle went off on a world of its own with only one hand controlling its power. The 0.338 bullet was enough to kill an elephant at half a mile, at ten yards, it was the equivalent of using a sledgehammer to crack a peanut shell.

***

Alex and Nick caught sight of Neil in the distance as they tried to get themselves as far from the militia as possible. His sharp change of direction as he was about to exit the Base and leave them behind had them both picking up speed. He had spotted something worth staying for. The family.

"You go on ahead!" urged Nick, his dead butt cheek holding them back.

"You sure?" asked Alex.

"The militia are far enough behind us. I'll be with you before they clear the hangars. Go!"

Alex raced off, leaving Nick to realize just how much his injury had slowed him. Not feeling the wound was making him forget he had even been shot, although he felt sure the drugs in the injection were helping with that.

Alex cleared the restaurant as his rifle was fired. He still had over a hundred yards to run. If he'd had the shot he'd have taken it, but there was too much happening. The dog was falling on Neil and the boy, while the young man was spinning and crashing to the ground. Alex had his pistol up and aiming at Neil as he neared the scene. He kicked the rifle away as Neil struggled against the dog.

"You okay, son?" asked Alex of the boy who was scrambling to his feet while his dog had no plans to let go of the shooter's arm. Alex had the shooter in his sights and was ready to shoot.

"Drop the gun!" came the command behind Alex.

***

The sound of the shot from the doorway brought Kate to life. She had been completely caught up in her daughters; all three oblivious to the world around them as they took some much needed comfort from one another.

Danny and Zach were outside and neither had a gun. Kate was up and moving in an instant, racing to the doorway, her PPQ out and ready for action. She ran out of the door without a thought for herself, and seeing Zach lying on the ground, aimed her gun at the man standing over Danny and another man, who she recognized as militia. Only one man had a gun and the shot had to come from somewhere.

"Drop the gun!" she commanded. "Zach, are you okay?" she asked, not taking her eyes off the gunman in front of her.

"Fine, I think," he said, feeling himself. Somehow, the man had missed him. He had felt the bullet as it flew past him, tearing at the fabric of his t-shirt. Spinning to his side had save his life.

"I'm on your side! He's the danger!" The man raised his pistol high in the air, letting it spin on his trigger finger.

"Just don't move," she warned, her pistol aimed at the back of his head.

"It's true," said Zach, standing and somewhat in a daze joining Kate. "He ran over here and kicked the rifle away and pointed the gun at him."

"Can someone get this dog off of me!" howled Neil from the ground. Hank was still clamped to his right arm.

Everyone ignored his pleas while they worked out who was who.

"His name's Neil, he's militia, and he was our prisoner! My name is Alex. My partner who is following slowly behind is Nick!"

Kate didn't drop her guard.

"And who are you, Alex?"

"I'm sorry that I can't tell you, only that we are on your side."

"And what side is that?"

"Not theirs!" he said, pointing to Neil.

Kate turned to look back down the road. A man was hobbling awkwardly towards them, his pistol remained holstered.

"Is that Nick?" she asked, allowing him to turn and look.

Alex turned around, catching sight of the woman they had kept watch over for almost two weeks. She was just as stunning in the flesh as from a mile away through a lens.

He caught himself from staring. "Yes, that's him."

Kate kept her pistol in her hand, but lowered it. "Danny, stop Hank from eating that man. God knows where he's been. Zach, can you take them inside?"

Nick joined them and failed to stop staring.

"Is your friend okay?" asked Kate. "He's staring at me, it's a bit weird."

"Drugs. He got shot in the butt," explained Alex, although he wasn't sure it had anything to do with the drugs. Nick was smitten and had been for two weeks.

"We should get inside. There are more militia men coming," suggested Alex.

"What about your prisoner?!" she spat. He had put his hands on her son.

Nick reached down and helped him up with one hand, while throwing a punch straight into his face with the other. Neil crashed to the ground. Alex reached down and flipped him over and bound his hands behind his back.

Kate approved of their tactics and held the door open as they pulled their dazed prisoner unceremoniously into the empty hospital.

"Everyone, this is Alex and Nick. They're on our side," announced Kate as she pushed past the men and rejoined Ava.

While Alex dealt with Neil, Nick caught sight of the family scene across the room and a clearly very ill young girl. He rushed as fast as his wound would allow to their side, pushing Sophie and Kate aside. "What's wrong with her?" he asked, checking her temperature and feeling for her pulse, clearly knowing what he was doing.

"Sepsis, she was cut last week and it wouldn't heal. We've got no antibiotics. She's called Ava." Tears were streaming from Kate's eyes, the look of worry on Nick's face was not helping the situation, which she already knew was dire. Having it confirmed by someone who knew what they were doing was not unexpected, but she hoped she had been overly worried.

"Throw me that pack!" ordered Nick of Alex. It slid across the floor and was quickly joined by Alex. Both men looked at Ava with great concern. Nick rummaged through the pack, producing a syringe pack. He broke the seal, checked the instructions and promptly ignored them. Injecting every fluid ounce of the contents into the young girl.

"What was that?"

"That was all the antibiotics we had. Every drop. It will buy us a little time, I hope."

"How much?" Kate's voice was cracking as it spoke.

Nick shrugged. He wasn't even sure it wasn't too late. He had never seen anyone that far gone with sepsis before.

"Wait a minute! You're the guys with a phone!" she suddenly remembered what she had seen earlier in the day.

Before they could think of an answer, the windows exploded around them in a hail of gunfire.

"Get down!!!" screamed Alex unnecessarily.

Nick ushered them all into the room at the back of the ward, a storage cupboard with no windows.

"Wait here," he instructed as Alex awaited his partner.

Kate rose to leave with them.

"Leave this to us!"

"Three guns are better than two and no offence, but as my family's life is on the line, there is no way you're stopping me."

She picked up her Remington and slung it over her shoulder. Alex had his Dakota and all three had a pistol each. At close quarters against seven men with automatic rifles, it wasn't great odds.

"How long until darkness?" asked Nick.

"At least another couple of hours," replied Alex.

"What difference would that make?"

"We own the night!" winked Nick. Kate had no idea what he was talking about and put it down to the drugs as Alex had explained earlier.

"So what's the plan?" asked Kate as another hail of bullets tore through the hospital. Fortunately, the walls were thick enough to stop the .223 rounds, unlike the windows. Keeping low was key.

"They'll be moving closer each time they fire."

"So what do we do?"

"Start shooting when they come in!"

"Great plan!"

"Thanks, thought it up all by myself," smiled Nick.

"We just want the woman!" shouted Trey as the onslaught ended.

"That's Trey," explained Kate. "He's the cousin of Bob Jackson, the leader of the militia. He's got a thing for me, crazy, he met me outside the supermarket and…"

"Not the only one," mumbled Alex quietly to Nick, receiving a punch in the ribs.

"What?" asked Kate, spotting the punch and the smile on Alex's face. "It's not funny, the guy's a psycho. It's his fault that Ava got cut in the first place. That son of a bitch is responsible for killing my…"

"Hey, we'll get you out of this. We'll save Ava."

"How? You said it yourself, that was all the antibiotics you had. There aren't any more. The world, in case you hadn't noticed, is fucked!"

"We'll work it out," Nick looked at Alex, who shook his head.

Nick stopped himself from saying any more.

"You promise me you can save my daughter?"

"Yes!" said Nick with a sincerity that Kate believed.

She stood up. "I'm coming out!" She dropped her Remington and walked out of the door, catching both Nick and Alex by surprise.

Before they could stop her, she was gone.

Chapter 67

"What the hell is she doing?" shouted Nick in frustration, watching the door swing closed behind her.

Alex looked at the floor where she had dropped the Remington. Only one weapon was there.

"Shit, she's still got her pistol."

"It wasn't in her holster?"

"She must have tucked it under her shirt…you don't think?"

"That's exactly what I think. She blames him for her daughter's condition. She's a mother, she'll give her life for her kids!"

"Not on my watch!" said Nick, racing to the door. Alex knew he should stop him but didn't, he raced after him. He had stood by and watched far too much to stomach over the last two weeks. It was now time to act, time to do what they had both trained their entire adult lives to do and what their country had spent millions of dollars training them to do. Kill the enemies of the United States of America.

***

Trcy's mouth exploded into a grin as Kate burst out of the hospital with her hands in the air. Finally, she had seen sense.

He waved for his men to lower their weapons. The last thing he wanted was for someone to shoot her by mistake.

He stepped forward and scooped her up in his arms. She recoiled at the smell of his stale sweat, pulling her face as far back from him as the curvature of her spine would allow. His arm was wrapped around her waist just above where her pistol was lodged in the small of her back in her beltline. Although he wouldn't feel it, he was stopping her from getting anywhere near it. Her arm not long enough to go over his and dig out the handle. She was stuck in his grasp. Her plan, as much as she had thought it through, had failed. Although, beyond killing Trey, her plan was fairly fluid.

A crash of the door followed by gunfire had her flying through the air as Trey unceremoniously tossed her aside to get to his rifle and return fire.

His men were caught with their rifles facing the ground, as instructed. Two fell as Alex and Nick exited the hospital their guns blazing, both rolling in opposite directions, shooting and moving. Another two fell.

Kate landed awkwardly, her head whipping into the tarmac of the parking lot. An audible crack as her skull hit the hard surface, sent a wave of nausea through her. Her mind began to swim, everything felt surreal, as though nothing was real. A haziness began to envelope her. She fought against it. She knew she had to save her kids. Her hand reached behind her, the butt of the pistol felt natural, she pulled at it, it felt as though it were floating away from her as she pulled it around in front of her face.

The element of surprise was gone. The militia men had their weapons to bear and the bullets were beginning to spout from their rifles. Nick and Alex looked at one another, a last nod as they fired their final rounds.

Kate was barely holding onto consciousness, only the booms of the guns firing around her were stopping her mind from completely shutting down. Her hand appeared in front of her, the pistol pointing at a man who she could barely see. She was struggling to even remember why she was holding a pistol.

Bang, bang, bang, the explosions were like an electric shock, bringing her back to life with each shot. Her mind focusing briefly as each bang shocked her back into the moment. The sight on her pistol rested on a face she recognized, a man she hated like no other. She pulled the trigger, feeling it break, just as her world went black.

***

The shooting stopped. Nick opened one eye then the other. He was still alive. A searing pain emanated from his right shoulder, but he was still alive. He looked across to where he had last seen Alex. He looked away quickly, it was not a sight he wanted to remember. He wanted to remember the sly nod they had given to each other as their last memory together.

He looked around at the militia men, two were moving, the others were dead. Trey, the man who had wanted Kate was one of those still moving. She had shot him, hit him in the head, but he was coming to. Nick could see the wound. It was on the side of his head, probably removed a small portion of his skull but had not penetrated the brain, not that there was probably much in there, he thought, as he tried to reach for his gun. His pistol lay next to his right hand. Nick sent the signal to pick it up, aim it at Trey, shoot, and kill him. His hand, despite his brain telling it to, didn't move.

He sent the same signals to his left hand, it reached across his immobile right arm. The pain exploded in his shoulder as he moved, sending him backwards onto the ground in agony. He looked over helplessly as Trey was pulling himself to his feet. His AR-15 was still in his hand. Blood poured from the wound in his head, but he was clearly fully conscious as he stalked towards him, an inane grin of achievement fixed to his face.

Nick tried again to reach his pistol, but the pain was debilitating, his body fighting against the pain to protect itself, not realizing it was doing the exact opposite.

Trey glanced over at the unconscious Kate. "You can only imagine the fun I'm going to have with her!" he cawed, raising the AR-15 to Nick's head.

Chapter 68

Zach waited for a few minutes of silence before venturing outside the storage cupboard.

"Wait there!" he instructed, closing the door behind him. He carefully worked his way to the window and took a look outside. Not one person remained standing, all were on the ground, including Kate. He grabbed her rifle, chambered a round and rushed to the door.

He stopped dead in his tracks. In the time he had taken to get the rifle, Trey was on his feet. Trey, the man he fully believed had killed his parents, stood over Nick with a gun to his head, laughing in his face. Zach raised the rifle. He had never fired one before. He had never killed anyone or anything before. Nor had he ever wanted to kill anyone more in his life. He fired. The rifle propelled him backward. He wasn't prepared for the amount of kick and had not rested the stock on his shoulder. His shot flew upwards. Had he been any more than a few yards away, it would have been a catastrophic error. Instead, his body shot became a headshot. Where Kate had failed with her pistol, Zach had succeeded with Kate's rifle. The massive bullet obliterated the laughing head. The headless body crumpled to the ground.

Zach pulled himself back to his feet and racked another round into the chamber. The only other living militia man stopped moving. He had no intention of ending up like Trey. While he covered the militia man, Zach helped Nick to his feet.

"Can you pass me my pistol?" he winced.

Zach bent down and picked up the pistol, reloading it with a fresh magazine at Nick's request.

Nick walked over to the last militia man and without a word, shot him cleanly through the temple.

"What the…" Zach jumped back in shock.

Nick turned to Zach. "I'm sorry, but that was necessary. You'll understand soon enough, don't worry."

As crazy as it was, coming from a man who had just executed a wounded man in cold blood, Zach believed him.

Both went to the aid of Kate, a pool of blood was spreading from the wound at the back of her head. Nick checked her pulse with his one good hand, wincing with every movement. It was weak, but steady.

"Okay let's get the hell out of here and get you guys to safety!"

Zach looked around. They were in the middle of nowhere with six exhausted horses that weren't going to move another inch for at least twelve hours.

"Look at the state you're in. Absolute agony and that's standing still, never mind what it'll be like on the back of a horse. And Kate and Ava are in no state to move anywhere."

"You're absolutely right," smiled Nick. "Can you drive?"

"Can I what?" asked Zach.

"Help me," said Nick. "That way." He pointed towards the housing estate.

"I don't know what drugs you're on, but…"

"Just help me, okay!" commanded Nick in a tone that demanded respect. Zach walked him across the Base and into the housing estate.

"Here," pointed Nick towards one of the homes, indicating for Zach to take him in. Like everywhere else on the Base, it was empty, everything was gone, every piece of furniture, including the kitchen cabinets were gone. Holes remained in the floor where the cabinets had recently stood. Nick pointed to the door at the back of the kitchen which led to the garage. As twilight was falling, the light in the house began to fade. As Zach reached the doorway, he intuitively flicked the light switch. Unsurprisingly, it didn't work. The light stayed off. Next to the light switch. a black panel the size of a small iPad was affixed to the wall. Nick pushed past Zach and with a cry of pain, pressed his right hand onto the panel, his left hand pressing his useless arm until a small click sounded. The door to the garage opened. Its wooden façade was exactly that. It was a solid steel door, more like a safe. Nick stepped back to allow Zach to go in first. Zach looked around, not going in.

"What are you doing?"

"Looking for a match or something, it's dark in there."

Nick pushed the door open and a fluorescent light automatically triggered and bathed the darkness in light.

Zach's mouth dropped and he walked forward in awe of something as simple as a light. He pushed open the door. An SUV sat in the middle of the garage. He rushed in and pulled open the door. It was much heavier than any door he had opened before.

"Armored!" explained Nick, seeing the quizzical look on his face.

A key sat in the ignition. Zach turned it, the lights ignited on the dashboard.

"But…how…I mean…how…" His mind was so full of questions, he didn't know which to ask first.

"Help me in and I'll tell you what I can," suggested Nick.

Zach helped him into the passenger seat before starting the engine. It fired up the first time. A clicker on the dashboard opened the garage door. It rose just as every garage door had for the majority of Zach's life but it somehow, was the most amazing thing he had ever seen.

"This was our last resort. I really never thought for a second two weeks ago that we would ever need it, nor did I think I'd be leaving here without Alex."

"Are you saying that some of the country did survive the attack?"

"Oh God, you have no idea," sighed Nick, shaking his head. He looked out of the window, he couldn't bear to look Zach in the face. "I'm sorry, but there's only so much I can say. It's best we just get the others and get moving."

***

Bob's eyes opened. Not gingerly, not slowly, but wide as the sound of the powerful engine roared nearby. He sat up and followed the sound. It was coming from the Base. A flash of light escaped between the buildings. Headlights. He wasn't dreaming, he wasn't going mad. There was a vehicle moving within the Base.

He looked around him. The fading light offered a less gruesome image than before. He stood up, his legs less stable than normal, his head swimming slightly. He had been out for hours. It had been mid-afternoon when he had been caught in the explosion.

He watched the Base. Off in the distance, the headlights were pulling out, driving south. What remained was darkness. He started a slow walk towards the Base. There was a chance if one vehicle worked, then maybe others did too. His mind raced as the implications of what he had just witnessed impacted his Boise, his Idaho, his country. He had plans and what he had just seen had fundamentally altered his thinking. Bob 'the Duke' Jackson had some planning to do.

Chapter 69

Two days later

Kate opened her eyes.

"Mom!" shouted Danny excitedly. Kate lifted her hand to her face, the light above her bed was blinding her. Whether it was because of the headache she had or the fact she was looking into a light at all, she wasn't sure.

Danny hugged her regardless. She moved her arm and hugged him back. She looked over to see a smiling Sophie and Zach. They stood by her bed. Sophie was obviously waiting for Danny to get out the way to get in and hug her too. Behind her in the next bed lay Ava. Numerous drips were hooked up to her and machines bleeped around her, but she smiled over at her mom. Kate burst into tears. Her baby was alive. They were all okay.

She looked around through her tears as she tried to come to terms with where she was. Clean, crisp, white bed sheets, a pristine hospital room. Lights, medicines, everything she would expect in a normal hospital, even a television. She took a second to look at the television. It was on, pictures were on the screen. CNN was on.

"You don't remember what happened?" asked Sophie, hugging her mom tightly.

Kate thought back. She remembered hitting her head. A truck, she remembered a truck. Her memory faded in and out. She remembered a phone call, a man demanding the snipers be stood down. She remembered how bizarre it'd sounded at the time. The cordon they had gone through, a security area. The truck had been searched, the man with them, Nick, that was his name, had demanded they be allowed through and after they checked, they had been allowed to continue. A few miles further, another checkpoint, this one ablaze with lights, and then normality. Everything was normal. They were driving though a town, she remembered the McDonald's sign, lit up and people waiting at the drive-thru. Just snippets. No more as she had faded in and out of consciousness

"That's enough for just now," a nurse interrupted the reunion.

Kate drifted back to sleep. Whatever the nurse had given her ensured she slept the night. She awoke the next morning, far brighter and more alert. The snippets from the previous few days were still struggling to make any sense. The television was off. She began to wonder if she had dreamt everything, until a man hobbled into the room. His right arm strapped to his body. She instantly knew him as Nick, the man who had saved Ava.

"You're looking much brighter," he smiled, taking the seat next to her bed after checking on Ava who'd smiled warmly at him.

"I feel a lot better. The headaches have gone as well." `She looked at Ava. "Hey, honey."

"Hey, Mom."

Both reached out their hands and managed to touch fingers.

"You've got questions?" asked Nick.

"Hell yeah!" said Kate with some feeling.

"What do you remember?"

Kate ran him through the snippets.

Nick nodded a lot and as Kate finished, he asked "Do you feel able to walk?"

Kate nodded and sat up. Her headache had gone and sitting up felt normal, so she swung her legs out of the bed and stood up. Nick was by her side, his one good arm ready to help her if needed. She was fine. The floor was metal, not concrete. She looked at Nick and the floor.

"Come with me," he said, leading the way. "Watch the step," he advised as they left the small ward. The door had a large wheel in the middle of it instead of a handle and didn't stretch to the floor and, like the floor, was made of metal.

"Are we on a ship?"

"Yes," said Nick. He led the way without another word, down a short corridor and through two doorways. He knew his way around. A constant hum, a noise she had thought leftover from her injury suddenly made sense. It was the ship's engine, not a noise in her head. Nick stopped at a door and knocked three times.

"Enter!"

Nick opened the door and let Kate walk in.

"Thanks," said the man inside the office. Nick closed the door behind her, leaving Kate alone with the stranger.

The stranger walked over to a large window in his office and looked down. He waved for Kate to join him.

"Don't worry, they can't see you. It just looks like a black panel to them."

Kate looked down on a number of screens and three men in what looked like an operations center. Two men were at controls in front of screens while a third kept watch over them. Kate looked at the screens. She couldn't really understand what she was looking at until she recognized a couple of buildings from Boise.

"That man there, his name is Scott. He dropped a bomb that most certainly saved your and your family's lives."

"Please thank him for me," she gushed.

"I won't. It was against my express orders," he said matter of factly. "Please, Mrs. Wolfe, take a seat."

Kate hovered, she wasn't comfortable in the man's presence, his coldness was disconcerting. She looked at the door, wishing Nick would come back in.

"Please, you'll want to hear what I'm going to say."

Kate sat down.

The man pushed a sheet of paper across the desk to her and placed a pen on top.

"Before I begin, I'd like you to sign this."

"What is it?"

"It states that you are fully aware that if you disclose anything we discuss here today, you will be executed for treason. You will be shot immediately. There will be no trial, no second chances. It is non-negotiable. I should point out that you and your family already know too much to ever leave this facility without you signing this.

"So, if I don't sign this, you'll just imprison us here forever?"

"We have no space, nor need for prisoners." There was no attempt to veil the threat. Kate signed the paper. Not for her, but her children.

The man removed the signed sheet and secured it in his top drawer.

"Mrs. Wolfe," he began.

"Kate, please."

"Kate," he smiled, without warmth. "My name is Frank Henrikson. I am the Administrator of the Federal Emergency Management Agency, FEMA, and was appointed by the President. It is my job to direct the efforts in Boise and oversee the situation for the President.

"Well, if you don't mind me saying, you're doing a goddamn awful job. And they thought Katrina was FEMA's worst disaster..."

"No, no. You've got it all wrong," he said, shaking his head. "We've not been asked to help the disaster. We were asked to create it."

Chapter 70

Kate stared at Frank, unable to speak. She barely stopped herself reaching across the table and beating him to death. His face remained impassive. Emotionless, he had just admitted to causing the deaths of tens of thousands of people, probably hundreds of thousands.

"You what?" she stumbled. "So it is only Boise that was affected by the attack?"

"Well, Boise and the surrounding area, yes. But there was no attack."

"But the power, it went out, the explosion at the nuclear plant…" she was struggling to comprehend the enormity of what she was being told.

"Unfortunate timing. The explosion was supposed to coincide with the power outage as though it were the cause. We set off a number of powerful EMPs across the area."

"EMPs?"

"Electro Magnetic Pulses. They fry electronics, stop anything electrical from working. They worked better than we predicted. I believe nothing electrical survived."

"Nothing, not even a flashlight," she replied angrily. He seemed proud of his achievements.

"You know there are thousands dying needlessly. They need medicines!"

"I don't disagree. It is tragic, but I do disagree wholeheartedly that it is needless…"

Kate stood up, she couldn't sit and listen to his superior and arrogant attitude any longer. "The President is aware of what you've done?"

"It was his idea," he answered simply.

She was dumfounded, struggling to think what to say given his brazen admissions of what she could only see as one of the most heinous crimes ever committed.

"Why Boise?" she struggled.

"It's our most remote city. It allowed us to understand the impact on a city scale while minimizing the number of participants."

Kate began to pace rapidly. The more she considered what the man had told her, the more she wanted to kill him.

"And what, the rest of America just forgot about us?"

"There are barely a handful of people fully aware of what is being undertaken here and that it is in fact not a nuclear accident that flattened the city. To the world, Boise has already gone and the area is now uninhabitable. There's a fifty-mile exclusion zone. Again, it's the reason Boise was chosen. Any other urban conurbation with that scale of accident would have involved a far larger populace."

"We think the world as we know it has come to an end, nuclear Armageddon, whatever you want to call it, all hope has gone that things will ever get back to normal."

Frank struggled to hide his pleasure at what she was saying. "I heard reports that was the case. Alex and Nick had given that impression, but it is encouraging to hear it first-hand."

"Encouraging?!!!" she screamed, her fury building. The door opened and Nick stepped in.

"You knew this, you knew we were living in some sort of game? You watched what we went through, knowing it wasn't real? That the world was going on around us as normal while our world collapsed, our civilization fell apart?" Tears of anger flowed down her face.

Nick nodded. "But it wasn't a game, I promise you…"

"Nick is right, this is no game. It's much more than that, I can assure you. It's a trial."

"A trial…a trial for what?" she shouted, her face red with rage. The more she thought about her friends, the people who had died at the hands of the militia and the tragedy she had witnessed at the hospital and the wider city the angrier she got.

"To understand what happens when the power goes out and the world as we know it ends."

"So what? We can stop it ever happening? Well it already has!"

"No, so we can learn how to go on, learn what we need to do to prepare for when it happens. What we can do to save as many people as we can."

"You mean if it ever happens?" spat Kate.

"No," said Frank. "For when it does happen," he said, pointing to a clock on the wall behind Kate, a clock that faced his desk. It was counting down, not up: 348 days : 14 hours : 22 seconds.

Kate stared at the clock as the seconds ticked away.

"What?" Her mouth dropped open.

"Meteors, a massive shower of them. None big enough to wipe us out entirely but certainly enough by even conservative estimates to wipe out ninety per cent of the world's population. You're worried about a few hundred thousand, but by this time next year, over seven billion people will be dead."

Kate just stared at the clock as he spoke.

"Whether we'll suffer the same amount of electrical disturbance, we don't know, but it is unlikely that any power stations or in fact many structures at all will survive the strike. We are also likely to experience some darkening of the skies for a number of years due to the amount of debris that will be released into the atmosphere as the meteors impact the earth at extreme velocities. Each meteor will have the destructive force equivalent to a nuclear warhead and the earth is going to be hit by thousands of them. Tsunamis will wipe out pretty much everyone within a few miles of the coast. It is going to be like Armageddon but we believe we can plan a way through. Will you help us?"

"Me?"

"You lived it, and according to Nick here, you rose to the challenge. Of all the people in Boise, only you are standing in front of me, which tells me as much as I need to know. You understand better than anyone what we're facing and the little things that could make the difference."

Kate shook her head. She walked back over to the window overlooking the operations center.

"Why are you not evacuating the coasts? You have a year to get people to higher ground, you can minimize the casualties."

"First, the populace can't know what's coming. The world faced with this news would cease to function. Who would go to work or school or go about their normal lives? The world's economies would crash and anarchy would ensue. Wars, famine, chaos and ultimately widespread death would be inevitable, without any plan for a future. When the strike comes, few can know it's coming."

"You paint a pretty bleak view of humanity!"

"Do I? Look at what happened to one of our most civilized and friendly cities in just two weeks! Imagine it a year from now, but add in overcrowding. Forty percent of the world's population lives near the coast. Where are they all going to go in less than a year?"

Kate remained silent, trying desperately to think of something, anything that would make sense of what he was saying. There had to be something they could do.

"And second," continued Frank. "And perhaps more important. After the meteor strike, food production will be a fraction of what it is now, if there's any at all. Depending on the amount of debris, it may be years before farming can be restarted. We face the prospect of 8 billion people starving to death. Or giving a fighting chance to the few that survive the strike and spend the next year working to give them every chance possible to succeed through the chaos, thanks to what we have learned here."

Kate wanted to go back to Boise. She shook her head, wanting to un-hear everything he had said. The enormity of what she was hearing was unimaginable.

"Please, I don't want to be overly dramatic, but your country…" began Frank sincerely, pausing, rethinking his words. "…mankind needs you."

Kate looked at the screens below, the devastating images of Boise projected on the screens.

"On one condition," she said, not taking her eyes off of the screens.

"What?" asked Frank.

She turned to look him in the eye. "You've got all you need from Boise. End the trial now!"

THE END

Other novels by the Murray McDonald

Thrillers

Scion

Critical Error

Divide & Conquer

America's Trust

Traitor

The God Complex

Captive-in-Chief

Young Adult Thrillers

Kidnap

Assassin

Novella (Perseid Collapse)

Rockland

Please subscribe to updates on new releases and special offers –by visiting

www.eepurl.com/IaKZz

Printed in Great Britain
by Amazon

61233511R00201